First hardcover edition December 2022

Book design by Andrew Alonso

ISBN 979-8-218-12176-1 (hardcover)
ISBN 979-8-218-07714-3 (paperback)
ISBN 979-8-218-07715-0 (ebook)

Published by Guy McMonstermaker Publishing
www.thecreatureporium.com

The Leaven

Andrew Alonso

DEDICATION

I love you son.
Dad always says you can do anything you set your mind to.
This book is proof that I'm not a liar.

Prologue

May 18th, 2027

"You're the first soldier to give me a smile, Lieutenant," the journalist shielded her camera's LCD from the harsh Siberian sun. "You have nice lips."

"Too kind," Lance Shepherd replied, gazing out the window at his side, contented. "If it were any other day but today, you never would've seen it, ma'am."

"Why's that?"

"Because he's going home to his hot-ass wife," one soldier said with a chuckle.

The journalist glanced at the three other Marines seated around the lieutenant. Their sly smirks made her cheeks turn rosy and warm as she pretended not to notice Lance's ring. "More smiles, guys, whaddya say?" she asked, lifting her camera to her eye.

The troops threw up peace signs as she flashed another photo. "Here's to goin home, boys," Private Carlyle said.

"Not a damn day too soon, man. C'mon, gimme some," Private Hudson added, fist-bumping his brother-in-arms.

The journalist snapped her shot, shifting back toward the

front seat again. "Feels a little stupid getting assigned to you guys days before the Russians surrendered. Got a free trip out of it, I guess."

Lance grinned, "Don't turn too excited yet. The fastest way to get yourself killed out here is by making assumptions in wartime." He looked over at his comrades, and his peaceful demeanor melted into a somber fog. "We saw plenty of men who made plans five years into the future who were dead six minutes later."

"Jesus, Shep, yer scaring the photo-jockey," Private Mendoza said with a devilish grin.

"You know how this ride's gonna end?" Lance asked.

"No, sir," Mendoza replied.

Shepherd nodded, "Shut the fuck up, then."

The journalist reached her arm into the back seat, flicking on her audio recorder. "Anybody wanna gimme a quote? Commemorate the day the war ended? This is history."

Nobody spoke a word.

"What about you, lieutenant? You have some interesting things to say."

"Not really. I'm just a country-boy serving said country. The only thing I love more than the US of A is my wife."

Private Carlyle shook his head, "You sure as hell don't sound country with all that-there enunciation, Shep. You're doing real country-boys dirty."

Lance elbowed Carlyle in the ribs, nodding over to Mendoza. "This asshole doesn't sound wetbackish, and I don't see you giving him any shit."

"¿Por qué tuviste que ir allí?" Mendoza asked, flipping off his superior.

Carlyle grinned, "Now you sound country, brotha… That's more like it."

The driver chimed in, turning up the radio. "Guys, you hearing this? Shut up for a sec… Listen."

A staticky voice crackled through the speakers. "All stations on this net, be advised, we have reports of an unidentified flying object fifty kilometers off the coast of Gatang Bay. All units in the vicinity, standby and await further instructions. I repeat—"

The driver turned down the radio, "Fucking aliens?"

Lance rolled his eyes. "An unidentified aircraft's just that—an unidentified aircraft."

"Nobody said shit about an unidentified aircraft though," Mendoza said. "They said unidentified flying object... A UFO."

"It's some stealth jet we ain't paid enough to know about," Carlyle added.

Shepherd nodded in approval, "See?"

Mendoza stirred in his seat, leering out the window into the clear sky above. "They said 'UFO'. It's something they don't recognize. That's the exact definition of the word 'alien', pendejos."

"I hope you're wrong, Mendoza," Hudson said, chuckling. "We just ended World War Three! Game over, man!"

Mendoza socked Hudson in the shoulder, "You wanna be a dick right now? After the little green men come down here and get their asses kicked, I'll save some for you too. Don't fuck with a New Yorker, baby."

"To hell with that, don't fuck with a Texan! What y'all liberals think you gonna do if ET comes down here to start somethin? Cry 'em to death?" Carlyle retorted.

"Enough already," Lance barked, staring daggers at his men. "This ain't a movie. There are no aliens."

The APC fell silent, save for the chatter of the broadcast coming through the speakers up front.

"Sure about that, Shep?" the driver asked.

A baritone voice came over the transmission, deep and menacing, half-muted by static but still audible.

And inhuman.

"I am Khoth Vulgrell of the Kil'Durian empire. You have no cause to fear us, so choose your martial steps wisely if you seek a greater peace. Your world is soon to become so much larger than you ever thought possible, and in time, you will come to understand the nature of true harmony… Rejoice."

"Holy shit," Mendoza whispered, clasping his hands together in prayer.

"Aliens." Lance eyed the awestruck journalist in the front passenger seat. "You look white as a ghost."

The journalist's jaw dangled open a bit, "Alien life… How's that for not knowing where you'll be five minutes from now?"

KABOOM! The APC was airborne for mere seconds, but the IED it ran over waited in the Siberian sand for God knows how long.

Days.

Months.

It didn't matter.

It was where it belonged, when it belonged, taking who no longer belonged.

No second chances.

Chapter 1: Choices

May 18th, 2028

Crickets chirped in the grass snaking over the stone path to Elle Shepherd's chicken coop. Like the fat birds clucking in the evening chill, she wondered if this was all there was. The woman needed busywork. The closer it came to the anniversary, the less motivated Shepherd became. Their farm was beautiful once. These days, it only belonged when bathing in the light of long-gone suns spread across the sky.

Like the stars Elle watched every night from her dusty back-porch, this homestead was dead.

She took a steaming mug to her lips, but it's warmth brought no comfort. Hot cocoa was their thing, hers and her husband's. She didn't remember the last time she had any alone.

The thick cup clanged against the wooden coaster on the table at her side and she slid into her wicker seat. She wasn't thinking, or even feeling, but being. Numb and distant, trying not to wish Lance was beside her once more.

She looked over her shoulder through the kitchen window, squinting to see the stove timer. She'd be damned if she burned her roast again. The smell was horrible, charred and salty.

It reminded her of Lance's body, burning in the APC wreckage for hours. What little of it that hadn't jettisoned into the sand in bloody, tattered hunks.

Elle poured the last of her cocoa into the wilting succulent in her favorite terracotta pot.

She needed something stronger.

The den was awash in an amber glow, dancing within the brick fireplace as embers crackled and popped. Shepherd tossed in a few more logs, staring through the living room window. The driveway bled into the night's abyss. It seemed black as the vacuum of space, but it wasn't. A gentle wind made the tiny windmill affixed to the slanted mailbox jutting from the dirt spin.

She hated that mailbox.

All it ever held were overdue bills and heartache.

Elle leaned her steel poker against the fireplace, looking over her shoulder. A pamphlet dangled over the edge of her food-prep island, beside her perfect roast.

At Evanscorp Cloning, life is as precious when it starts at the end.

She dared not read it, yet she refused to toss it out with the morning coupons like usual.

Elle moved toward the kitchen, her heart beating faster with every step. She was almost upon the pamphlet when she veered left, stopping at her liquor cabinet. She uncapped her favorite Scotch.

Her hands trembled with hesitation.

Shepherd eyed the leaflet, setting the bottle aside in favor of Alka-Seltzer instead. After dinner, she and her second glass of fizz were ready for a little television. Somehow, that damn brochure tagged along. It rested on the end-table, basking under the lamp's glow, as if God's finger tapped on it, beckoning the woman to look it over.

She couldn't, terrified of what she'd feel if she did.

Elle didn't know if Lance was nothing more than a rotting husk or a patient angel watching over her. What if she was robbing him of eternal peace by bringing him back? How could she live with herself? How could he ever forgive her? What if he returned some ghoul deep inside, seething with hatred for the woman that adored him? Shepherd read enough horror novels to understand what happened when you defied God's law.

But what if this was God's will?

A second chance.

How many people got another shot at happiness with someone dead?

Of those lucky few, who did the appropriate thing for the deceased? What was the right thing, anyway?

The Scotch in the kitchen called to her, but Elle reached for the TV remote instead.

Terrible idea.

"Our guest is no stranger to controversy," the seated television host began. "Author of Hell From Above: A Year Of False Idols, and the most irreverent Reverend in modern history... I'm talking about Reverend Jack Tanner."

The crowd jeered and booed as a stylish evangelical strutted onto the stage. He couldn't have been over forty, but his thick horn-rimmed glasses made him look older. The man dropped into his seat with a smarmy grin, blowing a kiss to the gallery.

"Beloved, do not believe every spirit, but test the spirits to see if they are from God. Many false prophets have gone out into the world. John, four-one," Tanner said. He exhaled a self-righteous sigh, checking the gaudy Rolex on his hairy wrist. "Ya got ten minutes, friends. I can only take so much adoration."

The host glanced at his cue cards. His nervous smile bounced between the gimlet-eyed Reverend and the stone-cold public.

"Seems you're never in short supply of fans, sir. It must be difficult receiving such—love."

"I'm blessed, ain't I?" Jack shifted in his seat so he could see the entire audience. Their baleful faces brought him perverse satisfaction. "For every one uh these jackals at least a dozen angels will hear the Lord's truth."

"Fuck you!" a faceless member of the crowd shouted. "Hateful bigot!"

"Sam! Jesus, do your job!" the host barked. "You're head of security! Get that guy out of here!"

Tanner's hand shot skyward, "No! No, let the fellow stay! Let him stay..."

"We're live, Reverend..." the host whispered.

"I know we are. The world needs to bear witness to this..." Jack pointed square at his profane opposition. "These are the ones wanna shut out God. These are the folks tryin to silence my words, America... Well, I'm here to tell ya it won't work!"

Claps rose from the dead-air, growing into a confident, defiant, applause. A few people lifted out of their seats, unafraid of how they looked to the opposing majority surrounding them.

"Yes!" Tanner cried. "Yes, my flock! Rise! Be proud uh yer faith!"

The host loosened his tie, "Reverend, we should continue with the interview if you please."

"When yer right, yer right." Jack motioned for his sheep to settle, shifting himself in his seat, legs crossed. "Shoot, partner. Let's get this show on the road. I'll even talk proper for ya, how bout that?"

"That'd be a switch," Elle whispered, disgusted by the sight of the hate-monger on her screen. So much of her terror stemmed from his unending reach and influence.

She hated him for it.

"Thank you for coming on such brief notice," the host added, itching to put the awkwardness behind him. "I understand the book tour's taking you all across the nation."

"All over the world, brother," Jack replied, straightening his lapels. "God's message doesn't stop here at home. No sir... This is a global movement."

Elle tapped the brochure against her thigh, sipping her Alka-Seltzer.

Tanner winked at the host. "I was reluctant to accept yer invitation at first, but publicity's publicity. Even if it's on this joke of a program."

"That hurts, Jack," the host chuckled, fanning himself with his cue cards. "You didn't want to do the show? Care to tell me why?"

"We're grownups," the Reverend said, slapping the host's knee, gripping it like a pit-bull playing with a bone. "I know what y'all say about me on this tabloid network... You, in particular, ain't spewed nuthin I can't handle. Some uh yer cohorts—they can take their lies about me and my cause and stick em where the sun don't shine."

The host's face was awash in a dumbstruck flush of pink that made his widened eyes pop a vibrant white. "I apologize, Reverend. We try to be fair, sir."

"We on a delay?"

"Yessir. Five-seconds."

"Then cut the bullshit, friend," Tanner said with a grin. "Y'all had it out for me ever since that liberal-Jew president y'all got took over. This network turned into Satan's commode, lemme tell ya."

The host cocked his head, offended, which the Reverend enjoyed. "You make it difficult to agree with your worldview, Jack. Some might even say it's—hateful... My liberal-Jew network president included."

"You wanna get real?" Tanner asked, leaning forward like a

cowboy in a rickety seat at a saloon poker table, eye to eye with the host. "The Kil'Durians ain't the benevolent saviors you think they are, you blind idiots. They're demons from the stars, come to do Satan's bidding and make y'all forget who's got true dominion over life and death... God."

A single tear slid down Elle's cheek, spattering on the pamphlet in her hand.

She needed to turn off the television, but didn't.

What if he was right?

"They're golden calves from the black unknown. Poetic as that sounds, it won't be when you're sizzling in the pits of hell for partaking of their forbidden fruits. Put your faith in a race of freaks instead of your sovereign creator and see what happens. I dare you."

The host balked, unable to feign diplomacy any longer. Not with Tanner's pompous mug in his face. "Wiping out China's pollution was in the devil's name? The eradication of Ebola, AIDS, and HIV—was the product of Satan? You're serious?"

"As a heart attack," Tanner barked. "There'll always be concessions in war, even the holy ones."

"On the subject of wars... The Kil-Durians brokered more treaties in one year than man has in all of human history. You mean to tell me the burgeoning world-peace we enjoy today is the work of the devil? Future generations may never have a clue what nuclear proliferation is."

"Yeah, well those people are blind sheep."

"Your worldview astounds me."

Tanner lorded over the host in full-on preacher mode, turning to the audience. "Let's not forget their greatest contribution! Clones! What a blessing, right? Please! Never was there a more abominable sin in all existence and y'all eat it up like starving dogs!"

"That seems unfair, Jack… Have you never loved someone so much you'd do anything to see them again?"

"Not if it meant falling from God's grace, no! What're a few decades to wait if you end up seeing them again forever in the afterlife? Who's that damn impatient? Don't be such crybabies."

The host looked out into the audience, "Any clones in the studio tonight?"

Over a dozen people raised their arms, some more hesitant than others.

The host presented the Reverend with these nameless faces, "What do you have to say to these individuals given a second chance at life? What do you tell these clones, Jack?"

Tanner inched toward the gallery, scanning the lifted hands in the crowd. "Frankenstein's creation didn't ask to be born, but he was still a monster, wasn't he?"

"Jesus! Have you any decency?"

"More than these abominations, friend!"

"That's it! I'll not have you insult my audience!" the host asserted. "Cut the feed!"

"Only God has dominion over our souls, not these fucking aliens! Y'all are headed for hell, those of you stupid enough to think you have a say in His divine plan! You will burn!"

"Go to commercial!"

"You're the monster," Elle said, awash in tears. Her lips glistened with the salty slickness of self-loathing. She'd grown disgusted with herself for letting Jack Tanner get inside her head. Like Evanscorp, he was everywhere. A moral counterbalance to an amoral technological giant. Or so the Reverend would assert.

There was no escaping the prison of their influence.

Elle wanted to tear up the brochure, but her heart refused to let her pass up the chance to see Lance again. She set it down on the end-table at her side, sliding her fingertips across the polished wood finish. Her digits brushed against a framed photo of her and her handsome beau on their wedding day. This picture was her favorite. Lance's enormous hands cradled Elle's delicate smile as they kissed for the first time as husband and wife. She sensed his touch at that very moment, reliving the memory staring back at her through the frame.

So much promise and hope.

Their possibilities once seemed endless.

Could they ever be again?

Hours passed and Elle grew no closer to dozing off. The oscillating fan, driving stale air across her king-sized bed, sometimes helped lull her to sleep once upon a time. Lance lived then. He'd run his fingers along her skin, inducing the sweetest of dreams she no longer remembered. They vanished, as did the hands sliding toward her every night to show her how much she mattered.

"I can still feel you," she whispered, lost in thought, running her hand across his side of the sheets. They were wrinkle-free enough to make Elle long for a little disarray in her lonely, ordered existence. She yearned for chaos.

Chaos meant motion.

Motion was life.

And death, to the widow with a tucked flag in a blanket-chest at the foot of her empty bed. Her knees pulsed with the phantom pain of collapsing on the front steps that morning. It was the first and last time her senses came into contact with that folded symbol of sacrifice. She could smell his casket (or whatever it was they stored him in back at the base) across the fabric. It forced her to think of him as no spouse should ever have to see their loved one in their dim mind's eye. Elle sought refuge in the moonlight that night.

Tonight was no different.

She sloughed off her bed, sauntering outside, leaning over the balcony. The blades of green blanketing her land looked almost purple in the early morning haze. The moon was a lavender flower frozen in the sky, surrounded by diamonds blinking in and out of existence. Still, it wasn't enough to lift Elle's spirits.

She closed her eyes, and the world soon followed.

There was nothing at first, but when she concentrated with more than her mind, she sensed Lance's touch upon her skin. His warmth caressed her face through the icy breeze. In life, he used to comb through her soft hair as she inhaled his woody musk by starlight. That same comforting scent wafted through the air now.

It brought her peace.

So many of her tears dried upon her skin that last year, but something unseen wiped them away for her at that moment.

Elle could have told herself it was the wind, but she knew it was Lance. She believed it was his soul working through the elements, desperate to be at her side. It made her realize an ineluctable truth she'd been running from since the day he died.

He never left.

Not even in death.

If her Marine was in heaven, he was miserable being there without her. She was certain of it, knowing him better than she knew herself. They were two sides of the same coin. If roles reversed, Lance would not have passed up the chance to hold his wife again, even if it meant going to hell.

Elle Shepherd understood what she had to do.

May 22nd, 2028

A foul stench belched from the overflowing sink. Hugo, the Strunk family's mangy cat, pawed at a piece of moldy pepperoni floating in the muck like a meaty lily-pad. The poor thing was so hungry. Her wet-food was bone-dry and her dry-food soaked in water dripping off the counter.

Hugo was nimble once, but years of malnourishment made her weak and uncoordinated. She slipped on a bottle cap as she stretched over the murky pool. Never was a feline so desperate to dig their claws into a rotten hunk of meat.

She almost had it.

"Git!" Barry Strunk barked, seizing the cat by the scruff of her neck. "Fuck's wrong with you, girl?" He set the animal on the floor, tossing the muddy dry-food atop the mounting trash by the back door. He poured her a fresh dish of stale munchies. "Ain't nobody but me do shit in this dump, Hugo, fuckin swear to God."

The pet *MEOWED* in agreement, burying her face in her bowl.

Barry grabbed a half-empty carton of milk from the fridge, pouring a thick sludge over his cereal. *PLOP.*

He punched the table in a teenage rage, "Fuck me, man!"

"Shut up in there! It's four in the goddamn morning! Some of us got actual jobs to go to in a few hours, fuckin ghoul!" an angry, exhausted, voice slurred.

"Suck it, Joe! Just cus you bang my mom don't mean you can screw with me too, prick!"

"Get yer twenty-year-old ass outta my house if you don't like it then, ya ungrateful little shit! Keep it down in there!"

Barry said nothing, stewing in his rickety kitchen chair. He knew Joe was right, even if he hated the guy. If he wanted a better existence, he had to get one on his own. After so many years subsisting under his druggie mom's thumb, the kid decided he'd had enough.

There comes a time in every person's life when their lack of choice forces them to choose what they're willing to lack.

Barry's guidance counselor said that when he earned his GED. It sank in three years later.

"Text message muffukka!" his phone barked, vibrating through his dirt-covered Dickies.

Supposed to be here four minutes ago, dumbass. Get a move on or you're fired in ten, his shift supervisor texted.

The chair flipped on its back, almost crushing Hugo as Strunk shot to his feet. "Fuck me!" he exclaimed.

"What did I say, Barry?" Joe hollered, banging against the wall with his (presumably) enormous fist. "Yer askin for an ass beatin, boy!"

"I ain't my mom, motherfucker. I'll hit you right back!"

There was no reply.

Strunk set his seat on its legs, ramming it against the dinner table. "What I thought… Bitch," he grumbled, about to take his bowl of rotten milk to the sink. He looked down at the putridness, returning it to the tabletop with a cruel grin on his stubbly face.

"Yo, breakfast's waiting for ya, dick!" he screamed, slamming the back door shut on his way out.

Barry sprinted over the knoll, hardhat slipping out from under his arm when he saw his boss. He was a pudgy guy leaning against a lifted pickup idling beside an excavation crane that dwarfed it. Their skinny coworker, Raul, was in the middle of a very animated story by the look of his expressive hands.

The supervisor looked over his shoulder when he heard footsteps over the hill. He tapped on his watch with a stern finger. "What's it gonna take to light a fire under your ass, Strunk?" He backhanded Raul's concave chest, "Even this fuck-up arrived on time, kid!"

"Why you gotta be like that, jefe?" Raul mumbled,

massaging his sore, tatted-up pecs. "We was bonding n' shit."

The supervisor slapped on his hard-hat, tossing Raul the spare in his truck-bed. "Don't be a fag, son… Enough talk, let's haul this sumbitch up already. Got a breakfast date at sunup, ladies, so hustle."

Raul's nose crinkled. "Who goes on a date in the morning, yo?"

"Someone tryin to fuck by the afternoon," Barry said, snickering.

"Whatever." The supervisor walked up to his boys carrying three shovels, handing out two. "I dig this one. Gotta do the whole shit-shower-shave deal. Ever get close to a broad when you smell like the Cryptkeeper's taint? Not pretty."

"Don't pretend you some saint, yo. You'll be screwing her by brunch," Raul said. "That's what white people call it, right? Brunch?"

The supervisor shook his head, amused. "I'll settle for fucking by nightfall if I gotta. Besides, goin for the breakfast. You ain't lived till you had steak and eggs at this joint, I'm tellin ya."

Raul gave his boss a slow once-over, zeroing in on his waistline. "You know you a fat-fuck when you trade pussy for food… Priorities, jefe."

The supervisor winked, "Never said I didn't plan on eating both, son."

Raul whipped a ghetto finger-snap, chuckling. "This muffukka dirty, yo!"

Barry inhaled the chilly, pre-dawn air, staring down at the job a few feet away. "Can we get this guy out uh the ground already? Freezing my nuts off out here."

The men suited-up, securing winch-straps to the headstone jutting from the dewy grass. It was in the shape of an American eagle with USMC etched above the name carved into the stone. It didn't appear as old as some others surrounding it.

"Start shoveling topsoil," the supervisor said, turning to Raul. "Pay attention for once, son. Almost ran you over with the crane last time we were out here, ya damn…" He hesitated for a moment, scratching the side of his temple. "Whaddaya call a dumbass in Mexican again? Ben-day-hoe?"

Raul smirked, "Yep, that's it, jefe… Ben-day-hoe." He gave his boss a salute, waiting for him to get far enough away before turning to Strunk. "Pendejo."

"Thought he'd never leave," Barry said, tossing a tuft of grassy dirt over his shoulder. "Ain't no way in hell any woman's fucking that guy. He's dreamin, bro."

Raul leaned close. "Wanna buy more shit? My cousin came back from Tijuana, yo. Got the hookup; whatever you need. Weed? Blow? H?" He glanced at the shaved scalp beneath Barry's filthy hardhat. "Some fuckin Rogaine?"

"I shave my shit, dickhead," Barry said, tossing another hunk of grass over his shoulder. "Bossman's the one goin bald, not me. He needs that shit bad."

"Homeboy needs alotta things, yo."

"Except more food; backwoods-Santa-lookin motherfucker… Hey, will you dig already, ya lazy spic?"

Raul drove his shovel into the earth, leaning against it instead of digging. "So no drugs for my man, Barry, then? Serio?"

Strunk's leer was as steadfast as his reply. "No more… I'm done."

"Like, for good, no more?"

Barry stopped shoveling, following Raul's lead and driving his spade into the dirt. "For good."

"You're serious," Raul said, pained to lose one of his best customers. "Why, yo? How come? Is it my shit? Cuz I can always get better product, you only gotta lemme know."

"Look at us, Raul," Strunk growled, making sure the fat-man wasn't within earshot. "We dig up corpses for bullshit money then go home to nobody that gives a damn afterword… It's time for a change."

"My moms says these are the years we supposed to be stupid, yo. Why you putting all this, like, pressure on yerself n' shit?"

Barry resumed his digging, "She had you when she was twelve… Check you out now. I'm not ending up like her or you… Not anymore."

Raul flipped off his friend, burrowing into the earth with a smarmy grimace on his mug. "We got our whole lives ahead of us, yo."

Barry ran his fingers across the letters etched into the marble headstone at his feet.

Here lies Lt. Lance Shepherd, 06/16/2008 - 05/18/2027

Strunk couldn't take his gaze off the marker, resting his palm atop the Eagle perched over Lance's name. "Did this guy have his life ahead of him too? He was five when I was born… Five." He looked at Raul with somber eyes. "I'm not ending up like him… When I go out, I'm going out strong. I'm gonna be somebody."

Raul believed him.

A few hours passed by the time the trio exhumed the mangled corpse of Lance Shepherd. His remains were in such ghastly shape, it made Strunk awash in gratitude for the first time in his life. Here was a man about to get another shot at existence, same as Barry, but unlike Barry, he had to die in flames to earn it.

Strunk's choice to fight for a decent life was almost arbitrary by comparison, but he was eager for the chance in the same way this stranger was about to be. He could feel it.

No, he didn't survive two tours of duty only to be taken from everyone he held dear.

No, he couldn't know the abject loneliness of those left behind.

But that was only because he had nobody to leave behind.

Barry was alone, same as Lance, who had been rotting in a wooden box for over a year, stolen from his wife, the sun, and the stars. Like Strunk, this man became nothingness in an ongoing, busy world that didn't care if he existed. Anything and anyone who couldn't keep up with life's pace withered in the dust of its fleeting promises.

But soon, Lance would exist once again, and the gaps of time would have to catch up to him instead.

What a beautiful notion that must have been.

More powerful than any high Barry ever chased in his veins, that was for certain.

Strunk could never understand what that kind of purity felt like, but he knew how much of a gift it was. An immeasurable treasure infecting him with a sensation he'd never experienced before.

Ambition.

Strunk was about to turn his life around, but the corpse at his feet cemented his resolve to shape fate itself.

Though so many thoughts raced through Barry's mind, only four words stood out above all others. He looked upon the charred skull (peering into his soul) bearing one thought.

Thank you, Lance Shepherd.

Chapter 2: Worthy

It hovered in the black of space, drifting at a glacial pace so minute it didn't seem to be moving at all, but it was. A communication satellite orbiting earth slingshotted past, dwarfed by its monolithic, crustacean-like form.

The human eye could have mistaken it for some kind of technopod, but it wasn't alive.

This was the Thrakrah-Krikari, an expedition-class Xilan dwarfing the Kil'Durian fleet's most lethal War-Slykas. She was a peacekeeping vessel, the crown jewel of the Imperial Airmada, and home away from home to its ruling family, led by the great Khoth Vulgrell and his Empress, Qhan Unda of Aurell'Kah.

If a Xilan's aesthetic reflected its inhabitants, the sharp jagged forms of the Thrakrah-Krikari represented the deepest parts of Vulgrell's heart.

He was a fearsome warrior in his youth (still donning the war-braid he earned on the night of his blooding), long before his ascent. His cunning saw him catapult to the apex of power, but it was his ruthlessness that allowed him to preserve it. Vulgrell's darkness was his strength, matched by his terrifying muscularity and physical prowess.

But he was no fool.

Far from it.

As the Xilan orbited the planet below, the Khoth brooded in his study, focused on his secret task. His scaly brow furrowed as he scanned the human faces scrawling across the alien display in his massive clutches.

This kraith looks promising, Vulgrell thought, tapping on an image of a man with a sharp jawline and strict buzz-cut. The screen became awash in mammalian glyphs and symbols beside a 3D turntable of the male he selected.

Vulgrell's mouth contorted as he mouthed the words on the screen. "L… Lons Sh… Shep-hard." He squinted his milky-white eyes, snarling in frustration. "Bankrah gogih xabannitrakka!" *Fuck this blasted language!* he hissed, switching the interface back to Kil'Durian.

He scanned the kraith's readout.

Athletic.

Obedient.

Lethal combat knowledge.

The Khoth settled into his gaudy throne, relieved for the first time in a long while.

His search was over.

"Ni nisar… Zantrakka zutzan gih zangro," he whispered.

At last…

One who is worthy.

Burning tobacco enveloped the penthouse as Dr. Vera Wild stormed through the doors. Her heels bounced off the marble pillars like she was in a cathedral. Crystal-blue water streaming from a fountain on her left dampened her steps. She passed a grand-piano on her right, set beside a pool-table nobody ever used. They looked so pristine in her periphery.

It didn't surprise her, given who's office this was.

Like the man who worked out of this opulent waste of

money, this suite was rich, hollow, and all about appearances. From the golden trimmed tiles to the polished Italian shoes atop his stretched mahogany desk.

Sander Evans loved it that way too, chewing on his Cohiba as Vera marched down his ivory walkway. He hated his stepsister but admired her model-like stride. It was as lengthy as her temperament for dealing with his bullshit was short.

"What do you want?" Wild asked, arms crossed.

Sander chomped his cigar, "Aliens need us lookin after a special clone. Top priority shit."

"'Top priority' how?"

"How the hell should I know?"

"You didn't think to ask?"

"Correction: What the hell do I care? That's what I meant to say, my bad."

Sander's stogy wafted into Vera's nostrils, tickling the cilia in her nasal passages as it burned her throat. She abhorred cigars, and he knew it, but she refused to satisfy him by showing it. "Did the subject die of natural causes?" she asked.

Sander exhaled a plume of smoke, "Does it matter?"

"Very much so, yes... Did the subject die naturally or not?"

Evans nestled into his gaudy leather armchair, amused with himself. "If by 'natural causes' you mean the bomb that tore his ass apart 'naturally' killed him, then yeah."

Vera leaned over her brother's desk, fighting the urge to shove his putrid stogy down his throat. "You're a sonofabitch, you know that?"

Sander offered Wild a cruel wink, "You could say the guy went out with a bang."

"We need to stop this horrid cloning business altogether. Let these people rest. You said we'd discuss shutting it down in the coming months—five fucking months ago."

"Yep, well," Evans grinned, "never was the punctual type, Vere. Surprised you haven't figured that out yet." He jerked his sleeve up, checking his watch. "Our friend should hatch any day now. Might even imprint on ya if you get there in time."

Vera balked, washing her hands of the situation, turning her back on Sander and storming from his desk. "Find someone with the hours to waste, because I assure you, that isn't me. I'm a geneticist, not a damn babysitter... Not doing it."

"Yes. You are."

Wild skidded to an angry stop, rearing toward her abominable step-brother. "I am not going down there." She stormed up to Evans with authority in her voice. "I refuse to watch that man scream his lungs out all over again just so you can appease those creatures! It's reprehensible, Sander! Cruel!"

"It's business, like you said, sugar-tits," Sander fired back, angered by Vera's anger. "We're the only ones who handle it for em, and I plan on keeping it that way, understand? End of discussion! You're gonna take that ass of yours, the one with a big stick jutting out of it, straight to the lab, and you're gonna welcome this asshole to the world a second time!"

"I will not!"

Evans erupted out of his seat, fuming. "Do it or you'll be packing up before the days out! I mean it, Vera!"

Wild leaned over the desk, unflinching before her bully brother. "I'm part owner of this company, you amoral dolt."

Sander took his cigar to his lips, inhaling deep, and blowing a massive plume of smoke into Wild's face. "You sure about that?"

Chilled air separated the outside world from Agatha Wild's cliff-side grotto. A sweet aroma emanated from the rock-steps descending into the lower area. Eroding rapids and springs cascading against the cavern walls gave off a certain scent. It reminded Vera of her globe-trotting days, back when she was adventurous. A time before her career—and step-brother—

turned her into a boring misandrist. She loved the taste of nature, the cleanness of it, but that delicious odor waned the deeper she descended. Chlorine replaced the flavour of the rocks, and classical music drowned out the spring-water raining beyond her mother's Olympic-pool.

Wild helped herself to a martini shaker behind the liquor-bar to the side of the stairs as her mother paddled in the shallows.

A tall man in his forties led the frail woman toward the pool-steps. He said something to her before getting out and drying off his legs. Agatha smiled, watching her therapist walk over to the bar.

"How's she doing today?" Vera asked, pouring her shaken martini into a glass without a glance at the man.

The therapist set his towel on the countertop, scratching the side of his head with a sullen smirk. "You don't wanna know, Ms. Wild."

Vera nodded, sipping her drink. "Understood."

The man looked back at Agatha, "I realize she needs exercise and all, but I'm not sure how effective my services are anymore… Swimming's the last of her worries now."

Wild leaned to the side, peering around the man, eying her mother wading in place as she sat by the edge of the pool. The seventy-year-old was aloof, yet contented, unburdened by the misery of forgetting who she was.

"I'll decide when you're no longer needed," Vera said, looking square in the man's eyes as she took her glass to her lips. "She looks happy. Whatever you're doing is still working."

"She's forgetting how to breathe."

A sharp pain radiated from the side of Wild's jaw, below her ear. "I see," she said, unclenching her teeth. "I take it you don't mean only while swimming?"

"That's right."

Vera glanced down at her glass, exhausted and defeated.

"We'll discuss your departure at the end of the week. Does that work for you?"

The therapist sensed the anxiety and helplessness in Vera. He wished he could say something hopeful, but it would only make things worse by trying. All he could do was nod with pursed lips too tense to brandish a convincing smile.

Wild appreciated it. "Okay then."

"Okay."

An old voice cackled in the background, "Vera, darling, is that you? It's about time you came to visit me!"

"I'm here every day, mother," Wild replied, moving out from behind the bar, toward the edge of the pool. "You're so busy, you never see me, that's all." She knelt down, leaning in to kiss her mother's paper-thin cheek. "How was your swim, lady?"

"Oh my, good. Good!" Agatha answered, inching close to her daughter as if about to tell a secret. "I'm training for my first meet. Isn't that exciting, darling? Uncle Raymond will be there! He's bringing his new wife, Cindy."

Vera grinned despite knowing her great Uncle had been dead for twenty years, and Cindy, for eleven. "I can't wait to see her," she whispered.

"Who, darling?"

There was an uncomfortable silence.

"Mother, do you know anything about reabsorbing the shares of Evanscorp you left to me? Think hard, please... As best as you can."

"Goodness, Vera, I'm not senile. I remember. Sander and his sister brought up some excellent points."

"What points did he and Toni make?"

"Well, he suggested I hold on to your stake in the company until you had a child. Very savvy, if I may say. A lot of red tape, but trust us, it's for your own good, in case anything happened to you. Sander loves you very much. He doesn't want your shares falling into the wrong hands, and who can blame him?" Agatha tittered, covering her mouth like a schoolgirl. "If you think about it, this is a smart motivator to get you to give me a grandchild too, darling."

"That sonofabitch," Vera said through a gritted whisper.

"What's the matter, sweetheart?"

Wild cupped her mother's chin, almost leering at the woman who gave her life. "Sander knows I'm infertile, mother… You did too, once upon a time."

Agatha clutched her child's hand. "I know you are. Why bring up something so painful? Vera, sometimes I worry about you."

"The feeling's mutual."

The void is silent and cold. A vacuum in time where minutes and centuries are one. There is no life or death here. There is nothing…

A faint amniotic WHOOSH churns in the immaterial blackness, followed by a human pulse. The thumping is slow, gaining traction with every activating neuron. Something ushers the birth of a long-dormant consciousness.

An ember spark ignites in the aether, and as the flame grows, so too does the discomfort. It's like a bee-sting at first, crescendoing into an agonizing tear through a once-lost soul aflame. The raging fire illuminates the fallen. Charred faces smolder in the glow of incomplete memory, shrouded by the darkness of a nascent mind.

A voice wants to cry out, but there is no sound, only the terrifying gasp of searing lungs. A frustrated dead tongue beckons to relearn every word it ever spoke in mere seconds. Like an obese person with sleep-apnea jutting upright in oxygen-deprived terror, this soul fears the silent void of death whence it came. Words are its air, and it is suffocating.

It must live.

It must think and feel.

*It **must** speak.*

"It burns!" Lance hollered, jolting forth, tearing through his amniotic bodybag in anguish.

"Sedative. Now," Vera ordered, clipboard in hand as she stood before the birthing pool with a clinical eye on Shepherd.

Two nurses pinned down Lance's upper limbs as a third injected a fast-acting medication into his feisty forearm.

The drug hit him in an instant. "I love you, Elle... I love you, baby..." he slurred, fighting to keep his eyes open. "Wha... What's happening to me?"

"Welcome back, Mr. Shepherd," Vera said with a dry smile. "Try not to tense up, you're experiencing residual cognition. It should pass soon, but you can help the process by relaxing. I've seen people go straight into cardiac arrest right out of the womb."

"Residual-what? Cardiac arrest? Lady, where the hell am I? Who are you?" Lance asked, mumbling, shielding his eyes from the surgical light overhead. "Am I still in Siberia? There was a blast, that's all I remember... What about my team? Where's my unit?"

"So many questions to answer. Let's start with the pertinent ones." Wild swiveled the lamp away from Lance's face. "I don't know what became of your crew, but I can tell you you aren't in Siberia. This is Evanscorp Medical, Lieutenant, and my name is Dr. Vera Wild. I'm the senior geneticist here."

"The hell I need a geneticist for?" Lance asked, wincing when his new abdominal muscles contracted for the first time as he sat up. "My skin's on fire."

Vera nodded at the liquid in the birthing pool. "That amnio-gel is forty degrees. Give your hypothalamus a moment to catch up."

"Hypothalamus?"

"Just wait a bit, please."

Shepherd's eyes darted around the sterile room. "Where's Elle? Where's my wife?"

"Waiting for you at home, Lieutenant. I'm returning you to her, personally."

"How long was I out of commission? I don't remember a damn thing after the blast..."

"Before I say anything further," Vera cleared her throat, "there are some matters to discuss."

The drive home from Price Airport was a slide-show of faded recollections deep in Lance's mind. It reminded him of his great-grandmother and her dusty old picture-albums. The woman reeked of death and sweat, which alone was excusable at her age. It was only a problem when she sat too close, forcing him to look at photos of folks even older than her. It overwhelmed him with the most underwhelming of sensations.

Boredom.

Apathy.

Numbness.

That's how Lance felt riding shotgun in Vera's expensive rental-car.

"I don't belong here," he said.

"Not uncommon for someone in your situation to experience existential hardship," Vera replied. "Normal feelings, given the circumstances. Nobody expects you to come from a petri-dish and *not* question your identity."

Lance looked askance at Vera, "You're no therapist, that's for damn sure."

Wild grinned, "Never had to cultivate bedside manner before."

Shepherd nodded. "If I could handle getting blown up, I can beat this, right?" He shrugged it off. "None of it'll matter once Elle's in my arms. All this, whatever the hell it is I got swimming around in my head, she'll fix it. She fixes everything."

A bleak gaze washed over Vera's countenance. "She's lucky to have someone who loves her the way you do. Others aren't so fortunate."

"Takes little. Just gotta try, ya know? Pound the pavement, find that one workaholic you can't live without."

"Workaholic?" Wild asked.

"You sure as hell ain't the relaxing type."

"What makes you believe I was speaking about myself?"

"All in the eyes, Doc."

Vera cracked a half-smile, "I can see why Elle missed you. Thanks for the candor, Mr. Shepherd."

"I oughta be thanking you. I felt shitty before you spoke. No offense."

"None taken. I'm a workaholic, always have been."

"How's that going for ya?"

"Never been much of an affectionate person, not in my youth anyway. It allowed me the opportunity to get as far as I have, to be frank."

"Lemme guess… Being in love seems needy in your book?"

Vera said nothing.

"It's okay, I saw plenty of those types in my day. This kid in my barracks was the worst of em all, like a fucking lapdog every time he'd video-chat with his girl. I'm talking full-on emotional-parasite status. He loved her though, we all knew it… Little bastard wouldn't shut up about the ring he bought her."

"Did they last?" Vera asked.

Shepherd leaned his head back, staring out the window, beyond the passing trees. "He got ripped in half by engine shrapnel on a routine patrol. IED." He smirked, grimly, "Something he and I got in common, now that I think about it."

"I'm sorry."

"That's war." Lance ran a finger along his lips. "We buried him with a photo of her in his breast pocket… I'd like to hope they would've stayed together… Don't matter now." He turned to Wild. "All I know is I wouldn't wanna be alone when that hourglass empties again. Grateful for my wife in a way no man who hasn't died can imagine."

"Blame my parents for any shortcomings if it ever comes to that," Vera said, not joking.

Shepherd grinned. "You're a tough lady. Strong."

"Thank you."

"Be careful. Strength can become a weakness if you let it, trust me. Turns people too cold."

Vera shuddered, knowing how right the man was. "Wilds aren't known for their warmth," she whispered.

Lance sensed he'd touched a soft spot. His gaze drifted toward the minty-green grass and blue sky beyond the window. "My C.O. lived in Los Angeles, and for the life of me, I couldn't convince him these places still existed."

Relief washed over Vera, thankful to not be talking about herself anymore. "Looks like a living canvas out here," she said.

Beads of sweat dribbled down Lance's brow as they cruised past the old Kershaw Windmill.

"We're almost home," he whispered.

Chapter 3: Home

TINK TINK TINK. "Got it off!" Harry Kojimatsuo pulled away the air-conditioning vent cover, setting it beside his ladder. He yanked a rag out of his slender overalls, drying his forehead and neck down. Elle Shepherd came around the corner bearing a glass of iced-lemonade.

"Can't tell you how much I appreciate this, Hare," she said, handing the cup to Harry.

He grinned, taking the drink to his parched lips. "Keep these coming, and we'll be nice and square."

"No, I mean it. If it weren't for you and Kat, I woulda lost my mind by now."

"Enough," Harry said, descending the ladder. "Neighbors do this stuff, okay?" He looked up at the air-conditioner with a sly brow, "I would consider a warranty next time. This is fix number three? Four?"

"Five," Shepherd answered, embarrassed. "I'm gonna do something nice for you soon, I promise."

Kojimatsuo balked, shaking his head. "Will you stop with that crap? You see me standing here with a ledger tallying up all my good deeds, lady?"

Elle hugged him tight, her misty eyes soaking into Harry's shirt. "Thank you. With everything the *aliens've* done... Still feels like honourable *people* are scarce sometimes, ya know?"

"Yeah… I do," Harry replied.

She ambled back, wiping away her tears. "I'll go check on lunch."

Her neighbor nodded with a somber smile. He was no stranger to human ugliness. His name wasn't even Harry, it was Hariyuki Fukoshimi Kojimatsuo, but he changed it at the height of the war. Nobody took his calls because of a conflict with a different Asian culture. That doesn't matter to a racist. Chinese. Japanese. Ko-rean. They all looked the same to bigots in Jefferson Parish. The sad thing was, Harry was born in Louisiana. It hurt that his wife, Katya, was an Ukranian refugee.

It's a miracle they lasted in that backwater dump as long as they did.

The turning point came when Harry got a call from the owner of MARSHALL'S TAVERN. When he saw the big-ass Confederate flag hanging above the liquor cabinet, he knew he was in danger. Jobe Marshall and his three sons took one hard look at the gook and told him to git the fuck out of their fuckin bar.

Kojimatsuo never moved so fast in his life.

Unfortunately for him, Jobe's eldest son was a white-nationalist, eleven years strong.

Harry didn't see the truck, but after a few lane changes, he noticed the same puke-yellow high-beams in his rear-view mirror. Katya was home, so he couldn't lead this beast of a rig there.

He pulled into the Jefferson Parish Police department's parking lot.

It seemed like a smart idea.

"Witchu doin in ma spot, boy?" asked a deep, gruff voice.

"I was being followed, officer."

"Only police is allowed in'nese spots, citizens park onna street." The cop locked eyes with Harry. "You is a citizen,

aintcha?"

"Yes, sir. Born right here in Louisiana."

The officer eyed Harry hawkishly. "Cough up dentification," he barked. "Hurry it up."

Kojimatsuo hesitated.

"Somethin ta hide, son?

"No, sir."

The cop smirked. "So git to it then, I ain't got all night."

Kojimatsuo handed the officer his wallet, trying not to seem reluctant about it.

The cop shined his light on Harry's ID. "I'll be damned, you were born here," he said, perusing the man's photos.

"The hell you doing, deputy?"

"Cute little lady, Mr. Chan. Almost looks Russian. She Russian?"

You know goddamn well my last name isn't Chan, *Harry thought. His blood boiled like a teakettle on the stove too long. "I want your badge number!"*

"Don't wad yer oriental panties in a bunch." The cop flung Kojimatsuo's wallet through the window like a spent cigarette butt.

"Badge number, mister... Now!"

The cop whipped out his gun and put it to Harry's temple. "I'll give ya more'n that if ya don't shut up, fuckin zipperhead. You sacks uh shit murdered my grandpappy in Korea, Charlie. My niece lost her husband to you filthy nips in China a year ago last week. I should blow yer yelluh face off in their honor."

Harry pressed his forehead into the barrel of the cop's gun. "I'm Japanese, you ignorant asshole."

The cop brandished a wicked smile, "You got balls, Charlie. If you wanna keep em, I'd take yer wonton-lovin ass the fuck outta my town. Drag that hook-nosed Roosky whore uh yers with ya." The officer slapped the top of Kojimatsuo's car and tipped his hat.

"Drive safe now... Never—"

"—Can tell who's behind ya," Harry whispered, recalling that horrid night with vivid clarity.

He tightened the air-conditioner's bolts, thankful to be anywhere but Louisiana.

WHAM! An arm snaked around Kojimatsuo's neck, yanking him off the ladder. "What the hell are you doing in my home?" a voice hissed. "Who are you? Where's Elle?"

Harry's vision was blurring the harder his attacker squeezed. He glimpsed his neighbor in the corner of his eye. "Get out of the house, Elle! Run!"

"Lance! Lance, let him go! He's a friend!"

Shepherd recognized that voice, loosening his strangle-hold on the stranger in his clutches as he reared toward the woman of his dreams for the first time in his fresh life.

"Elle?" he asked, almost fearfully. "Please don't let all this be a fucking dream, God."

"If it is, we're dreaming it together," she whispered.

Lance idled, motionless, blind to everything but the woman standing before him. Her hair was so different now, and the frown-lines etched into her forehead showed a heartbreaking passage of time, but so much was still the same. The cute way she squinted when she was trying to hold back her tears was familiar, as was the red plaid sweater she was wearing. He made her wear it on their first date after a harsh evening thunderstorm soaked her cardigan on the way back to his truck. She never returned it and he never asked for it back, but he didn't want to.

She always looked sexy in his clothes.

Now was no different.

"Are you still the man I married?" Elle asked, echoing his fearful sentiment, uncertain of reality now that he was standing before her looking so handsome and alive.

A soft smile crept across Lance's lips, "Till the day I die—

again."

Elle dashed into his arms, "I missed you so much!"

"I'm here, baby," Lance whispered into her ear, clutching her tight. "I'm not going anywhere… Not this time."

"This is the great Lance Shepherd?" a hoarse voice asked.

In their rapture, Elle and her husband forgot all about the befuddled man panting in their hallway.

Harry got to his feet, a little wobbly but otherwise okay, massaging his throat. "I hear wonderful things," he said, coughing.

Vera waited beside the rental-car for an hour before Shepherd came to the front door.

"You forgot about me," she suggested, half-serious.

"Sorry… I was getting to know the neighbors," Lance said.

Chapter 4: The Sickness

Jan 3rd, 2030

Elle could tally the number of times she became ill over the last six or seven years on a single hand.

Waking up nauseated unnerved her.

She tossed over-the-counter cold and cough syrup into her grocery basket that morning. A memory in the back of her mind told her this wasn't a bug.

You listen to your Nana; the thought said. *Don't be messing around with them scoundrels the way your mother did. She was a straight-A student with a future before the sickness. You understand what that is, girly? God's way of preparing you for the hardships of parenting's what it is. You want the sickness? Have the sex like a little whore. You'll be knee high in baby vomit washing the stink of curdled cheese-shits outta your cloth diapers in no time flat, believe you me.*

Those words haunted Elle, unlike so many other insane things the spinster used to spout.

Out of curiosity, she picked up a pregnancy test even though she knew there was no reason to.

Clones were sterile.

* * *

Harry lumbered into Shepherd's backyard hauling a bundle of firewood. His spine felt like a shower pipe flooded with searing water. "You're killing me, brother," he said, dropping the lumber atop a pile five-feet-high.

Lance brushed the split wood off his hacking stump with the head of his ax, a satisfied grin splayed on his face. "I recall you owned a construction company once, Hare?" *CHOP!*

"Ever hear of *time off*?"

Shepherd wiped the sweat from his brow. "That's what sleep's for." He drove the cutter into his chopping block and looked down the grassy slope above his acre of land. "Think this is bad? Wait till Spring, buddy. Building a barn down there. Maybe a stable. Whaddaya say?"

"Dunno if I'll even have the time to help. Shop's been busy after the aliens gave that speech."

"What speech?"

"It was all over the news, how could you miss it? They addressed congress yesterday, man. Ever since their queen was awarded the Nobel Peace Prize, they seem to think it's their job to police the planet... They wanna co-author a bill to reduce firearms across the globe! They already got Germany, the UK, and Russia on board, it's on every network, brother!"

Lance yanked the ax from the stump at his feet. "Dunno if you noticed, but I like to be outside instead of plastered to the idiot box, Hare."

Kojimatsuo shrugged, "People are going nuts over it... All I'm saying."

"Good nuts or bad nuts?" Lance asked, breaking the seal on a fresh, cold, beer.

"A little of both, I guess? My shop's sold more guns the last week than I have in the last six months if that's any sign."

Shepherd chuckled, "This is Price Township." He chugged his drink in one massive swig. "Sure when babies are born here they're swaddled with a copy of the second amendment."

"I ain't bitchin, trust me," Harry said, reaching for a fresh beer of his own. "If the interstellar Gestapo comes a'knockin, I guess we'll be ready." He pounded his brew, and the brain freeze kicked in hard. "How'n the hell do you do that? Jesus," he grumbled.

"I doubt it'll come to that, Hare. The aliens are doing what they think's right." *CHOP!*

"So you agree with em? You were a Marine, for fuck's sake!"

CHOP! "I didn't say *that*, buddy… I'm pretty against it, I'm just saying I *understand* it." Shepherd wedged his ax into the block again, leaning his elbow against its knobby end.

"Don't see how you can be cool about it given what you did for a living."

Lance shook his head, "I'm not… The aliens've done right by us. I wouldn't be here without em, but if I'm gonna join the bandwagon and draw a line somewhere, it's at our guns." He pried his ax from the chopping block, checking the blade's edge. "Weapons'll always have their place."

"Says the guy who doesn't even own a gun," Harry said, arms crossed.

"Don't gotta own one to know everyone else has the right to."

"How patriotic."

Lance gave Kojimatsuo a slick wink, "Like you said… I was a Marine… Besides, what do I need one in the house for when my best friend owns a fucking gun shop? I'll just steal the ones under your bed if I need em."

Harry idled with a stern eye on his companion, recalling his life in Louisiana. "You'll be singing a different tune when you need one and don't have it. The world ain't as perfect as the aliens want us to think it is, Lance."

Shepherd set another hunk of wood on the chopping block. "I'm not saying it is." *CHOP!* "I know it's not paradise, but it's a helluva lot better than it was before they arrived. Safe enough to sleep with the door unlocked's good enough for me."

Harry crossed his arms, unamused, "I don't understand how a Marine can talk like that."

Lance grinned. "Get blown up sometime and you will."

"I'll pass," Kojimatsuo said, cracking open yet another cold one with a smirk.

"That the last beer?" Shepherd asked, parched.

Elle sat on the toilet seat, transfixed on the tiny device in her hand.

Lance strolled past the bathroom, stopping in his tracks when he saw his wife's tears. "Honey, you okay? What's with the waterworks?"

She said nothing.

Lance dashed to her side, "Baby, what is it?"

Elle cupped her mouth with a faraway look in her eye.

"Talk to me, beautiful," Lance whispered.

He gently pried her hand away from her lips, baffled by her wide smile.

"I'm pregnant," Elle said.

Jan 4th, 2030

Max Amhearst couldn't have been more uncomfortable if you gave him a chair made of razor blades. He hated fancy restaurants with a passion, preferring a greasy burger over kale. The guy had more money than most of the suits seated around him, but he was a blue-collar grease monkey at heart. A hot shower and cologne could never hide his signature fragrance: Parfum d'huile de voiture.

Better known by its common name, *the smell of car oil.*

Hard to imagine Vera Wild accepting a date with this guy, yet here he was, waiting.

And waiting.

And waiting.

Amhearst checked his watch again when *CLACKING* heels raced down the aisle. He poked his head out of the booth, spying Vera looking herself over in a framed painting's reflection. He slid back into his seat, recalling something his Uncle Gale once said. *If a hot-lookin woman cares enough to make sure she's good-lookin enough, that's how you know the broad's into ya.* Uncle Gale understood a thing or two about women.

Then again, he also used to say: *If you wanna shove it in, go for the Catholic broads, they never use condoms.*

"I didn't make you wait long, did I?" Vera asked, sliding into the booth, embarrassed.

"You're a busy woman, I understand," Max replied, smiling. "When did you get in?"

Wild flicked up her wrist, checking her Rolex. "About an hour ago."

"Oh, jeez. I would've taken a rain-check. You exhausted?"

"No, I wanted to," Vera said with an insistent smile. "Who wants to be alone when the hourglass empties, right?"

"Hourglass?" Amhearst asked.

Wild reached for her glass of water. "Nevermind," she said, taking a sip.

Max nodded. "How long are you in town?"

"Only for the funeral. I have to be back by Thursday."

"Shit, a *funeral*? Pardon my language… I assumed it was a *conference* or something. The way you spoke on the phone—you should be with your family right now—not on a date with this asshole."

Vera grinned. "Thoughtful, colorful speech, self-deprecating. Quite a first impression you've made and I've not even had time to order a drink."

Max ran a hand through his hair, astonished by Vera's cavalier nature. "Please say it wasn't someone close then."

"My mother," Wild said.

"Jesus-Christ on a stick, your *mom*? You gotta go be with your family, Vera."

"She was my only family. As for the others, they never cared about Agatha Wild."

Amhearst had a million questions that vanished the longer he looked into her gorgeous, but vacant eyes.

"It's the daddy-issues you gotta run from," he said with an awkward grin.

"I appreciate the concern all the same. Very gentlemanly, Max."

"Thanks… Still can't believe you said yes though."

"Why's that?"

"You're Vera Wild. You should be seeing someone like Hawking, or Tyson."

"Shouldn't you be dating a Knight? Or a Burnell?"

"I've had my eye on you for a while, so it's kinda surreal to be sitting here is all I'm saying."

"How long?" Vera asked. "Should I be freaking out?"

"First time I met you was at Julian Evans' country-club, a company mixer. Didn't expect you to remember, but we spoke."

"My step-father's been dead for four years."

Amhearst nodded, abashed. "Wonderful guy… Too bad I couldn't say the same for his kids."

"That's some crush."

"My mom always said the best things were worth waiting for."

"I'm a *thing* now, am I?"

"A thing of beauty," Max said, stone-faced and self-assured.

Vera stared down at the table, unsure what she thought while speaking. "Say tonight goes well—and against wise judgment, I went home with you. I wouldn't find an altar with my photo on it, would I? Or a lock of my hair in a box, or something horrific like that?"

Max smiled. "Haven't got close enough to snip off any locks yet, but there's no shrine... I *think*."

"Then we have no problem, other than your crippling procrastination."

"Well-put. That said, would you have accepted my invite had I asked you to dinner sooner?"

"Probably not. Your rugged features notwithstanding."

"At least you're not afraid to crush a man's ego... May I ask why?"

Vera pondered his question for a moment. She glanced at her bare wedding-ring finger. "Spent the last two years learning a lot about what it means to love. I've seen it in action. Figured I'd give dating a try if I wanted to reach that point someday."

"Never heard someone say that word so gravely before," Amhearst said.

"You're talking to a woman who's never *needed* anyone."

Max couldn't take his eyes off Vera. "At least you didn't wait till the second date to let that puppy slip out. You don't mince words, do you?"

"No more than you."

A flamboyant waiter sashayed up to the booth. "Ah, your date's arrived. Excellent. A minute longer and I was going to offer you a sympathy shot," he said with an obnoxious titter.

Vera sank into her seat, mortified.

Max simpered, admiring the beautiful genius across from him.

I don't give a shit what she says, I'm gonna marry this woman someday, he thought.

Chapter 5: Miracle

Sept 27th, 2030

"Another big push," the doctor said. "One, two, three."

Elle cried out in pain, the sharp wail of a newborn overtaking the chamber. She glanced at her spouse, who was dumbstruck by the sight of their second-old child in the doctor's palms. Lance loved children as much as his own dad, Calvin Shepherd, God rest his soul. Cal would have appreciated a grand-baby running around the homestead at Christmas.

When Lance discovered he would never be a parent, the initial person he thought of was his father. He would have given anything to stand beside Cal in the delivery room.

Cancer took him three months earlier.

Calvin Shepherd never minced words, making clear he didn't want to come back. He was glad to see his son get a second chance, but gray dogs like Cal had been around long enough. *Too damn long*, he used to quip.

A lone droplet leaked from Lance's eye when the doctor placed the baby in his arms. He didn't know if it was a tear of joy or sorrow.

Until he looked at his offspring.

The doctor smiled, "She's a healthy girl. Congratulations."

Wild studied the joyous couple, thinking of the nights she would cry herself to sleep beside Max.

How can a clone conceive a child, yet I can't?

"What's her name?" she spied the doctor asking beyond the mirror.

"Calla," she heard Lance answer. "Her name's Calla."

"Beautiful," Vera whispered.

BUZZ BUZZ. She reached into her breast pocket, reviewing the caller ID on her phone. "What do you want?" she said.

"Cute kid, or one of them uggos?" Sander asked.

"Unknown. I can tell you it's a *female.*"

"*It?* Jesus, Vera, I hope you didn't call her that to their faces."

"Don't be stupid, Sander."

"Only covering my bases. You're gonna be putting in a bunch of time with the kid. Can't have tension between you and her parents screwing things up now that the aliens need *her* watched."

Wild looked at the writhing baby in Elle's arms with a sense of longing teetering on torment. "Was this their plan all along?"

"Would you believe me if I said I didn't know?"

"Not a chance in hell, Sander."

"Guess it was heartless of me then, huh? *Oops.*"

Humans had numerous names for them, but they were *Kil'Durians.* All children of Kil'Dur had one name.

They called this being Acean, which translated into *the faithful attendant.* He lived up to his namesake, challenging all who did not adhere to the *Strodha,* Kil'Dur's ancient tome and truest voice of the Empire.

Sander didn't give two-shits about any of that. They could have been from planet Whogivesafuck for all he cared. "When am I gonna talk to the big guy? I'm done negotiating with mouthpieces, Ace."

"Khoth Vulgrell does not communicate with lesser minds, kraith."

"Whatever, ya cloaked gecko."

"Case in point. Such uncouth behavior."

Sander smirked, "Then take off that hooded bathrobe you're always slithering around in and show the world how pretty you are."

"My word should be your sole concern, not my visage," Acean hissed, tightening the sash at his midriff.

"Yeah, yeah, blah, blah. Don't fret, we're keeping tabs on your little heap of joy. We didn't screw up with the dad, did we? No, we did not."

Acean slithered around the desk, lording over Sander. "Kil'Durians do not relish condescension by lesser animals. Continue, and your tongue may yet reach my Khoth—after I rip it from your mouth."

Sander's smug grin faded, "No humor where you come from, is there?"

"Enough, kraith." Acean's predatory eyes fixed on the feeble being before him. "Observe the Leevahn and Khoth Vulgrell will compensate you per our arrangement. Do not and discover how distasteful these exchanges can be."

"That a threat, Ace?"

The alien leered at the human with stoic orbs. "Yes... I thought it was obvious."

Chapter 6: Proposal

Sept 28th, 2030

Vadim Volkov muscled his last push-up when his little girl, Afanasia, pounced atop his back.

The youngster was eight, but she had the spirit of her late grandfather, Baba Volkov. He was a steelworker who moonlit as a champion arm wrestler in the old country.

Baba would have been proud of his little vnooch-ka, Vadim thought. He carried his baby into the kitchen and sat her at his rickety table, massaging his lower back. "What's your mom been feeding you? You weigh a *ton*, baby cakes." He leaned down to give his child a kiss when he caught a whiff of something sour. "You smell that?"

"Smell what, Papa?" Afanasia asked, sniffing her armpits with a giggle.

Vadim shrugged it off with a bitter grin. Afanasia's mother wasn't the most attentive woman. She must have forgot to bathe the girl before dropping her off.

"Nevermind, vnooch-ka," Volkov said, opening the cupboard above his sink.

It was empty.

The Russian scratched his head, "What the hell? I went

shopping yesterday!"

"It's not a big deal, papa," his daughter replied. "Let's go play!"

"You need to eat something, honey. A growing girl needs food."

"Why do I need food, Papa?" The little lady's voice sounded withered. "I'm *dead*, remember?"

Volkov turned around, terrified by the mangled carcass reaching out to grasp him.

"I love you, papa," the corpse hissed.

RING RING!

Vadim darted upright in his bed, snatching his phone with a sweaty palm. "Thank you, whoever you are," he said, chest heaving.

"Afanasia?" Max asked, downtrodden.

"Yeah." Vadim wiped the beads from his brow. "Her birthday's coming up soon. It always gets worse."

"Sounds like you need a drink too."

Volkov checked the clock on his nightstand. "You know what time it is, right?"

"Rushing to go back to bed?"

"I got a spare room, don't worry about it." Vadim chugged the last of his sixth beer. "I say you dodged a bullet."

"We're not split up," Max said, his back against the booth cushions with his legs across the seat. "At least I don't think we are."

"How you figure? If you aren't great enough to marry, you're not good enough to live with in my book."

Amhearst ran his fingers through his hair, vexed. "Then I guess we are? Shit, I dunno. None of this makes any fuckin sense, Vad. One day, all's fine, she flies back and—"

Volkov flagged down the buxom waitress sashaying past

their booth. "Another round over here, please?"

The waitress pulled her notepad out of her apron pocket, "Hope you boys got a ride home."

"This man right here," Vadim had a solid grip on Max's shoulder, "this guy makes six thousand dollars a week. He has abs like my old mamma's steel washboard, and most important, a heart of platinum. Platinum, babe. If this guy—"

"Vad… don't," Max grumbled.

"Hey, you called me, remember?" Volkov eyed the woman's nipples, unabashed. "Knowing everything I told you… If this individual asked you on a date, what would you say? Be straightforward."

The waitress brandished a dry smirk. "I'd think there was something wrong with the dude. Dunno anyone dumb enough to walk away from all that. You some kinda basket-case?"

Max mustered a distracted nod. "I wasn't nine months ago."

His answer was just pathetic enough for the waitress. "You're hot, I'll give ya that," she said.

Vadim slugged Max's arm. "Nice! That calls for a brew." He shifted to the waitress. "What time you off, honey? He's got a huge rear seat. You can get to know each other."

Amhearst shook his head, "I gotta go home. This was an awful idea."

"One more round," Volkov said. "You're ready to leave but I ain't, boss. I don't wanna remember shit when I get back to sleep."

Max slipped out of the booth, swaying. "All we're doing is hiding, Vad. Your daughter wouldn't wanna see you like this."

"My little girl's dead."

Amhearst grabbed Vadim's shoulder, "I'm sorry my god-daughter's gone—but it's time to do more forgiving and less drinking, man."

"You make me sound like an alcoholic. I ain't no boozer."

"Great. Keep it that way… I'll see you Monday, brother."

"Boss, one more drink, man. Please," Vadim said, watching Max amble out of the bar. "One more drink," he muttered, reluctant to shut his eyes.

Vera slid a steaming mug of tea across the counter-top while Max held an ice-pack to his throbbing head.

"You wanna talk about it?" she asked.

"I do."

"Okay, then talk."

Amhearst set the freezer-pack on the table, bemused. "You reject *my* marriage proposal, and *I* gotta do the talking? You're impossible."

"Max—"

"During our relationship, you never once shared the *real* you. How do we fix anything if you refuse to open up and tell me what's broken? Our problems shouldn't blow up like fuckin balloons because you need me to be a mind-reader, Vere."

"May I speak?"

"Don't do that. Not the calm therapist voice. Why did you turn me down? Help me understand and then you can say whatever clever thing you want… Is there someone else?"

"Never," Wild answered, adamant.

"Then why, Vera? Why throw away all we've built?"

She mulled for a second, realizing how often it irritated Max to see her gears whir in silence. "I did it to protect you," she said.

"Protect me? From who? *You?*"

Vera nodded. "Yes," she murmured with quivering lips.

Amhearst combed his fingers through his locks, astonished. "What went on when you flew back to the Shepherds? Something must have happened… We were fine before you left."

"I can't dedicate myself to my research and a relationship."

"That's what you've done for almost a year!"

"And look at us!"

The kitchen fell mute as a crypt.

Max offered the woman a hollow gaze. "Did you ever love me, Dr. Wild?"

"No," she whispered.

It was the biggest lie she'd ever uttered, but she was certain he'd thank her for it someday.

Max deserved the family Vera could never provide.

Chapter 7: Deception

The sun's rays crept into Khoth Vulgrell's combat-hall as he held his child close, though, not out of love.

"Compassion nor honor wins wars, daughter. Trickery is your ally. Expect lies from everybody, including those you care for. Do this, and you will never falter in battle," Vulgrell said, wrestling his offspring into submission.

"Must we speak English? This is enough of a workout as it is," his daughter growled, standing her ground against her opponent.

"Your mother insists we learn their ridiculous tongue," the Khoth hissed. "Now focus!"

Khath Emthy of Kil'Dur was a fearsome and brutal combatant, but an insect compared to the Khoth, even after centuries fighting at his side. She kicked her muscular leg above her horned head, crushing into Vulgrell's serpentine face. The impact sent him stumbling backward in a daze as she tucked an errant strand of hair from her jet-black Mohawk behind her tattered ear.

She made her father bleed.

A satisfying moment for any Khoth.

"No mercy, no hesitation," Emthy said, hiding her exhaustion.

Vulgrell lifted her by the shoulders, proud. "Zanzan, xa' trakka sarkreh tt nigihzan, Khath." *Soon, you'll be leading my battalions, Princess.*

"I breathe to bring glory to Kil'Dur."

"You do, child. Few can claim they've knocked me back in comba—"

"—Did you expect I would not find out?" the indignant voice of Qhan Unda boomed. "Xa sargo-zan Leevahn?" *An earth-born Leevahn?*

"Where did you hear this news?" the Khoth asked.

"Does it matter?" Unda retorted, eying Emthy. "You may resume your horseplay when I am finished with your father."

Vulgrell kissed his daughter's forehead. "Leave us."

The Khath heeded her father's order, bowing to her mother on her way out.

Vulgrell's baritone growl shook the ground, "It is a necessary precaution."

"Kil'Dur needs allies, not more death!" Unda exclaimed.

"You dare shout at me? I am your Khoth!"

"Xa Gih, xa Qhan… Zantrakka trakkaban xa rotrak zangih goxa Gih, xa tru!" *And I, your Empress… None deserve your confidence more than I, you fool.*

Vulgrell strayed from his incensed wife, fixating on the blue orb beyond the chamber window. "We've given the kraitho more than they could have dreamed possible—yet they still distrust us, Unda. If their primitive ways lead to conflict, the Leevahn *will* rise."

"And what of the Akkan? Do the kraitho know of *them*?" The Qhan stood behind her companion with a palm atop his rippling shoulder. "Why should they trust you if you do not give them a *reason* to do so?"

"Have you forgotten how many Kil'Durians died because of your bids for peace?"

"Compared to the countless species wiped out by you and your beasts of war?"

"All I do, I do for Kil'Dur!"

"Zutni nixa no trakkazang zan Sargo?" *What about the people of Earth?*

"I will confess, if not for *you,* their transgressions would have led to annihilation by now. Filthy, selfish, and ignorant miscreants, the lot."

Unda wrapped her Khoth in a loving embrace. "The Leevahn's creation proves why the humans cannot trust you. It explains why *I* cannot count on you to do what is right for all species concerned."

Vulgrell held her tight. "Don't say such things, my Qhan."

Unda pulled away. "Then prove me wrong. Show me you can be the ruler both our worlds deserve. The Akkan *must* stay dormant, as does the Leevahn."

Losing his Qhan's confidence shook Vulgrell. Unda was his life, his most trusted confidant in all but earthly affairs.

He would do anything to preserve her faith.

Say anything.

"I will not release them," he said.

Unda mustered a dubious grin, "Pledge, my Khoth."

Vulgrell pulled his Qhan into his bulging arms. "I promise," he hissed, staring daggers at the world below.

The Thrakra-Krikari was a floating reminder of the life Vulgrell had not returned to in ages. He redesigned the vessel's chambers after architecture of old to remind him of home.

Na Tarriban Zan Groavad, the grand chamber where he professed his love for his Qhan, inspired the feasting hall.

The craft's library mimicked Na Gihbanni Zan Krekla. An architectural wonder built by Master Artisan Imhaga, an exile from the moons of Asha. It was a labor of worship, a tribute to the most brutal Empress in Kil'Durian history, Qhan Krekla.

She hated it so much she had him and his sons beheaded.

Vulgrell admired her bloodlust.

The chamber he now rested in was his study, a perfect reproduction of Na Zliagro, home to the Death Judge of Kil'Dur, someone he wished was in his employ at that very moment as his brother-in-law, Acean of Aurell'Kah, invaded the room.

The cleric knelt, "Xa banzantrakk rakka, tt Khoth?" *You summoned me, my Emperor?*

Vulgrell unsheathed the dagger strapped to his shin, gliding its sharp tip along his index talon. "You dare kneel before me like a trustworthy servant?"

"Whatever do you mean, my Khoth?"

"I know it was you who told Unda!" Vulgrell roared, driving the blade deep into the arm of his ornate seat.

Acean rose to his feet, "I was providing her with a status report. I had no reason to assume she was unaware of *your* plans... If I kneel before you—I do so out of allegiance."

"To your precious *text*!" Vulgrell boomed, looming over his brother-in-law, close enough to smell the nrakku on his breath. "You feel safe hiding behind your impotent tome, don't you?"

"No safer than a great and powerful ruler going around his bride's back, brother."

"I despise when you call me that."

"My apologies, brother."

Vulgrell smiled, "A lesser Khoth would have gutted you by now, if only to silence your gaping mouth."

"Praise the Strodha, that our Empire is in the grips of such a worthy being."

SHWACK! Vulgrell snatched the dagger from his armchair, holding it against Acean's gullet. "Mention that book once more and I *will* slaughter you." Vulgrell pried his blade from the cleric's throat. "You *will* stay in contact with the kraith, and you'll leave Unda out of *our* interests. *Nothing* changes. We proceed… Am I clear?"

"Clear as the crimson-sea, my Khoth," Acean said, unwilling to look his ruler in the eyes.

Vulgrell brandished an imperious and pleased smirk. "I knew I could count on you, Acean."

Chapter 8: Reluctant Relocation

Oct 1st, 2030

Wild unsheathed her scalpel, the glint of its razor tip sent shudders down Elle's rear.

"She won't feel anything, I promise," Vera said. "Set her down on the bed, please."

Shepherd clutched Calla against her breast, inhaling the pure scent of her baby-soft hair. "What will this thing do?"

Vera presented a chip no bigger than a grain of rice to Elle. "Using this, I can track Calla's growth and development straight down to the genetic level."

Elle mulled over Wild's comments before setting Calla atop the bed. "Do it quick, would you?"

Vera sensed the anemic defeat of a tired wife pining for a normal life again. She empathized with Elle while finding herself envious of her and her baby in tandem. "If you're ready, please lift Calla's arm for me?"

"Will she be okay? It won't hurt?"

"Only for a second," Vera muttered, making an incision between the child's breast and armpit.

Elle winced in empathetic pain, looking away when Wild reached for the chip.

An unnerving silence overtook the room.

"Extraordinary," Wild whispered.

Shepherd's voice rattled, "What is?"

"Look for yourself."

The mother turned her reluctant sights on Vera, who held the scalpel to Calla's flesh. The baby's wound healed itself within seconds, leaving no traces of scarring.

"My God," Elle murmured, awestruck.

Vera's eyes widened. "I've seen nothing like this."

From the RESEARCH LOGS of WILD, VERA Ph.D./Evanscorp Medical/Genetics Division

Entry Log: 011210 - Nov 8th, 2030

Specimen exhibits cognition uncharacteristic of a two-month-old child. It also possesses the ability to locate its father via pheromone signature. During a game of hide-and-seek, the hybrid could not find its mother six times out of ten. As for Lance Shepherd, the subject found him no matter the distance. When Elle Shepherd wore her spouse's jersey the specimen found her without fail. Curious.

Entry Log: 022882 - July 12th, 2031

The hybrid has entered its tenth month of development. At the time of this passage the subject is in pursuit of a butterfly it discovered in a nearby meadow. UPDATE: Subject accidentally stepped on the insect, eliciting an advanced empathetic response. It mourned for the insect.

Entry Log: 349876 - Sept 27th, 2037

Today is the hybrid's seventh birthday party. I believed this *presented an opportunity to review its social skills. No peers attended, likely the byproduct of the subject's refined nature. I also suspect parents of classmates may be to blame. I have met many adults concerned over the **freak in his/her kid's class**. There is an unpleasant number of Jack Tanner sympathizers in their midst.*

Entry Log: 554678 - March 15th, 2041

Mr. Kojimatsuo tasked the subject with watching his twin toddlers this afternoon. The eleven-year-old hybrid's first responsibility. Its parents have done an exceptional job raising an organism as strong as it is sympathetic. Strength being literal. I've seen the subject thrust a sixteen thousand pound dead tractor fifty feet up a hill by hand. I'm reluctant to admit these incidents no longer excite me. I now endeavor to understand the utility of such a specimen, which is daunting. Much like its father, there are no genetic aberrations I can attribute to its abilities.

Entry Log: 884643 - April 17th, 2047

Calla Shepherd has been in a car accident. Hariyuki and Katya Kojimatsuo are dead. Their nine-year-old son, Jason, is paralyzed from the waist down. The daughter, Wilma, experienced a minor concussion but should make a full recovery. The children would not have survived had Calla not sheltered them from the collision. She shattered one-hundred-and-seventy-three bones on impact. When the paramedics arrived, the total dropped to fifty. By the time the ambulance approached the ER, Calla's restoration was complete. UPDATE: The motorist who smashed into Kojimatsuo's minivan was a member of Jack Tanner's church. The organization has been gaining national traction ever since my discovery of Auton-One.

* * *

Sander flung Vera's research dossier across the boardroom table. "Seventeen years later and ya at long last acknowledge she's a girl. *I* gotta get nailed by a truck, then we can be friends too." He reached into his humidor, chomping on a half-chewed stogy and snapping his finger.

Sander's gorgeous biological-sister, Toni (Antoinette) Evans, swooped in to light his cigar.

"See? Why can't you be like her? *Obedient,*" Sander said, batting Toni away as if she were an indentured servant.

Vera fidgeted with the pendant around her collar. "These people are targeting her and her dad, you ineffectual prick. This isn't time for your jokes."

Sander blew an obnoxious plume of exhaust in Wild's face. "What if those redneck pieces of shit meant to hurt *you*? Ever think of that? *The tramp who discovered the Trojan-horse.* That's what Tanner called you, right?"

Toni slid her manicured hand across the desk and seized Vera's research dossier. "What Trojan-horse?" she asked, needling through the pages.

Sander grinned. "Look at you over there, pretending to understand what your reading. That's cute."

"Screw you, little brother," Toni retorted. "What Trojan-horse?"

"Auton-One, ya fuckin dope," her sibling growled.

Sander relished belittling both sisters, but even he didn't know what Auton-One was.

It was a sophisticated nanostructure uncovered during Evanscorp's annual physics conference.

Vera used microscope EC-022920 to spy Auton-One in the protoplasm of a cloned cell. It was so small she couldn't decipher if it was a nanobot or nanobacterium, but one ominous fact was clear.

It existed for reasons she lacked the means and technology

to analyze.

"Why would Tanner come after *me*?" Wild asked.

"Get real, will ya? Who hates Evanscorp more than that *fire-and-brimstone* fuck?" Sander handed Toni an empty glass. "Scotch on the rocks."

"Pour it yourself, *ass*," his sister snipped.

"Ugh, you're gonna end up a lonely cat-lady, I swear to God. Do us all a favor and get dicked, grouchy bitch."

Toni snatched the cup from Sander, "Who needs one uh those when they got you around, cock?"

"That's the spirit!"

"Want ice, your highness?"

"The hell you think *on the rocks* means, fuckin idiot?" Sander leered at Vera. "Hope ya left nothing important back in cow-town. Takin you out of the field, effective today."

"What? No… you can't," Wild scoffed, wide-eyed. "All my work!"

"That gets uploaded to corporate, which you know. Try again, sweetheart."

"And the family?"

"Fuck em. I'm not helping the aliens keep tabs on the Shepherds when my sister's in Tanner's cross-hairs. You're the talented one. I need you."

Toni slammed the glass down with a splash. "Jesus, I'm standing right here, Sander."

Her brother held the drink to his lips. "I know."

"You won't buy my cooperation with flattery," Wild said, rising from her chair. "Nothing you do will convince me otherwise. I'm not staying, and that's the end."

Evans smirked, reticent and self-assured while downing his scotch. He set the glass down, leering at Vera with malicious eyes. "I was hoping you'd say something that stupid."

He snapped his fingers, and six armed guards burst into the

boardroom, circling Wild with weapons drawn.

"What the hell is this?" Vera asked, lifting her arms in surrender. "This is insane… I'm your *sister*!"

"Oh, proud to claim the family-card when the shit hits the fan, huh?" Sander shoved his goons aside. "This may *shock* you, but I've despised you since the first day I met you and your gold-digging whack-job of a mom. If it weren't for all the red-fuckin-tape, you'd be drifting in a ditch somewhere by now." He caressed the tip of her chin. "Truth hurts, I know."

Vera's foot rocketed into Sander's crotch, knocking him to his knees, gasping. "Hurt as bad as that?" she hissed, spitting in his fuming face.

The guards retrained their rifles on Wild, but Sander waved his hand and they all lowered their guns.

"That was a good punt," he whispered. "Toni, the record for the hardest kick in the balls no longer goes to you."

"At least tell me *why*, you bastard," Vera said.

Evans cupped his scrotum, eyes attached to the handmade pendant around Vera's neck. "Calla make that for you?" he asked, savagely tearing the jewelry from her throat.

"You motherfucker!" Wild reached for the necklace, but Sander's forces pulled her away before she could clutch it. "You had no right, Sander! Give it back!"

Her step-brother raised the pendant to the boardroom lights, impressed. "Must hurt knowing you're about to lose the closest thing to a child you ever had. Can't imagine what that's like," he said, helpless to maintain a straight face. "Okay, I sorta can, and lemme tell ya… I waited for this day."

"Monster!"

"Don't misinterpret, I never expected she'd live this long. Was kinda hopin she'd get picked off by one of Tanner's goons so you'd feel the loss on a more visceral level, ya know? That aside, there were more pressing strategic reasons to pull you out, I'm sorry to say. Shame too because I wanted to see you suffer much worse than this." Sander let out a callous sigh, "Such is life."

Tears slid down Vera's cheeks. "All this to punish me?"

"Don't flatter yourself, sissy. Hurting you's a side-perk of conducting business." Sander dangled the necklace in front of Vera. "Kil'Durians are up to something, Dr. Wild. You're the only one standing between them and the Shepherds. Who they are. Where they live, what they look like; all that data's gone. Now, let's say I let you go back to Hicksville and Tanner puts you six-feet-under. Nobody wins. Got no *advantage* against the aliens if you're dead, my little human-treasure-map."

"What the hell makes you believe I'll do anything you say?" Vera asked, wishing the guards would let her go so she could claw Sander's face off.

Her step-brother wiped away her tears with his soulless hands. "Because if you don't," he dropped the pendant by his foot, tramping down on it with a hearty *CRUNCH*. "I'll do this to your fucking skull, but first, I'll send for Calla's head so you can watch me do *her* before *you* die."

He nodded, and the guards released Wild's arms. She collapsed beside the broken necklace, heartbroken. "Can I at least say goodbye to them?"

"Nope. Get her outta my sight, boys," Sander ordered, turning to Toni. "Have her lab up and running *ASAP*."

His sister's glare was biting.

"What? Why you lookin at me like that?"

"You are an incredible asshole. Let her say bye to these people," Toni snipped. She didn't care much for Vera, but seeing the woman scrounge up the necklace shards at her feet tugged at Toni's thin heartstrings.

Sander pulled his sister aside as the guards escorted Wild out of the boardroom. "Correct me if I'm mistaken, but wiping out the records was your suggestion. Her being here is your doing too, stupid."

"You catch more flies with honey's all I'm saying."
Evans rolled his eyes. "I think you meant *shit.*"

64

Chapter 9: Hares and Harm

April 24th, 2047

It sniffed the earth, knowing danger was afoot. The stink of death lingered in the soil, but it wasn't enough to keep the animal away.

She needed food.

With a wrench of its teeth, a plump carrot sprang from the dirt and into the critter's jaws. She bolted into the woodlands, scanning the treetops for hawks squatting overhead.

The woodland creature halted at a burrow beneath a decayed tree, toppled over by the last heavy gales of the season. Its nose wriggled in the air.

Something was out there.

SHWACK! An arrow bore through the hare's skull, but death was not immediate. The animal's eyes danced in all directions, her head locked in place by the projectile driven into the wood.

She watched her own blood dripping from the shaft jutting out of her forehead.

Then blackness.

Calla Shepherd lowered her bow, passing a mournful palm along the animal's matted pelt. "Sorry, little one. It's you or the crops."

The girl seized the fresh carrion by its hind limbs when a faint squeak came out of the burrow at her feet. She peered inside the den and found six fuzzy babies crawling over one another in the dark.

Calla's heart plummeted into the pit of her gut.

"Morning, pal," Lance yawned, drawing a strip of jerky out of his bathrobe pocket.

Ricardo the raccoon waddled up the driveway. He was a plump ball of fur with reddish-brown eye-bands and matted coat. Shepherd found him and his siblings in the shed behind the house three winters earlier.

He was the only one who survived.

"Hungry, friend?" Shepherd asked, bending down as the critter drew closer.

Ricardo plucked the jerky away with a grateful squeak.

"Enjoy that, sir. Made it myself."

The raccoon chortled, scurrying into the bushes with its meaty-spoils.

Lance smirked, "See ya tomorrow, fatso."

"Daddy," Calla called out, adopting the tone Lance only heard when she wanted something.

That's when the forty-minute conversation began...

"For the last time, no. I'm not making a hutch for a few kits that're gonna die anyhow, honey."

"Dad, we gotta do *something*."

"Says who?"

"Karma!"

"Would you give this much of a rat's ass if that rabbit didn't have babies?"

"Their mom's dead because of *me*," Calla said, impassioned.

"She ate our crops, kiddo, that's a death sentence no matter what vermin you are."

"That's so cold, daddy!"

"No. It's life, honey. Didn't you learn anything from all those nature shows we used to watch when you were a little girl? If you hadn't brought that litter here a snake would have eaten em by now, I guarantee it. Why aren't you weeping for the poor reptiles you stole food from?"

"*Daddy.*" The girl's tone shifted to that exact pitch father's can't refuse.

"Don't do the voice thing, I'm serious."

"You wanna reject these needy orphans? No problem... I'll make a hutch myself. And it'll be *marvelous.*"

Lance shook his head, amused. "Knock yourself out, kiddo. I got Ricardo, my orphan saving quota's satisfied, so build whatever you need to for those little critters. You'll produce a better hutch than I could, most likely."

"I bet so too, dad."

"Fine."

"Okay."

"*Good.*"

"*Excellent.*"

They each burst out in laughter.

Shepherd hugged his daughter tight. "You're a splinter on my ass-cheek sometimes, but you got the biggest heart of anybody I know."

Elle shuffled into the kitchen. Her stylish bed-head was a thing of beauty.

"Next to your mother," Lance added, seizing his wife's waist from the rear and snuggling close. "Good morning, sexy."

"Morning, handsome," Elle yawned, kissing her Marine. "Tell her yet?" She poked her head over Lance's shoulder, blowing a kiss to her girl. "Hey, baby."

"Did he tell me what?" Calla asked.

The parents traded uncomfortable stares.

"Vera's not coming back, honey," her father said.

A wrinkle crept across Calla's forehead. "What do you mean? She *told* me it was only two days."

Lance couldn't look in his daughter's sad doe-eyes. "I was waiting for the right moment to tell you, sweetheart."

"She left because of me, I know it."

"Whoa, now wait a second—"

"She saw what those men did to Uncle Harry and Aunt Kat because of *me* and split," Calla said, dispirited.

Shepherd sat beside his child. "Hold on, missy. Blame yourself for killing a momma rabbit till you're an old bat. That's fine, but I don't wanna hear you fault yourself for what happened to them ever again, understood? The folks that killed them were pure evil."

"Now's not the time to get queasy," Reverend Tanner declared, lording over his faithful flock. "Look at what we've grown into, my children," he said, scouring the pews. He glided out from behind his opulent pulpit, plunging into the aisles. "Behold the monument your sacrifice has built for the Almighty! Dread not when he calls on you to exact his will upon the apostates!"

"Amen!" the parish said in one voice.

"Are you ready to prove thy selves, my children?"

"Amen!"

"Are you willing to serve the Lord, no matter what the laws of man proclaim?"

"Amen!"

"Then join me in crushing the shackles of Kil'Durian oppression consuming our planet! Open your spirits and you will be rewarded for your devotion when the trumpets silence and the enemy is no more!"

"Death to clones!," one member shouted. "Death to the aliens!" cried another.

"Yes, yes!" Tanner roared, waiving his hands aloft. "The nukes may be gone, but the exploded souls of the undead still roam the earth! Nations may know peace, but our neighborhoods are corrupt as ever! There is no paradise! There are only lies from the wicked! What do we do with the wicked? Do we forgive them?"

"No!" the writhing congregation roared.

"Do we avoid them?"

"No!"

"No! We must smite them! Kill them! Kill the aliens and kill the nightmare-spawn they have littered upon our soil!"

The congregation ascended to their feet, raising their frenzied fists high.

Jack Tanner returned to his pulpit, gesturing for respectful silence from the indoctrinated.

"Return to your homes, collect your arms—and await the sign, my children. Prepare for the war to come. It's time to rise and reclaim the planet our Lord made—for us."

Wilma (she preferred Billy) Kojimatsuo poked her head into the room to check on her brother, Jason. She tiptoed to the foot of the bed, wiggling his toes to see if he would wake, but he didn't.

She kissed his cheek, startled by Calla behind her.

"Mom's cooking up eggs. Talked her into making them the way you like," Shepherd whispered.

Billy dashed into her arms and squeezed tight.

"Everything's gonna be okay, Billy. I promise." Calla knelt down to Billy's eye level, tucking an errant strand of long brown hair behind the child's ear. "Life'll be harder now that Uncle and Auntie are clones. There will be people who don't understand, but I swear I won't let anything bad happen to you again if I can help it."

Kojimatsuo nodded.

"I love you kids."

"We love you too."

Shepherd smiled, rising to her feet. "Better scoot your butt in the kitchen and eat them eggs before mom tries to scramble em."

Billy left Calla with Jason, paralyzed in the bed he and his sister used to jump all over.

"Forgive me," she said.

Chapter 10: Marv's Milkshakes

May 11th, 2047

Harry inspected the brakes while Calla raised the back end of his van off the ground like a human auto-lift. "A few youngsters at school are saying awful stuff about Kat and me—and we were hoping you'd talk to Billy, girl to girl," he said.

"Whatever you need, Uncle."

"You got no idea how much it means to us, how great you are with the kids, honey... Thing's haven't been the same for a long time now, and I have no clue what to say to get through to them anymore. Billy most of all."

"What do you mean?"

Harry rolled out from under the van. "You can set it down. The lines look decent, appreciate the help." He got to his feet and dusted himself clean. "I dunno, just don't want to weigh her down with paranoia, I guess."

"You're not paranoid, Uncle."

"I'm a talented actor. Everything Kat and I went through back in Louisiana prepared us for the evil shit haunting us now."

"Which wouldn't have taken place if not for me."

Harry swatted Calla with his oily rag, "Stop it."

"Just saying…"

"Knock it off, Calla, I mean it."

"Consider it knocked off."

"Good… *Anyway*, telling Billy it'll be okay's a damn lie after everything that's cropped up… Trying my damnedest not to let my bullshit influence her and Jason, ya know? I want em to grow up knowing there are better ways to handle the cruelty this world has in store."

"I'd say you're doing a wonderful job so far."

"Don't feel like it. I hope to God I'm not making my kids too soft. Am I? Should I be telling Billy to fight back more?"

Calla grinned, unsure how well Harry knew his daughter. "Billy just might surprise you, Uncle. She's tougher than she lets on, trust me."

"If she is I don't see it, honey."

"You claimed you were an excellent actor… Maybe the apple didn't fall too far from the tree?"

Kojimatsuo smirked, "Hope you're right."

"I'll talk to her," Calla said.

MARV'S MILKSHAKES was an institution, a watering hole for anyone with a soft spot for the fifties. Calla fell in love with the joint the moment she stepped in, way back on her eighth birthday. She valued tradition, so when Billy turned eight, Calla convinced Uncle Harry to throw her party at Marv's.

They'd been going there at least twice a month ever since.

This should not have been one of those days.

Stubbs Huxley and his brother Clyde were sucking down a couple shakes when Calla and Billy pulled up. Everyone in town knew the Huxleys: trouble-making boys with strict Bible-thumping parents.

Stubbs earned his nickname by having a finger lopped off

at the knuckle, or so the rumor went. The truth was even weirder. It involved an alligator, a bottle of whiskey, a drunken dare, and that's all anyone needed to know.

Billy sauntered into the diner, swiveling left toward their regular booth. She froze in her tracks at the sight of Clyde Huxley sitting in her spot.

"Something wrong, little lady?" Calla asked.

"I don't wanna be here if he's here," Billy replied, desperate and disgusted. "Every kid in class hates me because of him. He told me I should kill mom and dad in their sleep because they're clones bound for hell. He said that in front of the whole classroom."

Shepherd's face streaked red. "That's the boy Uncle Harry was talking about."

Kojimatsuo nodded, discouraged.

Calla's heartbeat rang in her ears. She balled her fists, fueled by predatory rage. "Someone should teach him a lesson, shouldn't they?"

Billy clutched Calla's fist. "Don't. You'll get me in more trouble."

"He needs a talking to. They can't get away with this, honey," Shepherd replied, loud enough for the two boys to hear.

Clyde reared his melon-head over the back of the booth, surprised to see Billy. "Holy shit. Stubbs, that's the girl I was talkin about! The one with the freak parents!"

"Excuse you?" Calla balked, stepping ahead of Billy.

"Shut it, Clyde," Stubbs barked, embarrassed. "He meant nothing by it, little lady. He's only playin."

"Playing?" Calla's face writhed with loathing. "You must be dumb as he is if you expect us to believe that, jackass." She put an arm around Kojimatsuo's shoulder, escorting her toward the double-doors. "We'll come back when they throw out the trash, Billy."

Stubbs rolled his eyes. "Don't gotta be a bitch about it," he murmured.

Calla stopped in her tracks.

"What did you call me?" she asked.

Clyde and the diner manager dragged Stubbs out of the street as passing cars crept past the front of Marv's, unnerved by the commotion unfolding on the sidewalk.

"Don't set him down yet, son," the manager huffed, kicking a patch of glass out from under Huxley. "Wanna cut yer brother up anymore than he's already been? Careful now."

"Wh—what happened?" Stubbs slurred, staring skyward in a daze, swaying from side to side before the chill of the pavement overtook his backside. He winced, "Ooh, that hurts... Something's under me."

"Yeah, a shitload uh glass!" Clyde chimed, wide eyed and indignant. "You got tossed through a window, big brother!"

"*Tossed* through a window?"

The diner manager pulled a clean rag out of his apron, handing it to Stubbs. "Got some blood on you, son... I tell ya, in all my years, I seen nothing like it... The strength on that girl —Christ, almighty."

"Girl?" Huxley asked, dumbfounded. "A female did this?"

"Momma used to say not to call em bitches," Clyde interjected, "now I know why! The older one with the pretty boobs dun lifted you off the ground with one hand! Tossed ya through the front window like it was nuthin! One hand, Stubbs! All cuz ya called her a bitch!"

"Simmer down, Clyde," the diner manager said. "We got enough of a scene goin."

"Whatcha mean *simmer down*? She humiliated my big brother! Made him look like a big ole pussy, and my big brother ain't no pussy!"

Huxley palmed Clyde's shoulder, "I dunno if she did all that, now."

"She sure did! She dun humiliated you! Made you look like some kinda Sissy-Mary's what she did, and she oughta pay!"

"I had it comin, lil brother…"

The diner manager shook his head, "Maybe a slap across the face, but being thrown out a window? A bit much, son… And I'm sayin that as someone who's been serving that young lady for years. She's always been a sweet kid, but this ain't right. It ain't right at all."

"Yeah! And she gonna pay!" Clyde barked, plucking a small camera out of his back pocket. "I did good, Stubbs! I took a picture of the truck they was in! Got the numbers on it n' everything!"

"Where'd you get that?" Stubbs asked, gimlet eyed.

"I borrowed it is all…"

"From who?"

"From Mister Gimley next door. It was sittin on his porch, so I figured I'd hold on to it so nobody'd steal it or nuthin." Clyde shook his head, as if shaking off a tick of guilt. "We gonna find this girl or not? Daddy won't be happy if we don't."

Stubbs swallowed a gulp of nervous air, dreading what awaited him at home if he didn't follow through on Clyde's lead. The little boy was numb as a box of rocks, but he was dead right about their dad. Humiliation was unacceptable to their father, and Stubbs had the bruises and scars to prove it.

Nobody crossed a Huxley.

Nobody.

Stubbs outstretched his shaky hand toward his dullard sibling, "Gimme the damn camera then."

Flecks of apple jettisoned from Sander's lip. "What's so damn important? I'm missing my afternoon massage for this."

Wild peeled off her latex gloves and removed her face-mask. "The foreign body vertically transmitted to Calla is not Auton-One." Vera picked up a remote and powered on her wall display. A nano-organism with many flagella-like tentacles skittered through the protoplasm on the screen. "She's host to this."

Evans moved closer to the scan, awestruck. "What am I staring at?"

"Elegance," Wild replied, drawing a capped syringe out of the mini-fridge by her counter.

"Watch out folks, she's got a needle," Sander said, taking another bite of his apple.

Vera opened the lid to a terrarium on her desk, stabbing a mouse with the syringe. "I'd move away if I were you."

Evans leaned closer, watching the rodent spasm in writhing agony before collapsing on its side, stiff as a board.

"I'm sure there's a point to all this?" he said.

"I told you to keep back."

SPLAT! The mouse exploded, saturating the enclosure in bone and entrails. Its flesh slid down the glass into a pool of crimson slush that made Sander want to vomit.

"What the *hell* was that shit?" he asked, chucking his apple into the dustbin by his feet.

"Calla's blood."

"Blood? What kinda blood makes you fuckin explode?"

"Her foreign-bodies were trying to function independently of their intended host. When unable to, they terminated the organism."

"Why?"

Vera shrugged, "No idea."

Wild looked like she wanted to say something else, but staid her tongue in futility.

Sander scowled, "What? Spit it out?"

"If I could see Calla..."

"Nope. Not happening. You know what my plan is, so forget it."

"If we could run a few more tests with her here, we could —"

"Speak one more word about the fuckin kid! Find out what happens!"

Chapter 11: Peacekeepers

The pickup truck sped down the winding back-road.

"You got those bastards, Calla! You got em good!" Billy exclaimed.

Calla smacked her palm against the steering wheel, "I shouldn't have done that, but he made me so furious."

"Fuck em!" Kojimatsuo shouted with potency. "You put the fear of God into those boys! I bet Clyde won't make fun of me anymore after what you did!"

"Folks like that are too stupid not to retaliate, honey," Calla sighed.

The girls drove the dark dirt trail for another ten minutes before hauling up to Billy's home. Shepherd slumped in her seat, drained. "One for the history books, kiddo."

"You're the one who needs cheering up now," Billy said.

"I'm fine." Calla allowed a modest grin to sweep across her lips. "You should see the other guy."

Kojimatsuo let out a low chuckle, half consoled, but half scared. "Expect you'll get in trouble?"

"I tossed someone through a window." Calla shared a melancholy glance with Billy. "If I do, I'll deserve it."

"But you were trying to help me."

"I should've walked away."

"Well, you're a hero no matter what you say."

"Belief doesn't always make something true, little one."

Billy nodded. "If you say so."

"I say so." Calla raised her hand for a high-five. "Try to have a good night, huh?"

"Don't worry about me, I'm gonna remember the look on Clyde's face for the rest of my life." Billy slapped palms with her idol and stepped out of the car. "Hope dad left the door unlocked."

"He's opening it now."

Harry poked his head out the door, waving hello to Calla.

"How the heck do you do that?" Billy asked.

Shepherd switched on the ignition and revved up the engine. "It's what I do, baby."

"Son of a bitch," Lance hissed, wrapping a rag around his aching thumb. "Where the hell are my cutters?" he muttered.

A manicured finger tapped him on the shoulder. He turned to find his trusty Milwaukee fencing pliers in Calla's hand.

"A wise man once told me to watch where I dropped my toys," she said.

"Har har har." Lance swiped the pliers away. "I remember where I had them, for your information. Vera's the one who moved everything into the wrong spots. She even broke my radio, all I get is damn static now. You understand how hard working without music is?"

Calla smirked at her petulant father. "How do you do it, Daddy? You're such a trooper."

Lance returned to his workbench. "How was your evening out?"

"I don't wanna talk about it."

"Something happen?"

Calla leaned around her dad's broad back, eager to change

the subject. "What you got going on over there?"

Shepherd shielded his project from his nosy child. "Shoo! Mind your own business," he said, swatting Calla away with an oily rag. "Beat it, will ya?"

Calla beamed with excitement. "It's my hutch, isn't it? Lemme see!"

Lance tossed the rag atop his workbench, "Dammit, Calla."

"I wanna see!"

"I'm gonna crap all over one uh your surprises someday. Watch me," he grumbled, stepping aside to present her with her new spruce hutch.

Calla's eyes lit up like firecrackers. "Daddy, I love it!" She squeezed her gruff father tight. "I knew you'd build it. Thank you so much."

Lance kissed her forehead, annoyed. "I was gonna give it to you tomorrow."

"You saved lives tonight."

"You know I'm just gonna eat them when they're big enough, right?"

Calla whacked his thick chest. "You wouldn't dare!"

"If you say so." He draped a sheet over the hutch, rounding up his tools. "Lemme reinforce some of this fencing and dab a little lacquer finish on it tomorrow, then she'll be all yours. Deal?"

There was no response.

"Deal?" Shepherd reared his head toward the other end of the barn. "Earth to Calla."

The young woman stood beside Vera's belongings with an open journal in her hands.

"Honey… What is it?"

Calla dropped the tome and ran out of the barn, sobbing.

"She loved you, honey," Lance said from the other side of his daughter's door.

"She called me a *specimen*," Calla retorted.

Her father poked his head into the room. "I'm coming in. We gotta talk about this."

Calla plucked a tissue from the box in her lap, wiping away her tears. "Is that all I was to her? Some hybrid-freak to study?"

Shepherd sat on the edge of her bed. "Vera wrote that journal seventeen years ago. Before any of us knew what kind of amazing woman you'd grow up to be."

"That supposed to make it better?"

A ponderous expression washed over Lance. "You don't gotta believe it, but I watched her change over the years. I saw the way she dealt with you in the beginning. Don't think I wasn't afraid she'd make you feel less than human too." He looked his daughter square in her eyes. "I'd be lying if I said you two didn't bring out the best in one another. I thank God she was around to foster your mind the way we never could. The same way you fostered her capacity to love people. Vera cared about you, honey. I know it."

The young woman jumped to her feet and seized a framed photo of her and Wild off her nightstand. "She played us," Calla said, dumping the picture into the trashcan beside her desk. "Did she take a sample of your blood before she left?"

"Matter of fact."

"Yeah—mine too," Calla replied, reaching for her doorknob. "She got what she wanted on her last trip." She opened the door, "Please leave me alone now. I feel like punching something."

Lance shook his head. "This attitude isn't you. This ain't the girl I raised."

"It *is* me, dad. My feelings can't heal as fast as my body, okay? I'm *angry* and I *have no clue* what to do about it. First the incident at the diner, now this. I dunno what's next, but I'm losing control and you don't need to be here when it's gone."

"What are you talking about, Calla?" Lance asked, confused.

The girl shook her head, "Something's wrong with me and I don't know what it is, but I know this... The world'll never accept us, you and I."

"Honey," Lance whispered, unsure what else to say.

But there was nothing he could say.

Calla was lost in her emotions, but she still knew some things would always be true.

Those you care about will leave you.

People will shun you.

Then they'll come for you.

The Huxley home reeked of Aqua Velva and stale cigarettes. Few noticed because of the heavy dust wafting through their snouts, or because they didn't give a shit.

Why should they have?

"Huxleys built Merica, ain't nobody gonna run into my home n' tell me how to fuckin live."

That's what Budrick Theodore Huxley said every time Grampa Georgie's social worker came up to the house.

He hated that snot-nosed Jew, always whining about health code violations.

Huxley loved getting the man's goat. He'd smoke beside his eighty-seven-year-old dad with *COPD* to piss the little faggot off.

Bud was a real fucker, but he wasn't shit compared to his scumbag brother, Kleg.

Klegland Adolf Huxley was a born-again ex-con, heavy on fire and brimstone and light on mercy. He and his browbeaten wife, Alma, moved their two boys into Bud's delapidated trailer after Grampa Georgie passed.

Their new dwelling was a roach-infested sardine-can. It reeked of bad whiskey and death, but those were minor gripes compared to living with Kleg.

Clyde got it the worst, often getting himself beaten, banged up, and locked in the utility closet for hours on end. All because he wasn't bright enough for his dear-ole-dad.

The boy's big brother did his best to defend the boy, but their father was king. He proved it by shearing off the young man's middle finger one night. Seems Kleg giving Clyde a bloody nose was excusable—but Stubbs flipping him off for doing it—was not.

Alma rushed her eldest son to the emergency room in time to sew his digit back on. When the authorities asked what happened to the poor kid, she dreamed up a lavish story. Something about a drunken dare and an alligator. If she'd told the truth, her husband would have put their sons six feet underground.

That was the night Kleg christened his eldest son *Stubbs.*

The same night Alma killed herself.

CREEK! The two boys rushed through Uncle Bud's tattered screen-door. "We gonna make that bitch pay!" Clyde said with clenched fists.

Kleg and Bud sat at the dining room table surrounded by firearms. Bud shoved shells into his Mossberg, chambering a round with a loud *CLACK.* Kleg loaded his Beretta with hollow-points he kept in an old MARPAT tackle box.

"Whatchu girls cryin bout now?" Kleg asked, more engrossed in his guns than his sons. He glanced at his eldest with a rumpled brow. "Fuck happened to *you,* Stubbs?"

"A crazy bitch got the jump on him, daddy!" Clyde said. "She tossed him through a window like a stuffed animal!"

"Shut it, Clyde!" Stubbs barked, embarrassed to imagine what his dad must have thought. "I can explain."

Kleg's yellow chompers glistened beneath the filthy

chandelier over his bald head. "You was beat up by a *girl*? You a faggot, boy?" He shared a chuckle with his brother across the table. "Hear this shit, fat man?"

Bud chortled so vigorously his belly shook. "Kids today ain't shit," he said, spittle running out of his greasy mouth the harder he snorted.

Kleg's grin soured into a venomous scowl. "Get a couple good scratches in, son? Yank on her hair nice and hard? Makes their eye makeup run... coulda landed a few slaps."

"It wasn't like that!" Stubbs retorted.

Kleg shot from his seat, red-faced and wide-eyed. "Raise yer fuckin voice again, ya little shit, see if I don't change yer name to *Stumps* afterward."

"She ain't a normal girl, pop. She, she was a *freak*, I'm tellin ya."

"It's true, daddy! The manager at the diner told us her old man's one uh them clones!" Clyde yelped. "That makes her part devil, don't it?"

Kleg and Bud shared a grave stare that sent shivers down the two boy's spines.

"Can't be coincidence, brother," Bud whispered. "This the sign?"

Kleg shook his fat head. "God does nothing without revealing his plan to his servants, the prophets," he preached. "Amos, three-seven." He turned to his children, who both looked pale with fear, tossing them each a handgun. "The Reverend's calling has come, boys."

Bud bowed his brow in worship. "Amen, brother. Amen."

Kleg slapped the hollow-point clip into his Beretta, admiring his weapon. "Blessed are the peacemakers, for I will call them sons of God," he said.

Chapter 12: The Quiet Qhan

May 12th, 2047

The Khoth cradled his royal staff while Unda scanned the earth below.

He never understood her rich fascination with the humans.

"Such enchantment over the vestigial overgrowth of the universe. How you amuse me with your innocence, my love," he grumbled.

The Qhan's gaze shifted away from the viewing portal and settled upon her husband's ornate weapon. "The Scepter Of Elders is not to leave this shuttle," Unda ordered, rigid and resolute.

"And if it does, my Qhan?"

"This is to be a harmonious meeting. End of discussion."

Vulgrell snickered in malign amusement, "I smell the stench of excrement," he snarled. "You would not have me shelter you from this?"

"Humans mastered plumbing centuries ago," Unda said, admiring the Washington Monument below.

A grin inched across Vulgrell's scaled lips, "I was referring to the humans *themselves*."

Swarms of reporters watched the shuttlecraft touch down,

eager for a shot of the aliens. A mousy-looking fellow in a wrinkled black suit received them at the foot of the craft's ramp. His was an unfamiliar face the Khoth didn't much care for.

"Who are you?" the Khoth hissed.

"Mr. Terrance fell ill, your excellency," the man reached out his hand, "I'm his replacement, John Smith."

Vulgrell looked down at the pink appendage. "What am I to do with that? Eat it?"

"A joke, John Smith," Unda said, shaking the man's small hand. "My spouse is not fond of human greetings."

"Something, your predecessor should have shared with you," Vulgrell grumbled.

John lingered, processing the Khoth's remarks. "We have a motorcade waiting. It'll drive you to the steps of the U.S. Capitol building." He opened the vehicle door for the Qhan. "After you, Kahn."

Unda smiled, "Your Kil'Durian needs refinement."

"I know what I said, bitch," John seethed, thrusting his Glock between Unda's unsuspecting eyes.

THWAP! THWAP!

"Unda!" Vulgrell caught his mate's limp form in his large arms before it hit the ground. Her purple blood oozed down his countenance like hot, sticky molasses. He swayed her body back and forth, begging her to open her eyes. "See what your precious humans have done!"

"Praise be to God for showing me the symbols of their deceit!" wailed a wild-eyed John Smith. "Even Satan disguises himself as an angel of light. Corinthians, Eleven-fourteen!"

Vulgrell's blazing orbs locked on John Smith, "You speak of *deceit*?"

The Khoth outstretched his arm toward the open shuttlecraft.

The Scepter Of Elders rocketed out of the vessel, *CLANGING* into his vengeful hand. "You *dare* call me *Satan*," the Khoth hissed. "Your tome paints him as the epitome of evil and darkness, does it not?" He pointed his ornate weapon at John Smith, "I am something *much* worse?"

TWHAP! Smith discharged his weapon. The bullet *PINGED* off Vulgrell's armored chest-plate.

The Khoth lorded over the assassin, discarding his cloak. Droves of photographers snapped photos of Vulgrell's gleaming battle armor. "Record your visions!" he roared. "Commemorate this day, kraitho! For this is the moment humanity declared war on the Kil'Durian Empire!"

PITCHOO! A surge of energy plasma from his lethal staff blasted John Smith into a puddle of red slop in the street. Flesh rained like bloody chum upon the throng of journalists, yet it did nothing to repel them.

This was the scoop of a lifetime.

"This cretin murdered she who offered you mercy." Vulgrell hoisted Unda into his arms. "Expect *none* from *me*."

The Khoth stormed into his vessel, withdrawing into the heavens with a heart as black as space. He cradled Unda's body, kissing her forehead as his ocular ducts streamed down his quivering chops.

She was his life, and they stole her from him. A sniveling race of undeserving insects that appreciated nothing.

They would pay the exorbitant cost her life was worth.

Vulgrell never contemplated life without his beloved Qhan. He found himself lost for the first time in his life. What would he do now? What was his purpose without her to conquer for?

He almost regretted lying to her, but seeing her corpse only strengthened his resolve.

In his agony, Vulgrell found one morsel of liberating solace.

There was no longer a need to deceive his beloved.

The Khoth was free to stamp out the lecherous humans on his own terms.

All he lacked was the Leevahn.

"Pop! Uncle! I got em! They live up the ridge, out past the Kershaw Windmill!" Clyde said.

Stubbs dashed to the tobacco-stained computer desk. "Bullshit. You didn't find nuthin with them blurry ass snapshots you took."

"I did too! Look!" Clyde tapped on a social media photo linked beside the plate numbers he entered. The little halfwit didn't recognize the older guy, but he sure remembered the teenager under his wing.

Uncle Bud shoved Stubbs aside, "Sure it's them, boy?"

Stubbs scratched the back of his neck, nervous. "Hard to tell."

"You blind?" Clyde balked. "That's the girl!" He swung to Bud, "That's her, I'm positive!"

"She's got curves on her. Hope ya copped a titty-squeeze before she whupped yer keester," Bud said with a toothy grin.

"Enough!" Kleg growled, passing a chamois cloth across his double barrel rifle. "An alien's dead, it's all over the news." He leaned in tight to the computer screen like a hunter studying his prey. "It's the sign."

"What happens now, Daddy? We, we *really* gonna go through with it?" asked Clyde.

Kleg looked at his little boy and drew a slow hand to his round cheek. "I will fill your mountains with the dead. I will fill your hills, your valleys, and your streams with people slaughtered by the sword. I will make you desolate forever. Your cities will be no more. Then you will know I am God," he said.

Chapter 13: Sander's Headache

Max's gut wrenched once he strode into Vera's lab, stumbling over her wastebasket. She didn't expect to find her former flame standing behind her.

"You frighten my crew," Amhearst said, smirking.

Vera studied his lips. "You look well," she muttered.

"You too," he replied, recognizing the veiled pensiveness on Wild's beautiful face. "My board downstairs said you paged an hour ago. I'm not disturbing anything, am I? Toni told me to have the lab up to spec, but she didn't say for *who*. Seems my crew scatters whenever there's a call from Bio." Max mustered a playful scowl, "I suspected it might be you."

"Frightened men remind you of me?"

"You have a way about you. Let me put it that way."

"Some things never change, right?"

A parched grin slipped across Max's rugged face, "Never occurred to you to come say hello?"

"I've been busy."

"Pistol to your head or something?"

Wild mustered a defeated half-smile, "Don't ask… Are your men doing any work on this level?"

"Always."

"Anything that can cause reverberating micro-shifts in my

samples?"

"We have safeguards against those kinda things, you know that."

Vera looked through the lens of her microscope, concerned. "All my specimens appear to have shifted position, and I don't understand how or why."

"Don't mean to challenge the remarkable Dr. Wild, but are you certain they moved?"

Wild stepped away and gestured for Amhearst to have a gander for himself.

Max peeked through the eyepiece. "What am I staring at here?"

"Can you spot the machine-like granule in the protoplasm?"

"There's a slight speck floating in a *bigger* dot."

"Three hours ago, the tiny specks were *all* zero-point-three microns to the left. They're now the nearest to the nucleus they've ever been since my research started."

Max backed away from the microscope, massaging his eyelids. "Wasn't me or my men, that much I can tell ya."

Vera nodded, "Thanks for showing up and checking, anyway."

She extended a professional hand to her former lover.

Max stared at Vera's outstretched palm, "You're as beautiful as I remember… See ya around."

Vera's tongue froze.

Amhearst walked toward the exit.

"Wait," she said.

Max looked over his shoulder at the only woman he ever cherished.

Vera wasn't the same. She wanted to tell him she still adored him after all these years.

"We should grab lunch someday," she said.

Amhearst smiled, "You buying?"

EEEER! EEEER! EEEER! Red lights spiraled to life, and the deafening emergency system roared on-line.

Max cocked his well-trained ear toward the speaker. "That's not an evacuation alarm."

Sander spit blood at Vulgrell's heels, "You need me! You want your precious hybrid, you better be willing to renegotiate!"

Acean lowered himself before the Khoth's feet and wiped away the human's blood with the end of his cloak. "None before you were industrious enough to discover the Akkan... Bravo."

Vulgrell stomped toward the mammal like a bipedal rhinoceros, "You will *not* keep her from me!" The large alien clutched the human by his shirt collar. "You suggest renegotiations?" he asked, tearing Sander's arm off in a cascade of crimson, striking the human's face with it. "This is how *I* negotiate!"

"My arm! Dear Lord Jesus!" the human cried, seizing the raw stump while the Khoth wailed on his skull. There was so much blood Evans wasn't sure if it was running from his nose or his severed limb. Gore trickled down his scruff and pooled in his bellybutton with every blow. "Please... please stop," Sander murmured.

"Do you feel in control, kraith? Is this going the way you intended?" Vulgrell cast the limb aside, "The Leevahn is mine!"

Acean leered at his ruler, uneasy, "You don't suggest harvesting her before she has *chosen*, do you?"

Vulgrell swiveled his head, "So what if I do?"

The cleric slithered toward his Khoth, "Protecting the Leevahn is sacrosanct. Indoctrination and coercion poisons all the Strodha teaches us."

Vulgrell balled his ham-fist so tight his knuckles cracked.

Acean backed away, "Forgive my petulan—"

"Holy shit," Toni muttered, frozen stiff in the entryway.

Vulgrell leered at the woman, "Who is this delicate creature? Another mammal come to negotiate, perhaps?"

"Shit," Max said, dumbfounded by the gore in Sander's suite. He held Vera's hand so she wouldn't slide over the mangled limbs.

"What the hell went on in here?" Amhearst asked.

"They slaughtered him," Toni whimpered, swaying back and forth beside her twin's headless carcass. "The aliens came searching for the girl, and they killed him… It's my fault!"

Vera knelt before her step-sister, peering into her devastated eyes. "They came for Calla? Did they say why?"

Toni shook her head, "When Sander told him we destroyed her records the big one said they knew where she was all along. He said they didn't need him anymore," she hesitated, "then the sonofabitch caved his skull in!" She cupped her face, bawling in anguish, "Sander!"

Vera turned to Max. "We can't let them get to Calla."

"There was something else," Toni continued, finding her composure. "The big one said the Akkan would wake up soon, whatever that meant."

"This got anything to do with your research?" Max asked Vera, rubbing his bloody shoes off on a detached leg underfoot.

"I dunno. Maybe?" Vera grabbed Toni by the shoulders. "We have to go, right now. You're gonna have to grieve later, I'm sorry."

"And I'm coming with you," Max said.

"You are?" Vera asked, perplexed.

"Can you pilot a chopper?"

Chapter 14: One Alien Eye

Calla couldn't recall the last time she stargazed. The porch swing Uncle Harry built was rickety, but it carried fond memories of her youth. She glared into the night sky, yearning to taste her childhood again.

Back when the world was not so ugly.

The screen door *SCREECHED* open. "If your father caught you sitting out here at a moment like this, he'd blow his cap," Elle said, two steaming mugs in hand. She parked beside her offspring, who looked rife with inner turmoil. "What's on your mind?"

Calla took a cup in her shivering hands, blowing on it and staring into the shimmering abyss overhead. "You and dad used to relax out here with me, remember? You'd name all the constellations, I'd make up some of my own, and he'd fart so loud it rattled the swing."

Elle nodded. "You were a little munchkin."

"Why'd we stop?"

"I don't know."

"Do you miss it?"

"Well, now that you've reminded me. Yeah, I do. Your father and I would sit outside and stargaze long before you were born, but it wasn't what it became till you showed up. I miss it a lot, actually."

Calla locked eyes with her mom for a fading moment, then glanced back up at the stars, downtrodden. "Me too."

Elle took both cups of tea and set them down on a narrow oak table beside the swing. "Honey, talk. This angst stuff isn't like you. Regular teenagers, sure."

Calla's lips quivered. "I wish I was a regular teenager instead of," she looked herself over, disgusted, "a *freak*."

"Calla Emery Shepherd," her mother balked. "Don't you *ever* say such a dreadful thing again, hear me?"

"But I am," the girl replied, sobbing. "I'm not human, not a clone. What, what am I? A freak!"

Elle clutched Calla's head against her breast, grazing the child's forehead. "Lance told me about the journal, baby. You can't let it get to you. I watched you two over the years. There's no faking the bond you and Vera had."

Calla wiped her eyes, sniffling. "You don't know for certain, mom."

"Yes, I do, honey."

"How?"

"Because it's the kind of relationship *I* always wished you and *I* had."

The girl fell mute, absorbing with her mother's lonely words.

"I'm a homemaker from the middle of nowhere, baby. Vera was a woman who could motivate you to do marvelous things. If you ever feel like I wasn't around enough, it was only because I wanted to give her the space to help you reach your full potential."

"Mom."

"I never meant for you to think I didn't want to be close to you if that's what you believed. I'd sooner die than want you to feel alone, or like a freak." Now it was Elle's turn to weep.

"You're my little g—"

BOOM! A twelve-gauge slug exploded half of Elle's skull across Calla's stunned face.

"I got one, Pop! I got one!" a child's voice squawked from the shadows with perverse zeal.

"Momma!" Calla bawled, clasping her dead mother in her arms. "You fucking animals! She wasn't even a clone!"

Four silhouettes emerged out of the moonlit field across from the house, crunching along the gravel.

"That her, boys?" a crusty tone asked, the shadow of an AR-fifteen's resting against a fat person's shoulder.

"That's the girl," a timid teenager's voice, responded.

A bulky body walked up and nudged the teenager. "Gonna stand there? Shoot the bitch!"

"Yeah, kill the freak," the child added, excited. "Let's show em all what happens when you fuck with a Huxley!"

A collective outcry of: "Shut your trap, Clyde!" rang through the night sky.

Calla laid her mother's carcass on the porch swing, "You're the boys from the diner. I know it is," her nose crinkled, "I can smell you."

POP! A nine-millimeter slug tore through her forehead, followed by two through her chest. *POP! POP!* Calla's vision dimmed, and she collapsed with a hard *THUD*, battling to breathe.

The Huxley clan emerged from the blackness. Stubbs looked at Calla's fallen body with a sense of dread. His big mouth forced the girl's hand back at the diner. Now two women were dead. His ilk trusted in hateful signs, but in his soul, Stubbs understood the women died because of him.

"Elle!" an inhuman voice roared.

A misshaped humanoid hovered over the half-headless woman. Its flesh blistered and pulsated. "What have they done to you?" the primordial voice hissed.

Kleg grinned, taking aim at Lance. "No sense crying for your sweetheart, friend. You'll be seeing her in hell real soon."

"Elle was a good woman!" Lance roared. "She was *kind…* She was… She was… *Tasty.*"

CHOMP! Kleg choked back vomit once Lance tore into Elle's belly like a starving beast. "Our father, who art in heaven! Hallowed be thy name!" Kleg sputtered in terror.

Bud cocked his shotgun. "The fuck y'all faggots waitin on? Shoot!"

"Hell yeah, Uncle!" chuckled Clyde, too simple to fathom the imminent peril. "Let's get em!"

"This ain't right," Stubbs rebuked. "We, we shouldn't have come here."

"Too late to feel bad now, boy," Kleg said.

"I always knew you was a pussy, nephew," Bud snickered, taking aim at the freak eating its wife's guts.

POP! POP! POP!

Gunfire ripped through Lance's back. Spikes jutted from his spine, trailing a bloody crocodilian tail snaking out of the crack of his rear. *POP! POP!*

The mutant's limbs stretched into grotesque stalks of scale and sinew. His metal-shearing talons poised for attack.

CLICK. CLICK.

Kleg felt-up his tac-vest in a frenzy. "I'm dry, boys! Outta ammo!"

Bud slipped his last clip into his Beretta-M-Nine. "I forgot my shotty in the car, brother. These alls I got left on me."

"Why the shit ya do that, stupid fuck?"

"Pardon, fuckin, me! Didn't expect we was gonna be shooting at Godzilla!"

"What do we do, daddy?" Clyde asked, sneaking a peep at the monster from behind his fat Uncle.

The Lance-stalker sampled the gunpowder-laden air, but something else caught its attention.

It lumbered toward the female laying in the driveway, nudging her with its muzzle.

She didn't move.

"You gonna eat her too, demon?" Kleg wailed, beyond disgusted.

The beast drew back its lips, exposing a sea of jagged teeth eager to take a bite out of Kleg and his ilk.

Then she moved.

The bullet pushed out of Calla's skull, extruded by regenerated tissue, but her brain was not the same. Darkness slithered through the recesses of her conciousness, icy and angry, beckoning her to wake up.

She opened her eyes and beheld a nightmare beast staring back at her. Calla didn't recognize the animal, even though the word Akkan-Gah rang in her mind.

She didn't know what it meant, only that this creature was one of them.

There was something else, a gut feeling invading her emotional conciousness It warmed her.

Daughterly love.

"Daddy?" she murmured.

The Lance-stalker strayed from Calla, dispassionate and thirsty for redneck blood. The Huxleys scattered, but the beast caught up to the fat one first, seizing Bud by the scruff of his neck. It drove him to the earth and sheared his head clean off with its gnashing teeth.

Kleg dove into the bushes leading to the dirt road, poking his skull through the leaves. "We gotta run for it," he mouthed, flapping his dirty baseball cap at the boys hiding on the other side of Lance's truck.

"Daddy, stop waving yer hat! It'll get ya!" Clyde said, dashing out from behind the vehicle.

CLOMP! The Lance-stalker pounced on the witless child, shattering Clyde's sternum under its heft. Blood spewed from the boy's mouth. The creature cocked its head like a bewildered bird. It wondered if it should bother eating such insignificant prey.

Clyde reached a shuddering hand out toward his cowering father in the shrubbery. "Save me, daddy," he sputtered.

The beast tore into the boy, silencing the little nitwit forever.

A hot stream rolled down Kleg's leg, pooling in his boot. He whipped out the mini-bible in his vest pocket, kissing the cover before clutching it tight to his chest.

A droplet of blood spattered on the book.

Kleg looked up, glaring straight into Clyde's lifeless eyes. The child's remains dangled in the monster's jaws, looming above the cowering patriarch.

"Forgive us our trespasses," Kleg sputtered, "and d-d-deliver us from eviaaaaaaaugghhh!"

The screams ended with a wet *CRUNCH* that held in the twilight.

Stubbs poked his head over the hood of the pickup. The beast's chops bored into Kleg's hairy stomach like a starving razorback.

WHAM! A hand swung in from behind, dragging Stubbs into the long grass beside the truck.

"Don't move," Calla hissed.

"I thought you were dead. I, I didn't shoot you, I swear," Stubbs whispered back.

"Quiet," Calla replied through grated teeth. "We gotta get outta here."

"Why are you helping me?"

Calla looked askance at Stubbs. "Wanna go into my house and find the keys to the truck?"

"No."

"Got a vehicle that runs?"

"On the other side of the hill."

"Then you're helping *me*," Calla said, moving up against the truck, peeping beneath the vehicle. She could hear the keyring fastened to Kleg's belt-loop jingling and jangling while the monster fed. "We need those."

Stubbs peeked over the hood, terrified. "How we gonna get em?" There was no answer.

Huxley glanced to his side, but his unlikely ally vanished. "Well that was a good talk."

"Here! Over here!" Calla shouted, drawing the beast's attention to the front of the house.

The behemoth licked its savage jaws, advancing toward the small female.

She stepped closer to the animal, unafraid of its ghastly design. "Are you still in there?" she asked, standing her ground.

The creature's snout drew near her. Its warm breath dampened Calla's cheek, but the young woman didn't seem to care. She held a delicate hand to the side of the animal's face, gazing into its inhuman orbs.

Stubbs pried the keys off his dad's mutilated body, dashing into the brush before the beast saw him.

The hybrid stroked her father's scaly snout. "Do you remember who I am?"

The creature nudged Calla's palm, smelling it with interest.

"We're not so different, daddy. Two creatures nobody understands," she whispered, stroking the side of his face. "If there's any part of you left in there," Calla said, "I need you to know I love you."

VROOM! The Lance-stalker swatted Calla aside like a rag-doll as Stubbs plowed into the beast with an SUV. Huxley put the vehicle in reverse, smashing into the giant once more. The mutant fought to free itself while Stubbs laid Calla in the back seat. Its claws ripped through the hood in ravenous fury.

BOOM! Stubb's clutched his ears when a twelve-gauge slug punched through the windshield. Half of the beast's skull rested over the front-end in a smoldering mound of glass and brains.

The smoky shotgun trembled in Calla's hands as she watched her daddy's mutated corpse slide off the hood with a *THUD*. She tossed the pungent smelling weapon on the seat beside her.

"This piece of shit still running?" she asked.

"What?" Stubbs yelled, still covering his ears.

Calla stepped out of the rear seat and opened the driver's door. "Move."

Stubbs slid into the passenger side, abashed. "You didn't have to save me, but ya did. I… I wanna say thanks."

"Shut it! Don't assume for one second, because you're alive, that we're buddies, okay? We are *not* friends. You slaughtered my mother!"

"Hey, I didn't kill *nobody!*" Stubbs retorted. "You're not the only one who lost someone tonight, my little brother's dead!"

"Because you came up here to butcher my family!"

Stubbs coiled into a ball in his seat. "I'm a loudmouth asshole sometimes, but I ain't no *murderer*." Huxley gave Calla a dejected glance, "And I ain't no crackpot fanatic like my daddy. He's the one who had it in for ya, he and my Uncle, not me." He hung his head, "I'm glad they're dead."

"That makes two of us," Calla whispered, firing up the SUV with a stony eye on Stubbs. "I don't know what the hell's going on, but if every clone's changing into one of these things we gotta make a pit-stop. Hope you like kids."

* * *

Ricardo scampered across the road, freezing when it saw the huge thing in the driveway.

It wasn't moving.

The animal inched close to it.

It was still warm.

Ricardo sniffed the body, coming to a half-intact face staring into the night sky.

He licked his chops.

SHWACK! The beast's talons impaled the portly mammal, dragging the raccoon toward its mangled maw.

Ricardo battled to free himself, glimpsing the stalker's one alien eye as he shrieked in the moonlight.

He almost recognized it.

Chapter 15: Extra Butter

Half An Hour Earlier

"You want me to make popcorn, sugar?" Harry asked from the kitchen.

"Sure," Kat answered, crocheting on the couch beside Jason, snug in his rocking-chair. She asked the boy if he wanted extra butter, but he was too engrossed in his video game to reply.

"Extra butter, please," she called out anyway, knowing her son.

"You got it," her husband said.

VRRROOM! An SUV led footed past the front drapes. Its bright taillights and abysmal country tunes vanished down the road in a flash.

Harry poked into the living room, a little jumpy. "Tell me that was the TV."

Kat shook her head.

"Door locked?"

"Top *and* bottom bolt."

"What's going on?" Jason asked, ill-concerned, but curious.

"Nothing, bud," Harry said, sharing an unsettled glance with his wife. "News has us worked up, no big deal. Popcorn'll be ready in a few minutes." He walked over to the staircase, "Billy, wanna share a bowl of popcorn with your brother or do you want your own? I know he loves to swamp it in salt."

"I do *not*," Jason snickered.

Harry grinned, "Like *hell* you don't." He shifted attention back toward the stairwell. "Whaddaya say, honey? Yeah? Nah?"

"I can't hear you dad! One sec and I'll be down!" Billy hollered from her bedroom.

"Make it fast," Kat said. "Movie starts when dad's finished. You miss the beginning, that's on you."

Harry returned to the kitchen, reaching for the microwave handle when a dizzy spell fell over him. He extended his palm toward the counter, but missed it by more than a foot, causing him to tumble forward in what seemed like slow motion.

His eyes rolled back in his skull as his temple smashed into the refrigerator on his tumble across the tile. The cool laminate beneath his skin heated with the pulsing warmth of blood pooling around his face.

After a few moments the man mustered the strength and coordination to lift himself off the floor, but his arms gave out and he dropped to the tile again. Dazed, and feeling like his entire body was aflame.

The pain was excruciating.

"Mom, you okay?" Jason asked from the living room, alarmed. "Dad get in here! Something's wrong with Mom!"

The kitchen was dead silent.

Jason yelped in dread, powerless to do anything as his mother clawed at her own flesh in writhing torment. Her back arched high, tearing her bodice down the middle, and her flawless skin sloughed off her body.

The child turned sallow once his mommy's azure eyes ruptured across his pajamas in a spray of spongy goop. In their place lived two sinister lavender-hued orbs fixed on his belly fat.

"Mommy, stop!" the boy bawled, but it was much too late.

Kat and Harry were dead, absorbed by a violet-eyed stalker and its crimson-fanged mate.

And they were starving.

The Crimson-stalker slithered toward its boy bearing its jagged glistening teeth, salivating as it closed in on the child.

Jason howled in terror when his mutated mommy chomped down on his right arm like a dog gnawing on a scrap of rawhide. He sealed his eyes tight, praying to wake up, but this was no dream.

He never felt pain in his dreams.

The boy unclenched his eyelids, glaring straight into the Crimson-stalker's undulating glottis.

Its jaws engulfed his collar, clasping shut like a bear-trap around his esophagus.

"I love you, Daddy," the child gurgled, seconds before his father's fangs broke skin. "I... lu-grgghhh!"

RIP! Crimson tore Jason's jugular from his neck with a savage jerk and an obscene cascade of gore. Blood gushed down the boy's shirt as his parents bored through his sternum, feasting on his organs.

He drew his last breath with the lung his mother wasn't eating.

Family dinner.

Billy slipped her headphones around her collar when she saw the mangled chair. The squishy sound of rapacious animals feeding made the girl's knees quake. She descended the stairwell, eying a streak of blood at the base of Jason's seat. It trailed further into the living room, out of Billy's sight.

She stooped low, sliding against the wall, peeking around the corner.

Her brother's torso rocked side to side in a grim tug-of-war between two monsters lapping up his organs. His entrails snaked along the carpet in glistening gray coils saturated in brick-red ooze.

Billy retracted her head in awestruck revulsion, gagging on the vomit swishing in her mouth.

The Crimson-stalker's snout slithered past the archway, enticed by the stench of puke. The girl fell backward across the hardwood floor when the beast crept out of the living room.

It locked on the squirming morsel in the hallway with thick strands of drool oozing from its jowls.

Billy's face numbed when she saw her father's family medallion dangling around the mutant's throat. "Daddy?" she wept.

Crimson unhinged its slathering jaws, ready to feed on the girl, when a figure rose behind it. *CRACK!* The freak's skull snapped backwards with a savage jerk, and it collapsed to the ground like a spasming rag-doll.

Calla lorded over its body with a finger to her lips. "Don't move," she whispered.

"Holy shit!" Stubbs said, blasting his shotgun into the living room. *CHA-CHAK! BOOM! CHA-CHAK! BOOM! CHA-CHAK! CLICK.* "Uh oh…"

Violet leapt atop Huxley, chomping on the barrel shielding his face. The beast slashed his abdomen with its hind claws, battling to pry the weapon away from its prey.

"You gonna stand there?" he howled.

Shepherd marched toward the creature. "What part of *quiet* didn't you understand?" She slipped her arm around the beast's throat and heaved it off Stubbs' chest, decapitating it in mid-air with her bare hands.

She dropped its spasming body to the hardwood, kicking it aside, helping Huxley to his feet.

"What the hell are you?" Stubbs whispered.

Calla pondered a moment. "I ask myself that every day."

"The way you handled with those things was ama—"

"Instinct."

"Huh?"

"Fight or flight… I fought. I know that's hard for someone like you to understand." Shepherd tapped Huxley's cheek, "Try it sometime."

"Calla?" a youthful voice asked.

Calla hoisted the girl into her arms, hugging her tightly, "Thank God you're safe!"

"They ate him," Billy whimpered. "Mom and dad… *ate* Jason."

"Those things were*n't* your parents." Shepherd leered at the Violet-stalker's headless corpse. "They may have changed into these things, but they weren't *inside* them."

"How do you know?"

"It's what I believe."

Kojimatsuo locked eyes with her surrogate sister. "Believing doesn't always make something true. You told me that."

Calla nodded, unable to argue with the girl. "Let's get out of here."

Billy gave Huxley an incredulous leer. "I'm not traveling anywhere with him," she growled.

"This one's not so bad," Calla said. "Besides, if he gets eaten it'll give us time to run away."

Stubbs crossed his arms. "That ain't funny."

"Wasn't meant to be," Billy retorted.

"Okay, let's hate on the Huxleys. I get it, my family's shit, can we move on now? Figure out what the hell we're gonna do? Where to go?"

An epiphany struck Calla, and she plucked up Stubb's mangled shotgun. "I have an idea where we can go," she said, nodding to Billy. "Uncle Harry still keep the extra key behind the dumpster?"

Billy's eyes swelled with hope, "You're a frigging genius."

Shepherd kissed the child's forehead, "I know… We'll take off at sunup."

Chapter 16: The Akkan

<u>The Three Hearts of Warfare: A Brief History</u>
(Translated from the Strodha and interpreted in English)
KK - Kahzanxa No Kahtrakxa (Before the Kil'Durian Empire)
NTK - Nogo No Trakkroh Kahtrakxa (After the Risen Empire)

*The **Akkan-Rah** roamed the coasts in quest of flesh, fit to eviscerate everything in their path.*

The first heart of the Akkan. Beasts bred for war by Qhan Meekra after the Battle Of The Three Suns (12,000 KK).

Land-stalkers.

*The **Akkan-Kah** took to the air, stripping meat from cartilage. Wraiths born to defend Mount Kuzoth against Izedian forces during the* War Of Ardoon (1500 NTK).

Their brutality earned them a place as the second heart of the Akkan.

Death-gliders.

*The **Akkan-Yah** were monstrous leviathans with bone crushing pincers and poisonous tendrils. They swam the oceans of Xyonrath during the* Blek'sha Raids (2500 NTK) *that destroyed Tar Wrom's* *pirate fleet.*

Their ferocity earned them a place as the third heart of the Akkan.

Sea-creepers.

The Akkan protected the Empire for generations, laying waste to all its detractors.

Not until Khoth Turko's infiltration of the Miri'Tak did the High Council seek to regulate the beasts.

Embedding the Akkan into clones instead of Kil'Durian warriors was a dishonor.

An abuse of the Strodha's most divine decree: Gihbantrakka Nizantrakka Gihzan.

Virtue Above Victory.

The High Council instated a shield against the three hearts of the Akkan in response.

*Thus spawned the first **Leevahn** and its protector, the **Akkan-Gah.***

Acean shut his sacred tome and seized it against his breast, idling over a holographic war-portal in disgrace. He watched millions of kraith around the world succumb to their cloned friends and family.

Every death had a tale to tell...

PIERRE GAGNAIRE Restaurant

Paris, France

Adalene Renaut hated her job, but it kept her and her cat fed while she waited to hear from LE CORDON BLEU. She was an apprentice to the executive chef at PIERRE GAGNAIRE, but had no certificate.

Adalene would never get a lead position anywhere without one.

LE CAMEO hired often, but that was the worst restaurant in France. She had standards, which is why she was still unmarried.

Last one into the kitchen every dawn, she strode through the doors to find not so much as a stove lit. She inspected the whiteboard, unsure if the eatery had closed that day, but Jean's smock was missing. He never took it home, which could only mean he was in the building.

She passed through the double-doors leading into the darkened dining area. "Jean, où es-tu?" *Jean, where are you?* she asked, scouring the blackness, wishing the light switch wasn't on the opposite side of the room. "Pourquoi les lumières ne sont-elles pas allumées? Ce n'est pas comme si vous étiez en retard. Ou êtes-vous paresseux?" *Why aren't the lights on? It's not like you're late. Or are you lazy?* she prodded with a wicked smirk.

A low vibration echoed through the black, surging into a feral growl drawing closer to the lady.

Adelene gasped when a land-stalker in a tattered chef's smock slithered toward her in the dark. She couldn't make out the beast's features, but recognized the oil stains on the smock's sleeves.

It was Jean's.

"Mon Dieu!" she screamed.

The stalker pounced atop the woman, cleaving her breasts with its long talons. Her blood spattered across the checkered marble in rhythmic spurts.

The stalker ate her alive.

Adelene glimpsed the sign above her head while the beast gnawed on her still beating heart.

It read: La soupe est en marche!

Soup's on!

UNITED FLIGHT 282

North Pacific Ocean

When Ezra Peterson discovered his twin had cancer, he resolved to overcome his fear of flying. That was the plan, at least. He was a wreck the second his ass plopped into his itchy window seat.

The irony was, he was an aviation engineer.

A damn good one too.

The plane Ezra was sitting in, however—forty-thousand-feet over the ocean—wasn't his. He prayed there were no loose bolts that got by B-Check back at Pudong International.

If there had been, he'd find out soon enough, along with everyone else plummeting to their deaths.

Peterson was an optimist.

"Care for a pillow, sir?" asked a thickset flight attendant wearing too much makeup. "I know an uneasy guest when I see one," she smiled.

Ezra wiped down his misty brow, "It's fine, thank you."

"You sure? They're cleaned after each trip."

Peterson mustered a soft grin, "I'm not a germaphobe."

The woman blushed, "Sorry... I saw you wiping down your palms earlier. I thought...

He showed her his hands, "Sweat."

"First time flying?"

"First time since I came back. My last memory of flying wasn't a harmonious one if you take my meaning."

The flight attendant nodded, "Gotcha... Understood."

"You guys offer complimentary Seroquel?"

The flight attendant shot him a peculiar glance.

"Bad joke," he muttered.

"Hang tight," the woman whispered, stepping away for a moment.

Ezra's heart galloped as he stared out the window.

The recollections of his death sailed to the fore of his mind.

Screaming women and children praying to God.

Flames and wind swirling through the suffocating cabin.

Metal panels breaking apart into shrapnel digging into his torso.

Peterson shuddered, clutching his gut as he relived the drop all over again.

His body felt like it was on fire.

"Have this," a delicate voice whispered.

Ezra looked up and found the flight attendant leaning close with a little tablet in her palm.

"It's diazepam. Valium." The woman offered Peterson a bottle of water. "I know how you're feeling," she said, "it'll take away the edge."

Ezra said nothing.

"You okay, sir?"

Violent tremors overtook the man's entire body, and the capillaries in his eyes burst.

Sinister red spheres locked on the panicked flight attendant.

"I need a doctor over he—agckkkkkughhhh!"

SCHLACK! A tentacle punched through Ezra's pullover, boring into the woman's ample gut. It wriggled beneath her skin like a thrashing snake in search of food, latching onto her spine.

A necrotizing toxin coursed through her body, melting her flesh from the inside out. She collapsed in blood-curdling agony.

Passengers writhed in their seats as Peterson's arms

mutated into thrashing wings.

The rest of him followed suit, transforming into a hideous alien raptor with a killer *CAW*.

Its shriek shattered every porthole in the cabin, compromising the plane's structural integrity.

The craft's tail broke off, plummeting into the sea.

It took a class of second-graders returning from a field trip with it.

The death-glider soared above hundreds falling to their deaths, dis-remembering their terror.

Ezra conquered his fear of flying.

BONDI BEACH

New South Wales, Australia

"Turn off ya alarm, ya battlah!" complained a blunt voice outside Bill Smith's bedroom. "Been up fer two goddam hours waiting for ya!"

"Gimme a break, will ya? I didn't get enough sleep last night!" Bill yelled, burying his head under the pillow.

"Stop playin with ya donger fer so fuckin long and you'd be fresh's a daisy," his old man, Jimbo, shot back. He trudged through Bill's door with a generous grin to match his lively shorts. "Where's yer board? I'll pack it in the truck while ya switch out yer grundies."

Bill moved the cushion off his skull, glad his father was in such high spirits. "It's behind the cab, ya goddamn earbasher."

The Smith men were avid surfers, always had been since Bill was a child. When his mother left, Jimbo fell into a severe depression keeping him out of the water for a good few years. Damn near killed his spirit.

Bill refused to see his old man fade away, moving Jimbo

into his flat, moments from their favorite shore.

The old sand-rat bounced back after a few months in the sun, surrounded by tits and ass.

The cruise to Bondi Beach took six minutes, but there was a traffic jam extending all the way to Park Drive.

Jimbo poked his head out the passenger window to better inspect the gridlock. "Fuckin cars backed up fer four goddam blocks!" He swung to Bill. "There a holiday we forgot?"

"The beach ain't that far," Bill answered, struggling to see past the field of cars ahead. "Why don't ya git out and find us a spot while I wait fer these fuckwhits to move along, yeah?"

Jimbo socked his boy in the arm and yanked on the aged door handle. "When ya gonna git yer door fixed? I swear, it's time ya retired the old clunker and got yerself a proper car, mate."

"I'll do it tomorrow," Bill winked.

"Fuckin hell, how d'ya turn out to be such a procrastinator like yer mum?"

"Pay me more if ya want it fixed so damn bad."

Jimbo gave the door a forceful thrust, snapping it open with a rickety *CREEK*. He stepped out of the clunker, "Wish in one hand, shit in the other. Find out which fills up first."

"See ya down there then, bloody-cheap-bastard."

Jimbo shut the truck door and wandered past the gridlocked cars and out of view down the road.

Bill thought he heard a girl screaming up ahead, cutting his radio and rolling down his window. A seagull's shrill cackle echoed overhead, but there were no screams.

He cranked the glass back up.

"Let me in, son!" Jimbo shouted, wrestling with the passenger door. "Lemme in the truck, ya fuckwhit!"

Bill lunged for the handle, struggling to pry it open.

WHAM! A giant blur leapt past the window, tackling his

father to the ground.

"Dad! Hold on!" Bill cried as Jimbo screamed in anguish.

SNAP! An obscene splat of crimson gushed across the glass, streaking downward in thick, viscous, blobs.

The son reeled in terror.

Bill reached for the blade in his glove compartment, trembling uncontrollably as his eyes darted around the cabin of the truck.

CRASH! A lobster-like claw exploded through the glass, clamping down around Bill's larynx. It pried him from the truck and into the flailing tentacles of an army of sea-creepers. Droves more slithered over the horizon of automobiles, swarming his body. Their barbed tendrils stung his flesh so much it caused his heart to burst in his rib cage.

In his last moments, he stared up and saw Jimbo's severed hand gripping the passenger door handle.

So much for fixing it tomorrow.

NIGER RIVER

Nigeria, West Africa

It had been seven years since Yewande could sink her toes in the water. She used to tell her baby brother, Okoro, all about the current that once flowed past their village. He never believed her stories until the stream flooded with tears from the sky before his eyes.

The elders said it was because of the supreme deity Oluwa that the rains came.

Yewande's distant gaze over the glistening sweep of water suggested she didn't buy it.

"Ṣe o nini won, aburo mi?" *Do you believe them, sister?* Okoro asked, sheepish. "Ṣe Oluwa n ṣe nkan yi?" *Does God do this?*

Yewande waded through the water till it was past her knees, pouring hand-fulls over her dry arms. She looked disillusioned, turning to her sibling. "Ọlọrun wa nibo ni a ni ọrọ yi nigbati a n gba adura fun awọn olopa pa? Òkunrin kekere, iṣẹ́ṣẹ́ ni." *Where's God when we pray for the warlords to leave? It is a lie, little brother,* she answered. She was only thirteen, but she was world-weary far beyond her years. "Nigba ti omi omi ti ṣẹ, o le pa ọna wọn lẹ́ẹ̀ tẹ. Pẹlú awọn ogun tuntun." *Now that the river is full, you can bet they'll be back soon. With more guns,* she said in a placid tone.

Okoro froze in the shallows. His sister moved deeper into the water. There was something about the unseen below the shimmering surface.

It haunted the boy.

Crocodiles swam the streams. He heard the new crop of missionaries talking about them. Ones the elders called "keji aye."

Second-lifers.

"Ṣe o ma wa?" *Are you coming?* asked Yewande, dipping her head beneath the water.

Okoro shook his head, scanning the river with meek eyes. He looked up, high above the stream to the hillside on the horizon, when he thought he heard a woman's screaming.

One of the village women sprinted over the crest, waving her arms in a panic. Her clothes were bloody and tattered.

"Ẹ jọwọ, ọkan ninu yin!" *Someone help!* the woman cried, looking back at something beyond the hill in horror. She fell to her knees in tears, staring down the face of the hill leading to the river. It was much too steep to roll down, and if she jumped and missed the water, the fall would kill her. The village woman rose to her feet and spied two children playing near the river's shore. She coned her hands around her mouth and shouted at the top of her lungs. "Di wọn! Awọn keji aye ni awọn ibeji!" *Run! The second-lifers are monsters!*

Yewande's head upturned in time to see the woman above get whisked off the hilltop by a massive winged creature. The woman's shrieks, so piercing at first, faded into nothingness in the sky.

"Lo ba omi, aburo mi!" *Get out of the water, sister!* Okoro screamed, pointing up at the hill and seeing two men clawing their way over the steep ridge. They were in unbelievable pain, hurling themselves over the rocky hill.

Yewande heard their bones snap when they hit the water.

She paddled to shore in a panic, clutching her little brother tight.

They expected to see two carcasses bob to the surface. but the ripples gave way to placid waves. There was no sign of the men.

It made Yewande's flesh crawl.

"Kini wọn ti ṣe?" *What the hell happened?* she muttered.

The children were so fixated on the water below, they didn't notice the land-stalkers on the edge of the hill.

If they looked up, they wouldn't have seen the gargantuan pincers erupting out of the water.

Oju kan?

The end?

Acean powered down the glowing war-portal with his veiled head at half-mast, too distressed to watch the honor of the Empire decay before his eyes.

He would do anything to preserve the glory of his people against Vulgrell's vitriol.

Anything.

It was time to ready his escape-pod.

Chapter 17: The Journal

May 13th, 2047

CLOMP. The jolt of Vadim's exo-suit jarred the earth once he hopped off the chopper. "Beautiful countryside. You used to live here, Doc?" the Russian asked, taken with the scenery. He spied Kleg Huxley's corpse rotting in the driveway. "On second thought—place could use a good HOA."

Toni picked errant burrs out of her sleeve as she eyed Vadim's exo-suit. "You make that thing on company time?"

Volkov meandered toward the house, "Yup."

"Sander never allowed an armor program… That's theft."

"Can't steal from a a business that's pretty much done for, sweet tits."

"Excuse me?"

Vadim grinned. "Loosen up, I'm not gonna abandon ya because you're a nobody now. You're in good hands." He cocked the shotgun connected to the arm of his suit. "I can blow a hole through a rhino with what I'm packing."

"Peachy," Toni snickered.

Vadim winked. "So can this *shotgun*."

News reports about monsters running rampant weren't

enough to prepare Vera for what she saw. She was on the brink of vomiting by the time she happened across Elle Shepherd's swaying body.

The woman only had half a skull, but the expression splayed on Elle's rotting face haunted Wild.

"Adieu, my friend," she whispered, tiptoeing over the mother's fly-covered entrails.

The barn was pristine when Vera first moved in. Lance raised it weeks before Evanscorp pawned the doctor off on his household. Back then, the sight of creepy crawlies would have given her fever dreams of plague.

How things can change.

She grinned when she saw her small friend, Mortimer the spider, still dangling above her cot.

"The same woman who freaked out over wrinkled bedsheets called this dump *home*?" Max asked.

"Surprising what you'll accept when there's no alternative," Vera replied, eying the rafters. "Thought I'd die of swine-flu when I first came here." She ran a palm along the side of what used to be her workstation. "Can't believe I missed this."

Amhearst half-smiled. "Home's what you make it, right?" He picked up a hammer laying beside Vera's bunk. "Should that be insulting since you dropped me for this dump?"

"I was waiting for that."

Max set the hammer in a cherry-red toolbox hanging off the edge of Lance's workbench. "Place is *too* utilitarian, even for *you*."

Vera pressed the toolbox back onto the counter. "This isn't how I left it. Lance wasted no time reclaiming what was always his." She nodded to the cot, "*My* things are over there."

Max stepped over to the bunk, noting a tattered journal atop her bundle of possessions. "I gave this to you, didn't I? I did. For our six-month anniversary."

"Where did you find that?" Wild asked, her tone harsh and taken aback. She dashed to the cot and seized the journal away from Max's prying eyes.

"Jesus, I didn't plan on reading it or anything; I recognized it."

Vera leafed through the pages, dismayed. "It's not *you* that worries me. If Calla read this, the only other person I've ever loved besides y—"

Wild halted, reassessing her words.

"There's a high probability she assumes the last seventeen years of her life were a lie. I must find her," she said.

Amhearst looked into Vera's orbs, crestfallen. "Can't have her thinking you didn't care all this time, now could we?"

"Max…"

"You were about to say you loved me, Vera. What kills me is that you couldn't. There's gotta be a reason for it, and I pray to God I last long enough to find out." Amhearst ran a finger under his eyelids, sniffling. "We came to do a job. Let's do it. This town got an emergency broadcast system? Shelter? Anything like that?"

"That's it!" Wild snatched the radio above Lance's workbench. "Get me a screwdriver," she said.

Max handed Vera a rusty multi-tool hanging on the wall. "What's up your sleeve?" he asked, cleaning the cobwebs off on his pant leg.

Vera popped off the chassis, digging into the components, "Reception's dreadful here. I had to alter Lance's radio to calibrate a back-channel frequency from my workstation to the company. If I use these pieces to invert Calla's bio-chip transmission to my laptop—"

"—You can change it into a tracking device," Max interrupted. "Not bad."

Vera plucked a phone-sized transmitter-module out of the radio. "There's one more thing I need."

* * *

"This is a fucking mistake, boss," Vadim huffed, watching Max wrench open his exo-suit's energy-bay.

Amhearst set his tool down on the kitchen counter. "If it's the only way to recover the girl we gotta do it, Vad," he said, pulling off the exo's back-panel.

Toni uncapped a bottle of beer she discovered in the fridge. "What if it doesn't run?"

"How many beers left?" Vadim asked, eying Toni's brew, looking parched.

"Don't even think about it, Vad. We need you clear-headed," Max said, shifting to Toni. "And *you*... When have you ever known your sister to be wrong, Ms. Evans?"

Evans swigged her beer, "Step-sister."

"Thank God," Vera whispered, snapping the Exo's energy-board into the radio's transmission-module.

She installed the components into the side bay of her laptop.

Vadim snickered. "What happens now? Your computer gonna save us from whatever's out there, Doc? You heard the reports, you've seen your friend on the porch."

"Cool it, Vad," Max said. "You know the chopper has a weapon cache."

Toni twisted the cap off another beer, leaning against the counter, amused. "Can the weapons in the chopper blow a hole through a rhino? Hate to admit it, but Volkov's right, even if he is a jackass."

Max looked askance at his former employer. "Maybe lay off the sauce, Toni?"

"Give her a break, her brother's dead," Volkov interjected.

Evans lifted her beer to Vadim. "Thank you, jackass."

"That's enough!" Max shouted, turning to Vera. "How we doin over here?"

"Moment of truth," Vera replied, typing into a flashing prompt. A second window popped on the screen that read: CUSTOM COMMAND OVERRIDE = PRESS ENTER.

She pressed the key.

A three-dimensional topological grid of Price Township overtook the display.

An apple-green dot pinged one klick south of the mall.

"She's on the move," Vera said.

Toni pounded her beer, banging the bottle down and dragging her forearm across her mouth. "Let's go get the little darling."

Chapter 18: Stay Down

The DALTON MALL was an institution in town. A place the whole family could enjoy.

It was fun.

Hip.

Alive.

"It *stinks* in here," Billy declared, scrunching her nose.

"Keep your eyes on me, honey," Calla said, treading over the mangled-dead littering the food court. "There's a—puddle —up ahead. Careful."

"You mean blood… Gross."

Huxley offered a hand to the girl. "Need me to set you on my shoulders?"

"Not a chance," Billy snipped, clutching Calla's arm tight. "I'm sticking close to whoever has the shotgun."

"Let me know if you change your mind."

"I won't."

"Look, if I could take back all the nasty shit Clyde did to ya I would, Billy," Stubbs said.

Kojimatsuo simpered, "If someone threw me out a window, I'd regret being a jerk too."

"Enough, the both of you," Calla hissed, nodding toward the west junction. "This way."

*****

"Son of a bitch," Stubbs groaned, raising his leg over the shattered front window. "So much for needing a key."

"I see nothing missing, none of the expensive things at least," Billy sighed. "Couple flashlights, portable filters, some potassium… uh… pomegranate tablets." She walked around the shop-counter and unsheathed a curved blade on the wall. "Wonder why they didn't jack the cool stuff?"

"Only pack what you need. As much as you can," Stubbs said.

Calla nabbed two rucksacks off a shelf, tossing one to Huxley. "Uncle Harry kept the ammunition under the knife-display." She nodded toward the back room, "Rifles and pistols should be there.

Stubbs grabbed a machete off the wall, slipping past the draped archway, "Let's see what we got."

CLICK. The business-end of a cocked forty-four magnum dug into the back of his skull.

"Drop the blade," someone hissed.

"You don't wanna do this."

"I said drop the fuckin blade!" the voice demanded, driving the tip of the gun into Stubb's sweaty flesh.

"What's going on?" Calla asked from the showroom.

A large handgun jutted out from behind the drape, followed by Huxley and…

"You got taken hostage by a kid?" Billy asked, slightly amused.

The boy's arm coiled around Huxley's throat as he dragged him toward the smashed window. "Keep back! I don't wanna kill this guy! All I came searching for was bandages, I swear!"

A shudder jolted through Shepherd's body, leaving her breathless and wide-eyed.

"Let me go and this asshole lives, okay? No trouble!"

The fuzz on Calla's neck stood on end. "Too late," she whispered, reaching for Billy's arm. "Trouble's found you."

"What's that mean?" the boy asked, pointing the gun at Calla.

"Billy... Hide... NOW!"

CHOMP! The conspicuously intact Lance-stalker lurched through the window, engulfing the boy's head in its jaws. The boy let go of Stubbs, clawing at the teeth shattering his skull, crying out in blood-curdling pain.

Huxley scrambled to distance himself from the creature, but the monster's tail knocked him through the jagged glass, into a giant wishing-well outside the store.

The beast choked down its young victim like a saltwater croc tenderizing a raw chicken down its gullet, setting its sights on the mammal in the pool next.

"You want me?" a voice called out behind the animal. "Here I am!"

The Akkan-Gah reared its heaving body, eyes locked on Calla like a bird of prey.

"I know you won't hurt me," she said, sidestepping around the creature. She pulled Huxley out of the water, pressing two fingers against his carotid artery.

There was no pulse.

"Don't you leave me, dammit!"

The Lance-stalker cocked its head as the Leevahn pressed down on the prey's ribs. It snarled when she yelped in pain, jerking her fist away from the boy's trunk.

"Shit!" Calla growled, prying a three-inch shard of glass out of her palm. She ripped open Stubbs' shirt, accidentally spilling a drop of her blood into the gash in his torso.

She almost thought she saw his eyelids shudder.

GASP! Huxley shot upright, clutching his sternum. His wild orbs met Calla's. "What the hell happened? How long was

I out?"

Shepherd swatted Huxley's hand from his chest.

His wound disappeared.

"You, you were dead..." she said, dumbstruck.

"What do you mean dead?" A heavy growl beckoned Stubbs to rear his head. "No! No! Get the fuck away from me!" he screamed, recoiling at the sight of the advancing Akkan-Gah. "Run Calla!"

"No, no, no. Stop," Shepherd shushed, leaping between them as the monster curled its gore-smeared lips into a hideous, hungry, grin.

"Are you insane?" Huxley grumbled, afraid to set it off. "You've seen what it can do."

Shepherd stood her ground, "He's no threat."

"You don't know that."

The tiny female ran her hand over the bridge of the beast's nostrils, slow and gentle. "I do," she said, looking into the creature's soul. "We're the same. Two beasts trying to understand the world. Difference is, I knew I was a monster from the beginning."

The creature shook its hide, nudging the Leevahn with the tip of its muzzle. It sniffed her skin like an obedient, curious, guard-dog.

"Can you talk to it?" Stubbs asked, stumbling to his feet, a little less weary.

"Hard to explain," Shepherd said, running a hand along its protruding teeth. "I doubt he even remembers being my father, but my instincts say he's here to protect me."

Huxley stepped closer, "From what?"

The Lance-stalker sniffed the air, disinterested in Stubbs.

A terrible epiphany occurred to Calla.

She stared down at Huxley's chest.

"From anything that doesn't share my DNA," she said.

The creature's snout drifted toward the small mammal peeking around the pillar behind it.

It looked appetizing.

"Billy!" Shepherd shrieked, reaching for the animal's barbed tail as it pounced toward the pillar, crashing into it with a terrible rumble.

It snapped to the left, then the right, circling the thick structural support as Billy evaded its famished jaws. The monster's tail whipped the pillar, cracking it down the middle as the girl fell backward onto the bloodied tiles outside her father's shop.

The creature was upon her, drawing near enough for Kojimatsuo to smell the rotting flesh between its teeth.

In a panic, the child thrust a curved blade into its neck, "I'm sorry, Uncle Lance!"

ROARR!

The beast lunged at its attacker, who braced herself as its gaping mouth enveloped her squinted vision.

CHOMP!

What the hell? Is that it? Billy thought to herself, expecting death to hurt. She couldn't open her eyes yet, too afraid to see what had become of herself, but at least it was painless.

Blood didn't spew from her lips.

Her body wasn't cold.

There was nothing at all.

"Run," a voice said, and Kojimatsuo looked down to find Calla's armor-plated forearm locked between the beast's jaws. The girl ran her hands along her entire body, thankful to be alive as Shepherd sent the Akkan-Gah crashing into a storefront window with an inhuman uppercut.

The monster exploded out of the rubble, burying its talons into Calla, and impaling her on a stalk of rebar.

For a moment, their eyes locked, and though Shepherd felt

its rage, she found no venom in the beast's gaze. If the creature could speak, it may have said: *Stay down. For your own sake, stay down.*

Calla's head slumped to the side, her shoulders sank, and she slipped into darkness. "I don't care if you were my father," she muttered, wincing in pain and choking down her own blood. "You'll die before I let you get to them."

BLAM! The beast's skull exploded into a plume of red mist. The lumbering mutant collapsed into a pool of its own brains beneath Calla's limp body.

"Ask, and you will receive," a gruff voice said. "I'll take this one, you round up the other two. If they give ya any shit, shoot em."

Chapter 19: Jaded

"We can't leave them here," a silky female voice said.

"There comes a time in every person's life when their lack of choice forces them to choose what they're willing to lack, Muriel," a surly tone retorted. "Dunno about you, but I *choose* to lack another mouth to feed."

"How can you be so cold? They're kids."

"They let our son die. An eye for an eye, woman."

"No, *you* took your eye off of him, don't dare blame these kids."

"Oh gimme a break, will ya? You saw what the girl can do, she ain't no kid, she's a freak. For all we know she's in cahoots with those fuckin things. The other two kids were with her, that makes em enemies in my book."

"This isn't right, Barry!"

"Shut the fuck up, before they hear," the gruff voice hissed. "These hangars echo like a sonofabitch; use your head. I say we put these little shits out of their misery now. That, or leave em alive for those things to eat. I don't give a shit either way."

"You're a monster sometimes, you know? Why not bring them? It's the Christian thing to do, Barry."

"You think I'm gonna let that freak bitch on my train? You lost it, woman, you've gone insane—and you can forget about the other two. Who the fuck knows what crazy disease she gave em? What if they infect you and me, huh? Then what?"

"Then that's Lord's will!"

WHACK! A slap echoed through the void. "I told you to keep your voice down, Muriel. I won't repeat it, you get me?"

"Yeah… I get you," the silky tone muttered.

A volatile silence enveloped the darkness.

"Did you catch that?" the woman asked.

"Catch what, Muriel?" the gruff voice replied, exasperated.

"She moved."

The pungent stench of spent oil stung Calla's nostrils. Her eyelids fluttered open.

Someone chained her to a concrete pillar amid a vast industrial Quonset hangar.

Muriel Strunk stepped out of the shadows. She was a meek but well-attired woman with bruised arms and an inflamed left cheek. "You're in the train-yard," she said, polite but apprehensive. "My husband felt it might be a good idea to secure you. We both saw what you did for the girl… How your arm — changed. We couldn't take any chances."

"Hey, cut that out," Barry Strunk hissed, yanking his wife away from Shepherd. "Nothing you need to say to her."

"Where are my friends?"

Strunk loosened his mottled necktie, "They're around."

"We're right here," Kojimatsuo growled, chained to a pillar behind Calla, Stubbs bound beside her. "Mind kicking this guy's ass now?"

Barry swiped a pistol out from under his shirt, aiming at Billy, "Better shut up, ya little shit."

"She's just a child, man, relax!" Huxley shouted.

"So was my boy! Where were you when that thing tore him apart? Where were you when he needed you, hero? What were you doing before he died, huh?"

"He was begging your kid not to shoot him, dick-brain!" Kojimatsuo retorted.

Stubbs leered at Billy, "I wouldn't say I begged…"

"Dude, you begged."

"Shut it!" Barry barked, "the both of ya!"

Muriel tugged on her spouse's shoulder. "Will you stop yelling? The noise, remember?"

Strunk pulled away from his timid wife, clicking back the hammer of his gun. "I don't give a shit if those things hear me or not, these ingrates oughta pay for letting our son die. He was a decent kid! He was everything I wasn't, and you cowards watched him get slaughtered!" He collapsed to his knees, weeping. "I struggled to be a somebody instead of a gravediggin nobody so that boy could have a shot." He eyed Muriel, "So we *all* could."

Muriel's wistful eyes wandered from her husband, "We have each other."

Strunk nodded, drying his tears and rising to his feet. "That's about as reassuring as being Mayor of a city full of corpses."

"You're the Mayor?" Kojimatsuo asked, mortified. "No wonder Price Township sucks so bad."

"Billy please, you're not helping," Calla said.

Strunk stared daggers at the little girl, scraping the side of his head with his pistol. "Better listen, before we lose another innocent soul."

"Your kid broke into my dad's store and stuck a gun to my friend's skull, he wasn't innocent," Billy replied.

"He was desperate and scared! We told him to stay with us, didn't we, Muriel?"

The woman nodded.

"He wouldn't listen, insisting we needed supplies and shit.

Next thing I remember, I'm on the ground, my useless wife at my side, and the kid's run off with my piece."

Billy rolled her eyes, "Real honor-roll material."

The Mayor gave his spouse a pleading glance, "I can't listen to this anymore, Muriel. We kill em then get on the train.

"You can't leave us here like this," Shepherd balked. "You don't wanna do this."

"Like hell. My wife and me, we're headed for the promised land, kid. You think Reverend Tanner's gonna welcome us with open arms if we got you and your freak-lovin friends with us? They'll fuckin kill everyone!"

Calla looked up at Muriel, "At least take my companions. Nobody has to know they were with me… Please. I can handle myself, but they need your help."

Barry shot his bride a threatening glare, "Damnit, woman…"

The woman backed away from Shepherd, "My husband said no, girl. My hands are tied."

Calla glanced at the woman's wrists, disgusted and dissapointed. "Are they?"

"Good girl. Muriel," her husband grumbled, tallying the number of bullets in his clip. "I got enough to put three in each of em." He cocked his head toward Calla. "This thing heals though, so I guess I can save three, huh?"

"She's no *thing*," Huxley asserted, bracing himself for death. "Her name's Calla Shepherd and don't you forget it."

"Well," Barry chambered a round, "for that, you die first." He marched up to Stubbs and pressed the pistol between his eyes. "My son's name was Larry Strunk, and that's the last name you'll ever hear."

"No!" Shepherd roared, tearing through her titanium bonds in an adrenaline-fueled frenzy.

A *BOOM* rang throughout the hangar.

"Huxley!" she cried.

Barry idled over Stubbs with a vacant expression on his face. He glanced down at a crimson stain radiating from his femur.

BLAM! Another bullet ricocheted off the side of a steel table, boring into the concrete above Billy's head.

The homicidal Mayor collapsed to the ground.

Muriel didn't move a muscle.

CLINK. An empty cartridge sprang out of Vadim's Remington M-Forty. He pulled back the bolt from atop the hill, laying in the grass with his eye pressed against the scope. "Target's down, boss."

"Do you see a girl?" Amhearst asked, putting on a tactical-vest he found in the chopper's weapon cache.

"We got three hostages and one unarmed woman, two hostages are female."

"That's good enough for me." Max slung his AR-Fifteen over his shoulder and handed Vera a loaded handgun. "Hope you don't gotta use it, but just in case." He turned to Toni, "No weapons left, so stick close to us, got it?"

Toni lifted her shirt. A familiar looking forty-four magnum rested at her tight waist. "Found it at the mall while you guys were looting."

Amhearst nodded. "Suits you."

Muriel knelt beside her fallen husband, stroking his stubbled cheek. She wished he would turn blue before her eyes so she could be certain he was dead.

The woman's heart sank when his chest inflated with air.

Barry looked up at the only woman he'd ever loved in his own twisted way. He would never know how close he came to bringing her genuine joy for once.

In the hours since the invasion began, Calla saw more human ugliness than she cared to stomach.

Father's leaving their sons to die.

Children turning feral in the face of catastrophe, ready and willing to kill anyone in their way.

Wives heartbroken to see their husband's alive.

Alive.

Shepherd felt so alien, unable—or unwilling—to understand how volatile humanity was.

It jaded her.

"These chains gonna undo themselves, or what?" Billy asked Stubbs.

"Hold your horses," Huxley grumbled, untying Kojimatsuo.

WHACK! A foot kicked open the emergency exit door behind Calla. "Hands up," Vadim said, pressing the barrel of his M-Forty into her back.

Max strafed into view, an eye down the sight of his AR. "Nobody moves and this situation gets much less tense, okay? We're looking for Calla Shepherd."

"Who is?" Calla asked, arms raised.

Volkov nudged her with the end of his rifle. "We'll ask the questions, got it?"

Shepherd snatched up the weapon, breaking it in two and chucking the pieces over her shoulder. She grabbed the enormous Russian by the collar, hoisting him off the ground, one-handed.

"Calla don't!" a familiar voice cried out. "He's on your side."

Shepherd lowered the Russian to the ground, aware of who was speaking. "What the hell are you doing here?"

Vera advanced on her surrogate daughter with open arms. "You don't know how glad I am to see y–"

SLAP! Calla backhanded Vera across the face, splitting her lip. "Save the lies, bitch. This *specimen's* done being your pet project."

Wild wiped the blood from her mouth. "Suppose I deserved that."

"You do," Calla fired back.

Amid all the tension, Vadim couldn't help chuckling. "Nothing like a heartfelt reunion."

Chapter 20: Kekerah Riash

Volkov dumped a rucksack full of weapons atop a welding table, cleaning his MC-Six with an oily rag. When he finished tidying the weapon, he fished a flask out of his boot.

He took a hasty swig.

"That vodka, comrade?" Billy asked.

Vadim twisted the cap back on, embarrassed. "Whiskey," he said, looking over his shoulder. "You been sitting there a while?"

"Long enough to notice your drinking problem, buddy."

Stubbs gave the girl a nudge. "Don't piss off the guy in charge of the guns, numb-nuts."

Volkov grinned. "It's cool. She has moxie, I admire that... Reminds me of my Afanasia. Got names, or should I call you kid-one and kid-two?"

"I'm Billy," Kojimatsuo said, backhanding Huxley's chest, "this is my friend, Stubbs."

Vadim donned a curious, amused, leer. "Your name's Billy? With a B?"

The girl nodded, proud.

Volkov turned to Huxley, "I know I don't seem as smart as I am, but you expect me to believe your name's Stubbs?"

"It's what people call me," Huxley said, abashed.

"Okay then. Stubbs, Billy, my name's Tittyshits Finkywinkle."

"Seriously?" Kojimatsuo asked, resisting the impulse to erupt into laughter.

"Your name Billy?"

The girl rolled her eyes, "Wilma, okay?"

"Vadim Volkov," the Russian replied, extending his hand to them both. "Nice to meet you guys."

Huxley gave Volkov a firm handshake, "Back at ya."

"Easy kid, you got a grip like my grandmamma."

"Ouch," Billy said.

"Ouch is right. That old woman strangled bulls with her bare hands. I would've been proud if my daughter turned out half as strong as her."

"Where is your little girl?" Kojimatsuo asked.

Vadim uncapped his flask, but quickly twisted it back on. "She's not around anymore, Billy," he said, fighting the tremble in his lower lip.

"I know that face, me and my friend here both do."

Stubbs eyed Kojimatsuo curiously, "You know that's the fourth time you've called me your friend, right?"

"So?"

"You hated me not that long ago."

Billy shook her head, elbowing Huxley in the ribs. "Stop being such a bitch, Stubbers. You and Calla are all I got. If I could trade ya in, I would, but I can't... So, I gotta like ya instead."

Huxley wrapped an arm around Billy's shoulder, "Ditto, Wilma."

"Don't touch me."

Vadim's eyes darted between his booze, and the two kids. He tossed his flask of Whiskey in an overflowing trash bin next to Billy. "Who needs liquor when you guys are much more entertaining?"

Kojimatsuo grinned, "This one of them crossroad things? Did we just witness you make some life altering decision?"

"Maybe."

"Verenberg was the only installation broadcasting when we were airborne," Max said.

"Can we fly there?" Toni asked.

Amhearst shook his head, "We used up too much fuel. You'd be lucky to fly two blocks with what's left."

Evans slammed her fist into the table. "Damn you, Vera," she hissed.

"Hey, cut her a break. Even if Calla's transmissions updated in real time, we still wouldn't have had enough to make it that far west. We made a few stops, but at least we didn't come away empty-handed, Mrs. Forty-four Magnum."

Toni massaged her aching temples. "Ugh, whatever. What about a train then?"

Amhearst stared out the office window. A fleet of rusty and dilapidated train-cars cluttered the yard. "I doubt if any of them are even track-worthy."

"Not the ones you can see," Barry Strunk hissed, eavesdropping from a cot in the corner. "I got a train, hell it's more like a fuckin convoy."

"A convoy?" Max asked. "Where?"

Calla stood watch outside the Repair Bay. The whole operation was industrial and not a place the Akkan would flock to in their search for flesh.

It was peaceful.

She needed a little peace, a moment of silence.

"Can we talk? Woman to woman?" a voice asked.

"That's cute, coming from you," Shepherd replied.

Wild stepped closer, "You don't understand how hard it was to *not* come back to you and your family."

"Then why didn't you?"

"It wasn't my choice."

"Bullshit!" Calla cried. "I read your journal, you hated me!"

Wild idled a moment, cursing her past, "I wrote that seventeen years ago."

"I was a baby!"

"And I was wrong!" Vera roared, wiping away her tears. "I shouldn't have written that, and I couldn't be sorrier that I did! I wanted a baby so badly, and you were the miracle I could never achieve, Calla! So, yeah, I called you a specimen! A subject! It was cruel, it was petty, and I hate myself every day for it!"

She took a breath to compose herself.

"I love you like my child. You don't have to believe me, but it's the truth."

Shepherd listened to Vera's words, but she was nevertheless on guard, stepping closer to her surrogate mother. "You hurt me, Vera. You were supposed to be my family."

"I am, honey."

"Why should I trust you?"

"Because I've turned my back on those I loved before. You were never one of those people," Wild replied, inching close enough to embrace the young woman. "You're my daughter."

Calla wanted to say so much, but the hurt in her heart stayed her tongue. She resisted the urge to hug Vera, afraid to trust her even though she knew she could.

"I'm glad you came back while I was still—myself," Shepherd said.

"What do you mean?"

"There's something inside me, and it's getting stronger. Has been since the monsters arrived... I won't end up one of those things."

"Calla, look at me... Whatever's happening; we'll take it on together."

"I second that," Max interjected, leaning beside a light post near the emergency exit door.

Vera's face went pale. "How long have you been standing there?"

"May I borrow Vera for a moment?" Max asked.

CLICK, Vera switched on a lamp in a secluded corner, far from prying eyes and ears. "What's going on?" she asked.

"Mayor's got a train stored in Hangar Zero, but—"

"That's excellent news."

"Yeah, well—The entrance's key-code activated. Paranoid sonofabitch kept his codes in his phone—which Vad destroyed when he shot him. Only one other person had those codes."

"Who?"

"His right-hand man, a guy named Lars, his muscle."

"And where's Lars?"

"Dead, of course."

"Jesus Christ... We can't die in this shit-hole, Max."

"We won't. Barry says his codes are in a storage locker on-site. We grab them, get inside Hangar Zero, and ride the hell out of here. Bing. Bang. Boom."

Vera nodded, flustered, "Anything else?"

"Yeah," Max said, pulling her in for a kiss.

Vera didn't resist, withdrawing her lips as she gazed into Amhearst's eyes. "You were standing there longer than I thought."

Max touched his forehead to hers, "Why didn't you tell me you couldn't have children?"

"When I left, I did so knowing you loved me... I left knowing you didn't think I was defective."

"You aren't defective."

"I know you wanted a family I couldn't give you."

Amhearst caressed her cheek, wiping away her tears with his thumb. "I would have understood. All I've ever needed was *you*, Vera. That was family enough for me."

"That wasn't a risk I could take. I had no choice but to go. I hope you understand as much as forgive me."

"Do you regret it? Trying to *spare* me all those years ago?"

Vera pondered a moment, "No."

"No?"

She rested her head against Max's chest, "I'm sorry."

"You broke my heart that day."

Vera looked up at Max. "You asked me if I regretted it, not if I'd do it differently. I would have."

"No time like the present."

"No time, indeed."

"Touching," Toni mumbled to herself, spying on Max and Vera through a gap in a shelf a few meters away.

She had to move fast if she was gonna uphold her end of Vulgrell's deal…

"—Holy shit," Toni whispered, frozen.

Vulgrell leered at the kraith. "Who is this delicate creature? Another mammal come to negotiate?"

"This is the kraith's sibling, my Khoth. Far less obtuse than the male. She presents no threat to us," Acean said.

Vulgrell's face relaxed a little. "Sibling, eh? They say nobody can break a bond between brother and sister. Is this accurate?"

Toni looked down at her twin, whose arm outstretched in pleading despair. "Nope," she replied.

Her honesty intrigued the Khoth. "Not the answer I anticipated. I meant to leverage your affection for this animal so I may learn where the Leevahn is."

"I don't know where she is, but I know who does."

"You do?" Vulgrell asked, looking askance at Sander. "Then why do I need this one?"

Sander's eyes expanded in dread. "Toni... Toni, don't let him do this. Don't let him kill me! Please!"

"Say hello to mom and dad," Toni said, turning away when the enormous alien SPLATTED Sander's skull across the wall. She watched her brother's headless corpse slump onto its side with self-preserving satisfaction.

Khoth Vulgrell studied his handiwork, "I recommend you learn from his blunders."

"My father always said I was the agreeable one," Toni said.

The alien grinned, "You are most unusual. It is as though you are not afraid."

An appreciative tear trickled down Toni's cheek, "You took care of the one person I feared my whole life."

Khoth Vulgrell cocked his skull to the side, fascinated by this pathetic animal. "You remind me of a rat. Small and feeble, yet you thrive by any means necessary. A survivor."

"Suppose I am."

The alien nodded, "The Akkan shall awaken soon." Vulgrell eclipsed the chandelier above Toni's head. "If you wish to continue living, you will lead me to the Leevahn."

Toni choked down the lump in her throat. "I told you, I don't know where she is."

"But you know who does," Vulgrell hissed, planting a small alien device in her palm. "Use this when they lead you to her and I shall spare you from what lies ahead, little rat."

Toni studied the beacon in her hand, glancing up in time to spy Acean's disapproving scowl. "We have a deal," she said, tucking the tech into her back pocket.

Vulgrell lifted the tip of her chin with his clawed finger, "It is voice activated. When the time comes, say the words—"

"Kekerah riash," Toni whispered.
The device vibrated.

Chapter 21: Going Home

May 14th, 2047
3:23AM

Its tentacles ascended the shower wall like an army of sentient intestines.

A woman's half-digested head birthed from the beak beneath its gossamer body.

The creature clasped the firefighter's sizzling skull with its spiny pincer, flicking it out of the stall. It rolled to a stop beside a fly-ridden pile of human remains the beast didn't find appetizing. The pungent stench of rotting organs and old blood overtook the room.

The sea-creeper's fishy stink smelled worse than that.

It slid back into the thin pool of water at the base of the shower. The barbed cups underneath its limbs felt a subtle vibration. It had no ears, but its extremities were perfect echo-locators.

There was life nearby.

Food.

Like a squid darting through the blackened ocean on a moonlit night, the beast vanished.

* * *

Stubbs pushed open the glass door, Vadim at his back with his MC-Six locked and loaded. "How much farther?" the Russian hissed.

"We're in the dorm area right now. Apparatus bay's past the fitness center and the administration offices," Huxley said. He'd been on a tour of the place a few years before during Career Week at Price Township High. When he found out what it took to make it to the probationary stage, he tucked tail and ran. "Almost to medical if you wanna pick up supplies."

When they reached medical, Vadim handed his carbine to Stubbs, along with a walky-talky. "Stay here and lock the door behind me," he said, grabbing a hand-radio for himself. "I'm on channel six. Talk me through this dump. I'll let you know when I grab the codes."

"Why can't I go with you?"

"You're a kid, and kids do dumb shit… Nothing personal."

"None offense took… I guess." Stubbs extended his palm to Vadim, "Be careful, Mr. Volkov."

The Russian grinned, shaking his head. "Call me Vad." He nodded to his MC-Six, "Break it, I break *you* worse. Understand?"

"Sure you don't wanna take it?"

Vadim pulled a Beretta-M-Nine out of his tac-vest. "If this little lady doesn't get the job done," he brandished a live grenade, "my lucky boom-boom will. Lock the door behind me."

"You got it, Vad."

Volkov winked, "So the ladies tell me, kid."

Calla didn't expect to find Muriel kneeling beside the bathroom sink with her hands clasped in prayer, but there she was, lit candle and all.

"I'll come back later," Shepherd whispered, backing out of

the doorway.

"Wait," Strunk responded. "Please, come in."

"You sure? Looks like you could use some privacy."

The woman rose to her feet, straightening out her long skirt. "It's fine… I wanted to apologize to you."

Calla stepped into the restroom and shut the door, "How's your cheek?"

Strunk cupped a hand over her bruised face, "I'd rather not say."

"Ya know, it's not me you need to say sorry to… It's yourself."

"What do you mean?"

"You're the only one who can put an end to the way the Mayor treats you."

"He wasn't always so angry," Muriel replied. A fleeting glimmer of contentedness shined in her eye, dimming the longer she dwelled. "We used to be good together if you could believe it." A furrow etched into Muriel's brow, and she glanced at Calla as if trying to pinpoint a lost memory. "Your friend… Earlier today he said your last name was Shepherd, is that right?"

"It is, yes."

Muriel nodded. "That's a good last name to have according to my husband. When he was young, he worked as a gravedigger. Claimed it was a corpse named Lance Shepherd that turned his life around. He mentions it often."

"He does?"

"Barry used to say his biggest regret was not looking him up and shaking his hand. Lance ended up a clone, you see."

"They wouldn't have gotten along well."

"You don't think so?"

"Not if Lance knew how your husband treated his little girl."

* * *

Vadim's steps echoed in the dead hallway. His M-Nine trembled in his adrenaline fueled palms as he pushed through the swiveling double-doors leading into the apparatus bay.

The door *CREAKED* closed.

He scanned the area, counting two firetrucks, one ambulance, and a topless jeep.

There was a bloody hand-print on the jeep's hood.

Volkov spotted what he was after on the other side of the bay: a safe beside a red fire-pole.

He tiptoed against firetruck-A, stopping at a compartment at the rear of the vehicle.

It wasn't open when he first entered the garage.

The chainsaw was still there, but ax-two was missing.

KA-PANG! The gleaming steel edge of the second ax missed Vadim's skull by inches, boring into the side of the truck. The Russian tackled his attacker to the ground, knocking the weapon away.

"Don't fucking move," Vadim growled. He dug his gun into their cheek, the full weight of his body sandwiching his much smaller assailant against the polished cement. "What the hell you trying to take my head off for?"

"I didn't know you were a person, I swear," the mousy man said, bloody palms face-up in surrender. "Did you see it? The thing that killed my crew? It's *huge*, whatever the hell it is!"

"Your crew?" Vadim rose off the guy, hoisting him to his feet. "You don't look like a firefighter, buddy."

"I'm a probie. Transferred here with a couple others. One of em turned into that thing. He—or it—killed everyone in the station but me. I was hiding in the day room—that's how I survived."

"Good for you, scooter." Vadim's eyes darted overhead.

There were plenty of ducts and vents.

Tons of places to launch an ambush.

Volkov grabbed the ax on the ground and shoved it into the mousy man's arms. "Knock off the safe's padlock or you won't have to worry about some monster killing ya."

"Why can't you do it?" the little man asked, nervous.

The Russian nodded toward the ceiling above the safe, "See the open vent up there?"

"Yeah."

"Would you walk underneath that after what you just told me?"

The tiny man balked, "And I'm not worried about the same shit?"

Vadim plucked the chainsaw from the truck's storage compartment, "I got more common sense than you."

"Says who?"

"You were senseless enough to think you could get the drop on me, weren't ya? Look at you. You're a toothpick."

"With a fucking ax."

"Did you hit me with it?"

The small guy said nothing, but it was a begrudging silence.

"That's what I thought."

"What are you gonna be doing then?"

Vadim brandished the chainsaw in his massive clutches, "Whatever I need to. Shall I add beating the shit out of you for not doing as you were told to the list?"

"Dick," the little man grumbled, skulking toward his ill-gotten objective.

When he reached the safe, he looked back at the Russian, but the firetruck obscured him.

He inspected the padlock, muttering obscenities under his breath as his eyes skittered upward, toward the shadowy vent over his head.

An amorphous blob oozed down the fire-pole behind him.

"I don't hear any padlocks breaking over there," Volkov said.

A wet *THWAP* echoed through the garage, followed by an obscene oozing sound.

"Talk to me, little man."

There was no reply.

Vadim backed against the end of the firetruck, peeking around the corner.

What he saw made him shiver.

A huge octopus-thing blanketed the mousy man's body, but it was no ordinary cephalopod. It didn't just have a wide set of eyes atop its form, but a complete head with hideous serrated teeth.

The mousy man tried to crawl away, but the creature's tentacles pinned him to the ground.

Searing shrieks overtook the garage as the sea-creeper liquefied the man's flesh. It sloughed off in thick gobs of bloody muck the beast sucked up with its proboscis tongue.

Vadim watched the see-creeper's slimy branches slither, wondering how he'd bypass the thing. His chainsaw could kill it, but he would have to get close first, which wasn't something he was keen on doing.

His scanning eyes glimpsed a CO2 extinguisher hanging beside the double doors. If he got his hands on it, he could freeze the monster.

He had to be quiet.

"What's taking ya so long?" Stubb's voice crackled over the walky-talky.

The creeper's tentacles coiled against the cement, pinpointing the vibrations.

It slung itself against the side of firetruck-B, pressing into the surface.

No signs of life.

The beast slithered atop the rig, latching to firetruck-A beside it.

Something rhythmic pulsed nearby.

The sea-creeper snaked down the opposite side of the truck.

Still no prey, but it sensed reverberations close by.

Vadim covered his mouth, hiding beneath the firetruck.

A single tentacle whipped against the undercarriage, wrapping around the axle.

More arms slithered underneath like a faceless hydra closing in for the kill.

"Vad, answer me," the walky-talky said.

The beast knew where the sound was coming from now, springing off the truck and crashing into the desk by the front end of firetruck-A.

Volkov rolled out from under the vehicle, bolting for the extinguisher. He ripped out the pin and unleashed frozen hell on the flailing creeper, "I ain't getting done in by a fuckin booger!"

The monster was an iced-over statue by the time Vadim dropped the CO_2 canister, but its eyes still followed the human's every move.

The Russian revved his chainsaw.

"Let's see how you like being torn to pieces while alive," he said.

Stubbs checked the clock on the wall for the hundredth time when it became clear Vadim wasn't coming back.

That's when the panic set it.

If whatever's out there got a bad-ass like Volkov, I ain't making it out of here alone. The smartest thing to do is hunker down and pray someone saves me, Huxley thought.

It was a reasonable but terrifying plan of action.

If only he hadn't kept his finger on the carbine's trigger when the Russian pounded on the med-bay door.

4:15AM

"Get him on the desk!" Max barked, dashing out of the manager's office.

Wild shoved Huxley aside, cutting open the front of Vadim's shirt. Blood gushed from a gaping wound in the Russian's chest.

"I need a clean towel! A rag! Anything sterile!" Vera ordered, leering at Stubbs. "What happened out there?"

"It was an accident," the boy muttered.

"How do you *accidentally* shoot someone at point-blank range?" Max growled, storming into the office hauling a portable torching unit. "He counted on you! This man's been through more than your dumb ass could imagine! Now he's bleeding out because you got the jitters? Get the hell out of here, you fucking coward!"

Vadim's shaky hand draped around Max's wrist. "Go easy on the kid," he whispered.

"Conserve your energy," Max said. He wrapped the broken end of a broomstick in a strip of cloth from his shirt. "Bite down on this."

The Russian grinned, his teeth stained with blood. "Picked the worst time to quit drinking."

"Don't worry about it, when this is over, we'll polish off a bottle together. You and me, buddy."

Vera assessed the Russian's wound, concerned. "You can't cauterize this," she said. "If you try, the shock could kill him."

"We gotta do something! I'm not gonna watch him die!" Max eyed Stubbs, "Was there any Hemo-Proxy or Plasma-

Synth back at the firehouse?"

Huxley shook his head, afraid to speak.

"Fuck!" Amhearst roared, watching the life leave his pale friend's body. "No, no no... Vad... Vadim! Hang with me, brother!"

"It's okay, boss," Volkov mumbled, his drowsy eyes fluttering closed one final time. "I'm... I'm going—home—to my Afanasia."

"Stay with me..." Max pleaded.

But it was too late.

Chapter 22: The Beacon

Max... Max...

"Max!" Calla shouted from the doorway.

"What?" Amhearst barked, swiveling toward the young woman, catching himself. "Sorry, I... He was my best friend."

"I can help him."

"How?" Wild asked with a tinge of intrigue.

Shepherd grabbed a pair of scissors out of the desk drawer at her side and sliced deep into her palm. "Open his shirt again," she said.

"No!" Vera dashed in front of Vadim's corpse, recalling what happened to the rodents back at the lab. "I can't allow it, Calla, I'm sorry."

An inhuman voice rattled the windows, "Let the Leevahn do what she must."

The office fell silent.

Acean's lording frame slithered into the room, his hooded cloak shrouding him in mystery. The humans looked upon him in terrified awe.

"What the fuck is that?" Barry slurred; slapped awake by a mortified Muriel.

"It's the devil," she mumbled, clutching Barry's hand tight.

"He's dead is what he is!" Amhearst roared, aiming his

tucked handgun at the alien. "This is your fault!"

Calla clutched Max's weapon, crushing the barrel. "This one's not a threat."

"How the fuck do you know?" Max balked, shielding Vera.

Calla's eyes met Acean's, "I can sense it." She drew closer to him, unafraid and more than a little curious. "You called me the leaven. What does that mean? Is that what *I am*?"

Acean looked past the Leevahn, toward Volkov's body, "You haven't much time if you wish to save the kraith." The cleric reached for Calla's palm, slicing it open once more with his taloned fingertip. "Hurry, child."

"Calla," Wild pleaded, "you don't know what you're doing."

"Trust me," Shepherd replied, clenching her fist over Vadim's gory wound.

Three drops of blood squeezed out of her hand and into his cold vessel.

Vera clutched Max's shoulder, "None of us should be in here!"

"I'm not leaving Vadim in the same room as this—thing."

"Dammit!" Wild cried, pressing Amhearst's head against her chest in disgusted anticipation.

"The hell are you doing, Vere?" Max barked, trying to pull away.

"You leave me no choice!" she answered, bracing for the wet explosion with tightly shut eyelids.

But it never came.

"Mary, mother of God," Muriel muttered.

"You gotta be shitting me," Barry added.

"Vad?" Max mumbled. "How is this possible?"

Wild opened her eyes.

The big Russian cracked his neck from side to side with a hung-over grimace on his face, "Did I pass out or somethin?"

Amhearst bear-hugged Volkov off the ground. "Thought you were gone, brother!"

"I'm getting a super gay vibe from you, boss," Vadim said, surprised by Max's strength. "You wanna let me go now? My nuts itch."

Max released his jovial grip on the Russian. "Vad... You were dead, man."

"Dead?"

"Yeah."

"As in not alive, dead?"

"Fucking, eyes wide open, gaping hole in your chest, dead."

Volkov backed against the table, looking at the pool of blood smeared across the surface. "I thought the kid shooting me was a shitty dream."

"Did you see her?" Max asked. "Afanasia?"

The big Russian's face sank, and he shook his head. "It was black."

"My people call it the void," Acean interjected.

Vadim recoiled upon seeing the lording alien in the doorway, "The *hell* is that thing doing here?"

"Are all humans so hostile and ungrateful as the lot of you?" the being asked.

"They're afraid," Calla said.

"I am not the one to fear," the cleric replied, scanning the kraitho in the room. "There is a traitor in your midst, entrusted with a royal beacon leading to this exact location. If justice is to prevail, the Leevahn must flee. Now."

"I—I don't understand. Why are you helping me?"

"This is not the time, child. Others will be here soon."

Vera stepped in front of Acean, blocking his path.

"Who activated the beacon?" she asked.

Stubbs set Vadim's MC-Six-Carbine atop the welding-table

with all the other weapons. His head bowed in shameful mourning.

Billy walked up behind him. "You okay?"

Huxley turned around, "All he needed me to do was walk him through the fire-station and I end up shooting the guy. My Pop was right… I'm a useless coward."

Kojimatsuo angrily poked his chest, "Don't you talk about yourself like that! You're no looker, but you aren't useless! And a coward wouldn't stand up to those things the way you did!"

"Then why is Vadim dead?"

"You think Tittyshits Finkywinkle would want you to give up? I bet he wasn't a quitter, Huxley, and neither are you."

A slow clap bounced through the air, and Toni came ambling around the corner with a subtle limp in her stride, shoes in hand. "You got a career in motivational speaking, little girl… Assuming you live long enough to have one." She was surprised to find Volkov's booze in the wastebasket at her throbbing feet. "Must be my lucky day," she said, uncapping the flask. She winced as the alcohol sizzled down her throat. "Whoa, that's not Vodka."

"How's it that my boy here's more messed up over Vadim's death than someone who knew the guy?"

Toni grinned, taking another swig of the Russian's whiskey. "You can call me a bitch if you think I'm a bitch, ya little shit."

"Hey, back off," Huxley snapped. "She's calling it like she sees it, lady."

"That's right, bitch," Billy added.

Evans scoffed, "You kids make me appreciate not having any. Ugh, I need a foot rub."

"I'll put my damn hands on you…" a woman's voice said.

Toni swiveled around in time to see Vera's fist fly straight into her nose. *POW!*

"What the hell are you doing?" she cried, staring down at her shirt. "This blouse cost me six hundred dollars! Stain it and die!"

"Why did you do it?" Vera exclaimed, lunging for Toni's collar. "Where is it?"

"What are you rambling on about, you crazy whore!"

"The beacon!"

Evans licked away the blood tricking from her nostrils, "You're losing it, Vere."

Acean's lording silhouette revealed itself behind Wild, as if backing her up. "I disagree, kraith."

"You," Toni grumbled. She snatched Billy by the arm, pressing her forty-five magnum into the girl's temple. "Thought you aliens were all about honor, ya backstabber!"

Max, Barry, and Muriel advanced alongside Vera, and together they formed a serriform wall around Evans.

There was no escape.

"So you got a mob now, huh? Well, you can all go to hell!" Toni hissed.

"Judge not, lest ye be judged," Muriel shouted, "and let she who is without sin cast the first stone!"

"Good one, honey," Barry said, his arm slung over his wife's shoulder as she strained under the weight of his gut.

Evans smiled, "You're right, I shouldn't throw stones when I have led."

BLAM! Muriel's forehead flung backward and her brains spewed across Barry's face. He collapsed to the ground alongside her. "M—M—Muriel!" he cried.

Toni retrained the gun on Billy's head, "Any other takers? Anyone else wanna chat? Huh? I didn't want it to go down this way, but I'll shoot every last one of you if I gotta."

"Did the Kil'Durians even kill Sander?" Wild asked.

"Oh fuck you, Vera! If they hadn't, I would have, and so would you if given the chance. He was no better than those things. Difference is, the aliens promised me protection."

Acean snickered, "You've seen how my Khoth handles alliances. This will not end well for you, kraith."

"I'm just trying to survive. I don't wanna run the rest of my life, or worse, get killed by you assholes, like Vadim did."

A fresh wave of guilt sliced through Stubbs' gut when an impossible voice called out behind Acean. *"Sure you aren't a man, Toni?"*

Volkov stepped past his wall of friends, "Because you got some enormous balls calling us assholes."

Huxley's face lit up, "You're alive!"

Vadim winked, "Yeah, I get that a lot."

"Of— fucking—course you are," Toni said, tightening her grip on Billy. "One more word and she won't be, and I swear to God I'll make sure she doesn't come back."

"Either give this bitch what she wants or off her already!" Kojimatsuo hissed.

"Stop saying that!"

"Make me, bitch!"

"I will end you!"

"For calling you a bitch, bitch?"

"Billy, please!" Max exclaimed, stepping to the fore with his arms raised in surrender. "What's it gonna take to get you to put the weapon down, Toni?"

"Shooting this brat for starters!"

"With what bullets, ya dizzy broad?" Barry asked, still at his dead wife's side. "That's the gun Larry had on him when he looted the mall."

"So?" Evans balked.

"It only had one round left."

"Let's find out!"

CLICK.

CLICK, CLICK.

Strunk brandished a weary smirk, "I know my guns—

bitch."

POW! Billy elbowed Toni in the stomach, felling her to her knees. She reached for Kojimatsuo's leg, but the girl was too quick to catch, slipping behind the adults in a flash.

"Who leaves a single bullet in their gun at a time like this?" she gasped.

"He stole it before I could reload it, woman," Barry retorted. "If he hadn't, I would've used *that* to kill that big-ass freak back at the mall instead of my shotgun. More stopping power."

Vera's brow furrowed, "Freak at the mall? What are you talking about?"

"The thing, dammit! That big fucker had your girl pinned against the concrete before I blew a hole in its head! It was the size of a rhino, how could ya miss it?"

"We saw nothing like that."

Acean looked down at Wild, "Your weaponry will not easily kill what he speaks of."

WHOOSH! A volcanic tremor shook the I-beams overhead. Tools slid off the steel shelves, clanging to the ground. The Repair Bay's garage door buckled inward.

The whirring sound of a plane engine drew close, peaking into a mechanical hum. It idled over the dirt road beyond the structure. The hydraulic hiss of landing struts hit the earth.

Then silence.

Max crept toward a dusty window at his side when Vera latched on to his wrist, shaking her head. "Don't you wanna know what we're up against?" he asked.

"Nothing your feeble munitions can destroy, I assure you," Acean said.

Vera's heart pounded in her chest as she scanned the bay. "Where's Calla?"

"We got a bigger problem, Doc," the Russian answered.

"Where's Toni?"

Ten Minutes Later

Kojimatsuo peeked through the grimy front windows, "Uncle Lance is *eating* her… Karma's a bitch, man!"

"Get away from there, kid," Max said, stuffing a roughed-up Kevlar sack with as many weapons as he could carry.

"He's right, Billy. Don't wanna give up our position," the Russian added.

"Dude, she had a gun to my head. This is therapeutic, okay?"

Huxley watched Vadim fasten his lucky grenade to his vest. "Glad I didn't shoot *that* thing," he muttered, testing the waters.

Volkov looked down at the explosive on his chest, smirking. "It's luckier than I thought."

"I wanted to say I'm s—"

"—I forgave you already, kid."

"You—you did?"

Vadim slapped Huxley's shoulder, "What'd I tell you back at the station? Kids are fuckin stupid, remember?"

"Ain't that the truth," Barry added, still stroking his dead wife's hair.

Volkov turned to Max, "What do we do with him?"

Amhearst shouldered his Kevlar sack, nodding to Stubbs. "Help Vad carry the Mayor… Let's move."

"I'm staying," Strunk said, staring down at Muriel. "Leave me a gun, I'll handle the rest."

"Bullshit," Max scoffed. "If we're gonna make it through this, we need to work together."

"Maybe I wanna be with my wife and son instead of you assholes, boy-scout. Ever think uh that?"

"We need you. It's your train, dammit."

"You're an engineer, figure it out!

"You're coming, Strunk. That's all there is to it."

Barry clenched his fists, "Why do you even care?"

"Because giving a shit is the only thing separating us from the creatures," Vera said, tossing Strunk a crutch she cobbled out of a broomstick and some foam padding. "You heard Max... Get up."

CRASH! Two mechanical tentacles burst through the grimy pane, coiling around Billy's arms.

She shrieked in terror, "Let me go!"

The segmented whips hoisted her through the glass, into Emthy's waiting clutches.

"Billy!" Stubbs cried, about to dive out the window as Vadim swooped in to restrain him. "What are you doing? I have to help her!"

"This is where you stop being a stupid kid!" Volkov barked, shoving the train-codes into Huxley's palms. "Help get the Mayor to the convoy! I'll handle this!"

Stubbs forced the crumpled paper back into Vadim's hands, "My brother died because of me, even *you* did... Let me be the hero for once."

"Think Max's gonna give you a weapon after what happened? He ain't as forgetful as I am, kid."

"I know... But I need you to trust me."

Vadim stared daggers at Huxley, "You and Billy better make it to that fuckin train... I mean it."

Stubbs hugged Volkov a little too snugly, invading his personal space. He stepped back, pocketing something the Russian didn't notice.

"I'll have luck on my side," he said.

Chapter 23: Sibling Rivalry

Fifteen Minutes Earlier

WHOOSH! A volcanic tremor rocked the rooftop beneath Calla's feet as a predatory starship braked into a hover outside the Repair Bay; its spider-like landing struts, *HISSING* on impact.

Shepherd hid behind a mound of steel girders when a slender armored alien emerged from the Xilan below. It inhaled deep, crinkling its vestigial face slits in disgust.

"Father was right. This place reeks of excrement," Emthy said, looking over her shoulder, into the dark recesses of her ship. "Gih goxatre *xa* treka no." *And I thought* you *smelled bad.*

"She's here! The girl's here!" Toni cried, mad-dashing toward the alien.

"Excellent, kraith," the Khath purred, studying Toni's frail anatomy with spiteful curiosity. "This is my maiden trip to the Earth's surface. You are the first human I have witnessed up close. It appears the females of your species are quite—soft... No muscle at all. Disappointing."

Toni rested her palms on her thighs, panting. "That's what it means to be feminine here, sue me."

Emthy cocked her head, "Femininity? On my home-world,

we have another word for such an affliction… Prey."

She *SNAPPED* her finger and the Akkan-Gah limped out of the spacecraft, it's skull, still half-exposing its undulating brain as it unleashed a furious ROAR so loud it rattled the earth beneath Toni's already trembling feet.

"We had a deal!" Evans gasped, stumbling away from the behemoth stalking toward her. "The big one said I would be taken care of! That you wouldn't hurt me!"

The alien grinned, "Do you see me laying my hands upon you now?" The panic in the human's voice infuriated her. That a fellow female could be so pathetic made her three stomachs turn.

"We had a fucking deal!"

Emthy gestured to her menacing new pet with a grandiose wave, "Not enough space to spare, unfortunately. I picked up a guest on my way here. The poor thing was meandering in the streets, like a common Akkan-Rah. I could not leave this magnificent animal behind just to accommodate a feeble mammal such as you, could I?"

"Go to hell, you fugly whore!" Toni growled, tripping over her own feet, scrambling backward as the ailing Akkan-Gah trodded forth, stopping its advance when its massive half-a-head hovered over hers. "I didn't mean that! I'm sorry, okay!" she whimpered, backpedaling in a frenzy while the monster's breath beat down upon her sweaty skin. "Call this thing off! I'll do whatever you want! Anything!"

"What I ask of you, you can not provide," Emthy said, stone faced. "Dying with a warrior's honor."

CRUNCH! The beast's razor-sharp jaws bore down around Toni's blubbering face, tearing her beautiful skin away as she shrieked in blood-curdling anguish. She clawed at her bloody countenance, unable to cry as the creature gnawed on the part of her flesh containing her tear ducts.

The creature's wounds began to heal instantly, as if the

molecules made up of its victim restored its injuries in real-time.

Emthy snarled with glee, watching the human writhe and flail in searing agony underneath the rippling pillars the reforged Akkan-Gah called arms. "Fulfill my father's promise... Take care of her," she said.

The monster took a massive palm to the kraith's chest, pinning her torso against the dirt, exploding her heart under its colossal heft. It watched the woman's bloody mangled face spew even more gore before enveloping her entire head in its drooling maw.

Calla peered over the girders as the Lance-stalker popped Toni's skull open like a grape, licking her juicy brains from its scaled lips.

"What do we have here?" Emthy asked, shifting her attention inside the building.

Dual control handles jutted from her armored wrists, into her palms, as two tendrils telescoped out of her forearms. They snaked through the window like a pair of chrome pit-vipers, retracting with Billy coiled in their clutches, kicking and screaming.

"No!" Calla cried, leaping off the rooftop, hitting the dirt with a thunderous crash that caught Emthy off guard.

The alien pulled Kojimatsuo close, looking her opponent up and down, unimpressed. "We meet at last, sister... You are attractive, for a half-human."

"Let her go!" Shepherd roared.

"Is that any way to introduce yourself to a sibling?"

"You're no family of mine," Calla hissed.

"We are both children of Kil'Dur. Who am I if not your true blood?"

"An asshole!" Billy interjected, squirming in the alien's coils.

Emthy smiled at the girl, "So young, and yet so eager to die... You have a warrior's spirit, little one."

"Put me down and I'll *show* you a warrior's spirit!"

"I can arrange that..." the Khath replied, dangling Kojimatsuo above the Akkan-Gah's head like a human-sized dog-treat.

The beast sprang into the air after her, but she was too high above its salivating jaws, dropping an inch closer to its snout with every failed lunge.

"Are you certain you wish to be released, child?" the alien asked, eying Calla as she spoke. "Kraitho recant in the face of death, it seems."

SNAP! The Lance-stalker nipped at the tips of Kojimatsuo's shoes.

"If I die, I'll die knowing you're *still* an asshole!" Billy cried. "A coward too!"

"Bold words. I should allow him to eat you for that insult alone," Emthy replied, bobbing the child up and down above the gnashing monster.

SNAP! It caught Billy's left shoe, swallowing it whole as it lunged after the child's foot next.

"Dad, stop it!" Calla pleaded, but the beast continued to lunge after the morsel overhead. "That's enough, I said!"

"The Akkan are the Kil'Durian Empire's to command until a Leevahn is capable of *taking* command... You are nowhere near ready, sister," Emthy said, amused by her game. "If you want him to cease, I propose a trade: You for the girl."

An arm snaked around Calla's throat from behind, "Let Billy go, or I'll kill your precious leaven!"

Calla recognized the voice, raising her arms in befuddled surrender. "What the hell are you doing, Stubbs?"

"Not sure yet," he whispered, slipping back into character. "I mean, shut up, freak!"

The alien cocked its skull to the side, "How can you slay the Leevahn when you have no weapon, kraith?"

"Oh, I don't?" Huxley asked, brandishing the grenade he stole off Vadim's vest when he hugged him. "What's this then?"

"An Izeddian gorg egg, perhaps?" the Khath replied, slightly amused.

"No grenades where you come from, huh?"

"Explosives? You imbecile!" Emthy flung Billy aside (well out of the Akkan-Gah's reach) in a flurry of panic, reeling Stubbs in, away from Calla, with both tendrils. "The Leevahn is not yours to slay!" she cried, clawing at the grenade in Huxley's slippery clutches. "Give it to me!"

Huxley locked eyes with the Khath. "You want it? Here... Have it," he replied, relinquishing the explosive into Emthy's eager hands.

"Wise choice, kraith."

Stubbs gave Emthy a hateful grin, dangling the grenade pin from his middle finger. "You'll be needing this."

"No!" the alien shrieked, trying to shake off the human clinging to her armor with all his might.

"What are you doing, Stubbs!" Billy cried. "Get outta there!"

Huxley offered his friends one final smile. "My real name's Thomas..." he said, prouder of himself than he'd ever been before in his life.

KA-BOOM! An enormous fireball hurled metal and flesh into the sky as Calla shielded Billy from the blaze.

"Stubbs!" the child wailed, reaching toward the wreckage in tears.

"He... He's gone, honey," Shepherd whispered, searching for the Akkan-Gah out of the rim of her eye. A meter-long hunk of metal impaled the beast's gushing neck as it laid prostrated in a muddy pool of blood.

"The Guardian will not stay down forever," Acean said, jump-scaring the girls with his appearance. "We must flee before they awaken. Surviving an encounter with the Khath of Kil'Dur *and* the Akkan-Gah is not likely to happen twice in one's lifetime."

"Where the hell have *you* been?" Kojimatsuo asked, angry. "We needed you!"

The alien gave the child a serious glare, "I am of no utility dead. Do not mistake stratagem for cowardice."

"Well, what would *you* know of *heroism*, Uncle?" a fearsome voice yowled through the fiery debris. "Your presence is an affront to all my Khoth fights for!" Emthy said, rising out of the mangled remains of the front of her ship. She deactivated her form-fitting vitality-shield, trampling over the billowing wreckage. "How could you forsake your Empire this way?"

"My devotion is to the Strodha, Khath, not your cruel father. Do not let your intimate feelings distort the matter. Your mother died because of *his* acts, not mankind's."

"How dare you claim such things!"

"My sister wanted to bridge the chasms between both our races with unity. It was her husband who spurred humanity's vitriolic movement against our kind."

"Lies!"

"If I am lying, why did he send you to secure the Leevahn? You know the High Council forbids such an act. He means to dominate this world for *himself* by any measures necessary. Where is the honor in that?"

"The kraitho murdered my mother! These creatures don't deserve fair judgment!"

Acean shook his head, heartbroken by his niece's madness. "If you believe that, you are no better than your father."

"So be it," Emthy hissed, slapping a small button fixed to her chest armor.

EER! EER! EER! The Battle-Xilan's chassis detached in

incremental panels. A spherical craft the length of a dual escape-pod hovered above the dirt road.

The Khath pointed at Shepherd, "One way or the other you are coming with me."

Calla cracked her tense, exhausted, frustrated neck, "Get Billy out of here, Acean… Time to teach my sister here some manners."

"YAAAAGGHHH!" Emthy lunged at her opponent, flinging her through the Repair Bay window. The Khath leapt through the broken glass after the hybrid, but an unforeseen I-beam crashed into her torso, launching her skyward, through the ceiling.

CRASH! A black form exploded through the rooftop, landing a few meters ahead of Emthy, crouched and coiled. Its skin was spiny and hard; its face, overshadowed by two shining orbs glowing a fearsome blue. The being rose to its feet, exposing its lithe frame.

"Your move, sister," the Leevahn hissed.

"Shit!" Barry winced, staring down a semi-truck with two tons of lumber spilling off the bed, obstructing their path to Hangar Zero. His panicked eyes bounced between the row of buildings to his right, the mile-long concrete wall on his left, and the mountain of wood wedged smack-dab between both.

"Sonofabitch," Max said with an AR-Fifteen in his shaky clutches and a dozen more weapons slung over his shoulder.

"I second that," the Russian added.

Wild looked confused, "We can just climb over *that*, can't we?"

"You assholes may," Barry retorted, tapping the side of his crutch.

"No dice," Vadim said, pointing toward the wood at the top of the spill. "See the angle? Climbing that with the wrong weight distribution's gonna make the rest pile down on us.

That's a half-ton of trees, kids."

"Vad's right. We gotta find another way," Amhearst responded, backtracking along the dirt road a few steps, thinking of an alternate route and coming up short since he didn't know the area. "Suggestions, Mr. Mayor?"

Strunk's head dipped in vexed exhaustion as he scratched his throbbing temple, digging for a faded recollection of the yard locked away in his jumbled mind. "There's a concrete barrier twelve feet high, same as the one here, that runs flush behind these three buildings, so we ain't going around the structures."

Vadim snickered, "Whoever designed this place was a real asshole."

"Hey, what do ya expect?" Barry barked, pointing at the towering wall to their left. "There's shit for security on that side, that's why they kept the scrappers over there." He cocked his head to the right. "This side's got all the hobos and homeless fucks stealin whatever ain't bolted into the damn ground. We did the best we fuckin could!"

"Jesus, relax," Vera said. "It's not like you built the place."

"I approved the plans for it! Almost the same thing!" Strunk snapped, taking a breath to compose himself. "We could go around the back of Engineering-One if the bridge's down; but if it's *not*, we're screwed. There's a ravine down there; flows out from the water processing plant, which I'm guessing nobody's *running*. That means crossing a raging rapids worth of shit and piss."

"Where are the controls for it?" Wild prodded.

Barry grinned, "Right next to the damn building we're tryin to get into, lady. And on a day as lucky as this—that bridge ain't down, trust me."

"This is major league bullshit," the Russian said.

"Why the hell ya think I dragged you twats this way? It was the clearest shot! I didn't wreck the fuckin semi!"

"Wait a minute," Max interjected, scrutinizing the structure on his right. It was taller than the others on either side of it. "This building has a second floor."

"Yeah… There's a kitchen up there," Strunk said.

Max strafed a few meters to the left, trying to see down the narrow alleyway obstructed by the lumber. "Everything up to code?"

"What, ya wanna stop for a fuckin bite to eat or somethin? The hell's the matter with you?"

Amhearst lunged for Barry's collar, "The *building*, you idiot! If it's up to *code*, there's a fire escape up there. These buildings aren't spaced that far apart. If we make it to the roof we can jump over to Hangar Zero."

KLANG! Two steel pipes clashed in a torrent of blinding sparks.

"Why do you fight?" Emthy roared, drawing back her weapon as her opponent's reached its apogee. She parried the Leevahn's attack, dashing to the right, "There's nothing for you here!"

"And there is on your ship?" the Leevahn growled, yawing her metal pipe as her enemy danced around her.

"Such energy wasted," the Khath hissed, shattering the hybrid's rusty weapon with one adept slash. "You will never know the power that lies inside you, the influence your sheer existence yields!"

The hybrid grabbed the armored alien by the throat, uppercutting her into an open field.

Emthy rolled to the side as Shepherd vaulted over a mound of scrap-metal. *BAM!* The hybrid's spiked fist plunged deep into the earth in a hail of dust and stone, missing her sister's skull by mere millimeters.

"These animals do not deserve you!" the warrior-princess growled.

"That isn't for you to decide!

The Khath staggered upright, unwilling to yield, like her mighty father before her. "They'll never accept you the way the Empire can. My Khoth gave the kraitho all they could have dreamed of and they turned against him! Humans are barbaric animals! They will do the same to you!"

"No, they won't."

"How do you know, you fool?"

"Because it's what I believe."

Emthy's face contorted with insolent amusement, "Spoken like a true kraith… Breaking you shall be most orgasmic."

DHAK! DHAK! DHAK! Gunfire in the distance distracted the Khath. *POW!* Calla kicked her through the Engineering Bay's front wall.

Emthy crashed into a pillar, rolling onto her side in mild pain as Shepherd pounced atop her aching back, wrapping a thick chain around her neck.

The armored alien staggered to her feet with the Leevahn still clinging to the bonds at her throat, flipping the hybrid over her shoulders and slamming her into the concrete floor.

She perforated the armor fastened to her midsection, exposing three flaring nostrils pulsating against her shredded abdomen. "Think as a human does, and you will fail like one."

DHAK! DHAK! DHAK! DHAK! "C'mon, c'mon, let's move!" Volkov barked as Max shoved Barry's hind-end through the second-story window. He pushed Vera onto the fire-escape before diving out himself.

DHAK! DHAK! DHAK! The dozen Akkan-Rah the group encountered whilst breaking into the Dining Hall didn't go down easy. Vadim downed a measly three creatures by the time he slapped in his third PMAG, firing through the glass as nine monsters gnashed after him.

Vera and Amhearst helped carry Barry up the escape and onto the rooftop as the Russian took potshots at the writhing beasts on the ledge.

Max dashed to Vadim's side, unleashing hell on the land-stalkers clawing through the window. "I'm out!" he shouted, ejecting the spent magazine from his AR-Fifteen.

The Russian whipped his head back, blind-firing down the stairs, "If you're gonna jump, now's the time, Doc!" He kept shooting his weapon until that dreaded CLICK rang in the air, reaching for the lucky grenade pinned to his vest.

It wasn't there.

"Fuck me!" he roared, uncertain if he was angry or hysterical. *What the hell did the kid say? That he'd have luck on his side?* The Russian couldn't help but smile. *Clever little bastard!*

"Vad!" Max cried.

CLOMP! A one-eyed stalker bounded over its dying brethren on a collision course with Volkov. The beast bit down on Vadim's arm as he shielded his face from certain death. "Yarghhhh!" he wailed as it thrashed like a feral wolf-pup digging into its first kill.

CHOMP! A second joined the attack, fastening its jaws around the Russian's right shin with an agonizing *CRACK.*

"Vadim!" Vera shrieked, helpless to do anything as she held Barry upright at the edge of the roof. "Max, do something!"

Amhearst dropped to his knees, ripping a Remington-Eight-Seventy out of his Kevlar sack. A third Akkan-Rah mounted for the kill, but Max blasted its face off in a blizzard of gore before it could sink its teeth into his friend.

He swiveled the shotgun leftward, blasting a twelve-gauge shell through the one-eyed stalker's throat. A second slug obliterated the second stalker chewing on Vadim's leg.

"Five left, boss," Vadim winced. He struggled to shoulder

his MC-Six as Amhearst dragged him away from the edge of the fire escape. The Russian clutched his M-Nine when he saw the last of the creatures slithering up the escape, slow and cautious, forming a half-circle around their prey.

They were learning.

"Nobody moves," Max cautioned. "I bagged three, which leaves four slugs for five monsters... If anyone's got any ideas, I'm all ears."

Barry nodded to the Kevlar-sack, "Well, what else you have in there?"

"Nothing you'll grab in time."

Sensing fear, the land-stalkers closed the gaps in their half-circle.

"I have the gun you gave me earlier," Vera said. "Vad and I can get two, you handle the rest?"

Vadim shook his head, "Doc, I didn't pull out my Beretta to shoot *them*."

"Shut it," Max barked. "I ain't losing my best friend twice in one day."

"We're fucked," Barry declared, calculating his odds of jumping over to Hangar Zero on his own.

If I hit this bitch in the ribs with this shitty crutch, I bet I can get across while they're eating her before anyone even notices I'm gone... Meh, then again, her dickhead boyfriend'll shoot me. Fuck!

Vera's brow beetled as she studied Strunk's faraway gaze. "Something on your mind?"

The Mayor gave her a smarmy smile, "Thinking about how much I fuckin love you people, that's all."

The pack inched forward, a feral council of death closing in on their prey.

SCREE! A piercing sound sliced through the dead air.

Everyone honed in on the shrill noise coming from the Engineering Bay's imploding rooftop. A blinding beam erupted skyward through the smoldering concrete and rebar, slicing left, then right, wielded by some unseen entity.

Distracted, the pack-leader didn't notice the Kil'Durian war-blades on a descent through its torso. *SHWACK!*

"Go to them, child," Acean hissed, shielding Billy from the four remaining land-stalkers.

She dashed behind Max, who was himself shielded behind the seven-foot-tall alien about to save them all.

Volkov coughed conspicuously, nabbing Kojimatsuo's attention. "Kid didn't make it, did he?"

Billy mustered a somber smile, "His name was Thomas."

The Russian nodded, lost in a sliver of silent mourning as the unfolding carnage muted for a brief existential moment in time. "Good name," he said.

The cleric sheathed his blades before a pile of massacred Akkan-Rah, looking back at his human counterparts, slightly winded. "I have been among your kind long enough to recognize that a *thank you* may be in order, is it not?"

Barry's jaded mug grimaced, "So you killed your pets for us, big whoop. That don't get us on the other roof, pal."

FWOOSH! The alien whisked Strunk and Vadim over his shoulders, dashing across to Hangar Zero's rooftop. He set the Russian down with care, dropping Barry like a sack of potatoes.

"Thanks," the Mayor grumbled.

SCREEEEE! SCREEEEE! No human could wield the A-S laser-cutting system without crane support. It was a massive light gun designed for heavy welding jobs. The emission chassis alone weighted seven hundred pounds.

Calla discharged it through the Bay like a toy pistol, demolishing everything in her path.

Emthy evaded the beam at every turn, taunting the hybrid with her agility, slithering along the west wall as Shepherd stopped to catch her breath. "You are strong, yes, but still half-human... Your energy will wane soon enough, sister" she mused.

The Leevahn's eyes flashed red as Antares, "Stop calling me that! RAGGHH!" She swung the A-S upward, above the alien warrior, decimating the ceiling overhead. Massive hunks of rubble rained down on the Khath's battle-hardened frame in a billowing plume of destruction.

Exhausted, the Leevahn dumped the laser and fell to her knees.

POW! Emthy's fists erupted skyward, followed by her sparking torso. She shook her dazed head, prying off her damaged chest plate as she shuffled out of the debris. "I underestimated you, hybrid. You fight with the fury of a Glass-Knight."

"That supposed to mean something to me?" the Leevahn replied, circling her so-called sister.

"They are the highest order of warrior my people have ever encountered. So named because of their crystal-clear allegiance to whoever commands them... It is a grand compliment."

"If you say so."

"I do," Emthy replied, tiredly surveying the devastation surrounding them. "I am being complimentary hoping you may wish to cease this mindless battling."

"Don't tell the person you're trying to manipulate how you're doing it, stupid."

The Khath sighed, backing up against the last remaining intact pillar to catch her breath. "We can leave this violence behind us, here and now if you so choose... All you need to do is fulfill your purpose and the suffering may stop once and for all."

"What happens to the Earth if I do?"

"Does it matter? The Akkan will be yours, and you shall know power unlike anything you could dare dream of.."

"And if I don't join you?"

"Non-compliance means the destruction of everything you hold dear. A simple choice to make, is it not?"

"Not gonna lie, humans disappoint me. They're cruel. Selfish. Violent... But a few of them are decent when they aspire to be."

Emthy gave the hybrid a confused leer, "That description alone suggests they aren't worth saving. I cannot see the disadvantage in choosing their extinction."

"What a shocker." The Leevahn's hardened face regressed back into Calla's perfect porcelain skin, "My dad taught me never to rush into a big decision—*sister*."

The Khath leered at Calla with beetled brows, "And now he's my lapdog, isn't he? Pity his wisdom won't save you from kneeling before *my* father!"

WHIKASH! The alien's mechanical whips coiled around Calla, dropped the hybrid to her knees with a paralyzing jolt of electricity.

Emthy lorded over her sister, "First, you must kneel before *me*."

Calla's eyes rolled over white as she channeled her focus elsewhere.

"Ignoring the pain will do you no good, girl. Embrace it, for it shall be your sole acquaintance when this is over."

Shepherd flashed a cock-sure smirk through her electric convulsions, "I don't ignore pain... I *bring* it, bitch."

A faint rattle scattered the rubble beneath Emthy's feet.

Her eyes darted in all directions as the seismic activity increased.

A knowing scowl etched across her features, "You believe you are ready to handle him, do you?"

CRASH! The Akkan-Gah burst through the wall, leaping toward Emthy, but its heaving form smashed against an invisible barrier of telepathic command with the wave of her hand. She caressed the beast's snout, believing she felt it shudder, but that couldn't be possible.

He was hers to wield.

"I could rip out your father's heart right in front of you," she said.

Calla's fatigued vision flickered in and out of focus as she linked with the beast one last time, fighting to mask the desperation she refused to let Emthy take advantage of.

You may not remember who you were, but I do. You were a man with a family. A wife that loved you. A daughter that still *loves you and needs you more than ever before... Stop her, daddy. Before it's too late. I can feel your rage. The anger, the pain. It's all part of being* human, *just like love is... I know your humanity is within reach, and I need you to find it... If that means nothing to you anymore, then let her kill me.*

Emthy charged up her sparking coils, etching deep molten gashes into the glowing concrete as she lashed them across the surface. "Time to go, sister."

WHIKASH!

ROARR!

The coils snaked around the Akkan-Gah's granite-like forearm instead of their intended target. A raucous war-cry rattled the earth as the monster ripped the handles from the Khath's clutches. *WHAM!* It grand-slammed her out of the building with a devastating back-swipe of its massive hand, sending her crashing into the junkyard beyond the north gate.

The Lance-stalker nudged its child with the tip of its snout, sniffing her skin as the Leevahn-born flesh melted back into her pores, leaving her nude and unconscious.

It had to get her somewhere safe.

An unusual ideate for a creature as primal as the Akkan-Gah. Their kind was a species created to serve and protect, but thinking was not a priority for the Guardians of old.

But none of them had been human before.

And none had ever cared for a child the way this father adored Calla.

"How long's it been since you rode the rails with this piece uh shit?" Max asked from beneath the central console. "Looks like you ran her ragged."

Barry scratched his head, recalling as best he could. "Let me see, now. Last time I smuggled anything across state lines, I was already Mayor. Guess that means the last time this baby was haulin was," he snapped his fingers, "oh, that's right… None yer fuckin business."

Max grinned, "Fair enough." His hand jostled deep inside the trunking beneath the central console. He felt a loose cable coiled behind the operation board, reconnecting it with his thumb. The primary controls hummed back to life, along with all the bulbs overhead. "And then there was light."

Vadim sat in the co-chair while Vera bandaged his wounds, turning to Strunk. "Any disinfectants onboard? Anything besides these dusty wraps?"

"Jesus, do all you assholes got somethin to complain about or what? *Barry*, these bandages are filthy! *Barry*, the train won't run!"

"Barry, *shut the hell up*," Volkov barked with a playful wink.

The Mayor wagged his finger at the Russian, "I like you, ya Roosky fuck. You and me're gonna have a drink later."

"Don't count on it," Max muttered under his breath, typing the ACTIVATION COMMAND CODE into the key-panel on his left. The train's hum upgraded to an uproarious churn shaking the grates beneath their feet. "We're operational, guys."

TSSS. The hydraulic door at the rear of the car slid ajar and in entered Acean, scanning the room. "Where is the young one?"

A hatch behind the alien sprang open, "Relax, big guy, I'm checking out the digs. Ya miss me already or something?" Billy said.

The cleric almost smirked, "I am ensuring my earlier exploits were not in vain, child."

Kojimatsuo saluted him, "Gotcha, stretch… There's a crap-ton of vents and stuff down here. It's a maze."

"Don't get too comfy down there, please," Vera warned. "If you fit in those tight spaces, they may too."

"The female is correct," Acean said, clutching the scruff of Billy's shirt.

Billy swatted at the alien plucking her out of the hatch, "Hands-off ya overgrown salamander."

The alien lowered to the girl's eye level. "On my world, a pack of Akkan once stormed an orphanage on the outskirts of my home province of Ro'Thkha. They ate all but two of the children sleeping in their beds. The young ones woke to the blood-curdling screams of the damned flooding the darkness. There's no greater delicacy to the Akkan than youthful flesh, Billy of Earth."

"What happened to the two kids?" Billy asked, morbidly curious.

Acean brandished a genuine smile this time, "Zain of Aurell'Kah adopted them before his ascension to Khoth of the Kil'Durian Empire." His gaze listed, and the corners of his lips sank. "Only one lives today."

THUD! THUD! THUD! The plodding steps of something massive rattled the portholes, shaking the steel panels snaking along the wall as it advanced, stopping at the head of the train.

Vadim raised an eyebrow, "That don't sound good, do it?"

"He is out there," the alien said.

"Who is?" Billy asked.

"Lance Shephard."

TSSS. The conductor's hatch slid ajar and a janky stepladder descended to the gravel. Max went down first, trailed by Vera close behind, with Acean backing up the rear. The trio crept along the side of the train as the guttural growl rang through the air.

Max's hand jutted backward, motioning for a pause. He inched toward the edge of the car, beads of sweat trickling from his brow as he spied what was in the creature's arms.

"It's got Calla," he whispered, unholstering his M-Nine.

"It means us no harm, but it is still an *animal*, kraith," Acean warned, scowling at the weapon in Amhearst's hands. "Would you advance on a wild boar in such haste?"

"We have to do something, dammit," Vera snipped. "That's my girl in its clutches!"

"Leave this to me, kraitho. Wait here."

The Akkan-Gah's powerful snout sniffed out the tall alien drawing near. Vestigial remnants of its programming compelled it to growl in protest, but its hostility subsided upon glimpsing the small female skulking behind the cleric.

"My words were not clear?" Acean asked, eyes glued to the beast cradling Shepherd.

"I was family," Vera replied, halting beside Acean. "If there's any part of him left in there, he knows how much Calla means to me... If he doesn't hurt her, he won't harm me either."

The animal followed Wild's every move with its large, glowering orbs, but it made no sound.

She placed her palm against the Lance-stalker's neck. She could feel the animal's pulse racing beneath its worn hide. "Your baby girl's safe with us."

The creature exhaled a wheezing breath that could have been mistaken for a whinny of sorrow. Its bulging arm relaxed and lowered Calla to the earth. It nudged the girl with the tip of its rough snout, breathing in the sweet scent of her hair.

Memories flickered in the blackness of its mind, vanishing as fast as they came.

They brought the animal peace for a fleeting moment.

The Akkan-Gah's orange-yellow orbs welled with fluid as it backed away from Calla. It reared toward the north gate, trampling out of the train-yard.

Forever alone and without the courage to look back at its child one last time.

Chapter 24: Lost Without Her

The moon gleamed by the time Emthy opened her eyes. She clutched her aching torso, dragging herself through the junkyard in a furious daze.

The vista beyond the barrier ahead was black and mute and had been for many hours.

And her target was long gone.

She had to get back to her escape pod.

Smoldering pockets of fire still wafted beneath the craft's hull.

Emthy caught a whiff of something else burning under the midnight sky, shrouded by the mangled debris.

An unmistakable stench.

It smelled of opportunity.

May 15th, 2047
6:55AM

An erratic thrum reverberated through the steel exodus chugging across the tracks.

Hills to the left of me, flatness to the right. Here I am, stuck in the middle with them.

Strunk lifted his good leg atop the command console as the

dawning sun overtook the car.

"Shit!" Barry growled, squinting out the window in a half-asleep stupor. "Anyone upstairs wanna give a guy a fuckin break?"

There was no answer.

If Muriel were still alive, she'd know how to settle his nerves. She always did. It was a gift of hers.

But she was dead, like Larry and everybody else he knew personally.

It haunted Strunk to realize he'd never get to make up for all he did to the wife he claimed to care for. She was his life, but because of his frigid nature, she never believed it. It didn't matter much. Truth was, she would have abandoned him years ago if given half the chance to develop the courage to do so.

That's why he did his best to keep her down.

And still he fancied himself a *winner*.

Nobody ever left a somebody.

Barry collapsed to his knees beside his chair, realizing how alone he'd become in this mad new world, and it made his pulse rocket.

Holy fuck, I'm having a coronary…

It was only a panic attack, but it flushed Barry's sins to the fore of his mind with relentless vigor, as if the sum of his life's failures flashed before his eyes. He was grateful for it because so many of his offenses gave him various glimpses of Muriel through the ages, and he was already missing her face.

She was so delicate and beautiful.

Always had been.

Even in his hour of existential strife, Strunk lusted after his wife in her youth.

He hated himself for turning a nubile specimen like Muriel Wheatley into the lonely matron she became in marriage.

His memories of her faded like a flickering candle, replaced by the bright LEDs of loss and anguish as his mind forced him to look upon her prostrated body in a pool of blood again.

I abandoned her.

They forced me to.

Fucking forced me.

Barry Strunk rose to his feet, glancing askance at the console at his fingertips.

"They wanna go west… We'll go west-ish," he growled through gnashing teeth.

It's what Muriel would have wanted.

Max splayed himself along the chaise lounge in the corner, far across from the woman he loved.

He was so tired.

There were others around him, but they may as well have been invisible. All he could see, all he had the strength to focus on, was Vera. The hell he'd gone through to get to that fucking couch, breathing his shallow, exhausted breaths, knowing she was safe was worth it.

The man was lost without her.

Wild sat beside a California-King, running her fingers through Calla's locks.

Billy leaned against the side of the bed, worried.

Vera skimmed the back of her hand along Shepherd's pristine cheeks. "She'll be on her feet in no time. She's a warrior like you, kiddo."

Kojimatsuo smirked, "I wish I was as strong as her."

Vera's brows arched, "You are."

"How ya figure that? I'm just a regular girl; this chick's a badass," Billy balked, staring at Calla, longing to see her open her eyes.

"I remember this one day… Your parents asked the Shepherds for medication because you had a temperature high enough to cook an egg on your forehead. Scary stuff, in retrospect."

"In whatrospect?"

"It was snowing and I couldn't return to Evanscorp for an address on molecular biology the coming Tuesday. It was a good thing too."

"What's that gotta do with me?"

"Well, the Shepherd's had no medicine, so Lance recommended putting you in a bathtub filled with ice." Vera shook her head in humorous recollection. "One of the stupidest ideas only a male would come up with… I raced over to your house in time to stop Harry and Kat from burying you in snow shoveled off the driveway. If I hadn't reached them fast enough, you might not be with us now."

Billy glowered, "Dude, they almost did that to me? What the hell, man?"

"A desperate parent will do anything for their child if they think it'll help."

"More like *to* a child," the girl grunted.

Vera nodded; a downtrodden throb of remorse in her voice as she indexed her own shortcomings. "That too."

"This guy got any booze around here?" the Russian asked, dipped in a leather armchair scratching his bandaged arm.

Kojimatsuo sprang off the edge of the bed with a glower on her face. "I saw you throw away your flask, Tittyshits. That's the universal sign someone quit drinking."

"Says who?"

Billy shrugged, "I dunno… The movies?"

Vadim winked at the child, "This ain't a flick, little lady, and I'm thirsty."

"I'll bring you water."

"Different type uh thirst, dammit." Vadim's tone was less friendly as he minded the girl. "I *need* a *drink*."

Acean had been keeping to himself on the other end of the suite, staring out the window in deep thought, but the way the Russian spoke to Billy caught his attention. "Leave him be, young one. He quests after something a decanter will never provide."

"Swallow a bag uh dicks," Vadim growled. "What the hell makes you think I'm chasing anything?"

"I've encountered every emotion in the cosmos; you are remorseful and frightened."

The Russian's face loosened up, and a glaze coated his eyes as he stared off into nothingness. "What do I do about it then, huh?"

"Sleep—to detox your brain," Max barked, eavesdropping from the lounger.

"Hibernation will not quell his woes," Acean asserted, his long index fingers inching toward Vadim's temples.

The Russian batted the alien's digits aside, clenching his fists. "What the hell are you doing?"

"I shall examine your thoughts, kraith."

"You can do that?" Billy asked, wide-eyed.

The cleric smirked, "Tame your excitement. It seldom works on cognizant beings, but this one—given his current disposition—may prove receptive enough to penetrate."

Volkov scratched his face with his middle finger, "Think I'll deal with things my way, stretch. Keep your scaly mitts off me, got it?"

"Physical touch is superfluous. I extended my hands so your primitive senses could *detect that I was* initiating a connection," Acean said, cocking his head in fascination as he entered Volkov's mind. "You have lost something precious to you."

The Russian touched his forehead, confused by the sudden throbbing.

"A human..."

"Stop it…"

"A youth… A daughter."

"Stop! *You got no fucking right!*"

Consternation scratched at Acean's throat, "Someone stole her from you… A clone."

"Get the hell out of my brain!" Vadim cried, slipping off the armchair and tumbling to his knees, sobbing in intense agony.

Acean looked down at the distressed human with stoic features, but within, he was anything but cold. "It is not I who needs to flee the confines of your tortured mind, kraith."

Billy tugged at the alien's robe. "Let me try," she said, helping Volkov off the ground. "I'm sorry about your little girl," she whispered.

Vadim sloughed back into the recliner, "I miss her so fuckin much it aches."

"How old was she?"

"Six… Six years old when some drunk cloned fuck got in his car and ran her over." Vadim's voice shuddered, "She was playing in a cul-de-sac outside her whore-mother's apartment. Nobody, not even the guy that trampled across her body, found her until thirty minutes later… My baby girl laid there, afraid and dying under all the stars she and me used to count before bedtime. Coroner told me she'd bled out by the time my druggie ex-wife noticed she was fuckin gone."

Kojimatsuo set a skittish palm atop Vadim's shoulder, "What happened—to the guy?"

The Russian leered, "I handled him."

Billy slid her index finger across her throat, "Handled, handled?"

"More or less, kid."

"Whoa."

"Turns out he was coming back from a party in his honor. Celebrating his return to the living after dying in the line of duty. He was a cop. A decorated one, too."

"What was he doing drinking and driving then?"

Vadim smirked, "Wanted to make the most of his night's my hunch."

"And you murdered him?"

The Russian's stare dropped toward the ground. "He was rushing over to his mother's condo when he killed my Afanasia. The old woman was suffering chest pains. Called up her son and collapsed over the phone while he was sucking back way too much tequila."

"How do you know all this stuff?"

"Because he told me as he pleaded for his life." Vadim clenched his eyes shut, letting loose a dark and tortured sigh. "Not a day goes by I don't think about it, kid. Not one. Hoped if I went through with it there'd be some kinda closure."

"Was there?"

Volkov studied the girl, "No such thing as moving on."

Billy hugged him, "I'm so sorry."

Vadim clutched her tight, "Me too, kid." He pulled back his immense arm, mopping the tears from his face with a sympathetic grimace. "Sorry about Stubbs... Thomas was a solid dude."

Billy's voice trembled, "He turned out to be a hero after all... Even if he was a Huxley."

"You dug him, didn't you?"

"Yeah... I did," she whispered, as if struck by an epiphany. "A lot."

The Russian gave Kojimatsuo a bittersweet smile. "Enjoy the memories... Don't let what you lost—or what you *took* from someone else—ruin you. You'll end up a boozehound before you know it."

"Okay, that's enough... Billy, come watch Calla for me," Vera muttered, holding a fresh rag and a bottle of disinfectant.

"This discussion's becoming a little too heavy for you," she exhaled, unwinding the gauze around his arm.

A flash of confusion overtook her.

The woman stared into Vadim's distressed eyes. "How much pain are you in?" she asked, rolling his tattered pant leg above his tibia.

The Russian didn't bother looking. "It don't feel good, let's put it that way. Disinfect it already, Doc."

"Well, I would," Wild replied, tugging Volkov's pant leg back down, "if you were wounded."

Vadim glanced downward, staggered. "What in God's name?"

"Not his... Mine," Calla said, sitting upright in the California-king, a little groggy but otherwise okay.

Vera locked eyes with the hybrid, "I still don't understand any of this... I've seen what your blood does to living things... It should have *killed* him."

"This world, like the Akkan, is alive," Acean interjected, gazing through a porthole beside the bed, admiring the desolate vista beyond the glass. "The soils, the air, the oceans... They are all a singular entity. Dispose of one element and this sphere shall wither as so many others in the void of space have done countless times before. Earth cannot endure without synergy, and neither can the Blood-Akkan if detached from the Leevahn."

"Blood Akkan?" Vera parroted, as fascinated as she was confused.

Acean backed away from the porthole, slithering toward the slight female. "Khoth Vulgrell endows clones with the Akkan, but the *Blood-Akkan* belongs to Calla alone; a sentient nanotechnological life-form giving her dominion over the beasts roaming your lands. You speak of organisms perishing by the Leevahn's blood? Without her, there is no will. If there is no will, there can be no harmony."

"Only chaos…" Wild whispered.

"My people understood the risks of granting the Blood-Akkan to the unworthy. They took measures to ensure only a Leevahn may wield such power."

Billy's nose scrunched, "Otherwise the host—splats?"

Acean winked at the girl, "Liquification at the sub-atomic level."

"Not gonna lie, that's kinda metal."

The alien nodded, "Unpalatably metallic in taste, yes."

"I don't get it… What's separates Vad from Vera's lab-pets?"

"*Intent*. When the Leevahn's blood entered the lesser organisms, the Blood-Akkan self-destructed in response because there was no will."

Wild shot Acean a gimlet-eyed leer, "She *willed* Vadim to survive? Told them to save his life?"

"She instructed them to restore his damaged cells, yes. Once they have left her body, they will do only this task in perpetuity."

"Are they still linked to her?"

"No. Withdrawing from the Leevahn's body devolves the Blood-Akkan into mere machines. A shield against unforeseen —malfeasance. If they remained sentient, they would be lost without her."

Max belted out a modest chuckle as he spread out across the chaise lounge. "They'd be lost without her?" His tone sounded drained, but the longing glint in his eye twinkled as he gazed at Vera from top to bottom. "I was just thinking the same thing about you."

"Is that so?" Wild inquired.

Amhearst nodded, "Oh yeah."

The train's immutable rattle ricocheted off the steaming shower head. Warm water cascaded over Vera's body in pulsing waves as Max passed a bar of soap across her belly from the rear.

Wild intertwined her fingers with his, steering him over her creamy skin.

Amhearst fused himself into the only woman he'd ever loved. His thrusts, hurling into rapture as she braced her palms against the wall.

The shape, the thickness; all the familiar motions returned to her in undulating waves of sexual memory.

As they both climaxed, Max and Vera came to accept an ineluctable fact.

They were one anew.

Chapter 25: The Darkness

"You have an impressive vehicle here," a voice said.

Barry jerked to attention in his seat.

He knew it was Calla standing behind him.

"What the hell do you want, freak?" Strunk asked, resting his good leg atop the central console, too lazy to turn around.

Shepherd's fingers moved through the holo-map flickering to the right of Barry's filthy boot. "I wanted to offer my condolences. Muriel and I had a few words before she passed."

"The love of my life is dead because of you... Get the hell out of here."

A wave of indignation overcame the girl, and she clenched her fists so tight they bled. "I wasn't the one who killed her, asshole."

"Listen here, you petty bitch!" Barry roared, erupting out of his chair before realizing what he was doing. He collapsed, catching himself before crashing to the ground. His smoldering stare glimpsed the hatred in Calla's unflinching eyes as blood trickled down his injured thigh.

"You think you're tough, kid? That it? You ain't afraid of nuthin?" he asked, wincing in pain.

"Not you," she deadpanned.

Strunk clenched his jaws, grating his teeth beneath his

meaty cheeks. "I shoulda left you for dead back at the mall. Then my Muriel would still be alive!"

Calla's anger was overwhelming, but she knew he was right. She played a key role in Muriel's death. It infuriated her; always apologizing for things out of her hands, yet dependent on her existence all the same. She was so tired of feeling like a burden, and a curse, and as she stared down the arrogant pudgy bastard before her, she couldn't resist the need to lash out. Barry Strunk was the least human person Shepherd had ever met, and she'd be damned if he would treat her this way.

He didn't deserve her sympathy, or remorse, or guilt.

Or humanity.

"Muriel *never* loved you, she *feared* you," she hissed. The spiteful pleasure she derived from hurting the man made her guts churn, but the devastation on Barry's face satisfied an alien darkness inside the hybrid.

Attacking him felt good.

The Mayor's bloodshot eyes glazed over, and the hatred in his stare washed away, extinguished by the last sliver of honest reflection telling him Shepherd was right. The girl was a cunt, but one thing she was not, was wrong about his beloved wife.

"How the fuck did you know she didn't love me?" Strunk whispered.

Calla said nothing at first, realizing she never noticed how short he was.

Is that why he's such an insecure prick?

She inched closer, "What makes you believe a monster like you would ever find love?"

"Go to hell."

"You think you can do whatever you want and we women-folk are supposed to accept it? I saw the bruises on Muriel's arms... Her legs... Do what you say or get punched, right? Not on my watch, you sonofabitch!"

Calla clutched Barry by the throat, hurling him across the

car like a rag doll. He crashed against the wall so hard it put a dent in the steel.

"Get up!" she growled, heaving him to his feet as she cocked her fist back. "What did you call me earlier? A freak? A monster? I'll show you a fucking monster!"

BAM! Her hand pierced through the metal panel beside Strunk's skull, and a flurry of pressure flooded the car. Barry's thin hair flapped in the wind as the breach-slats activated and locked into place.

"Don't hurt me! Please!" Barry cried, panting in anxious exhaustion. A swath of self-loathing crept out of his mouth in the form of a blubbering whinny upon realizing he was terrified of an eighteen-year-old girl.

Calla drew back her fist as her battle-carapace oozed over her pink knuckles. "How many times did Muriel beg the same of you?"

WHAP! Acean's long fingers folded around Shepherd's wrist. "The youthful woman Vera Wild speaks so highly of would never harm a soul," he hissed. "Mind your inclinations or there shall be no difference between you and those you oppose."

"He's a pig! An animal!" Calla retorted. She tried to break away from the alien, but a fledgling Leevahn was no match for his strength.

"All kraitho are animals. Even you, child, are half animal."

"This fucker wanted to kill Billy! Stubbs! He beat his wife! Neglected his son! He doesn't deserve to live!"

Acean peered deep beyond the hybrid's seething eyes, freeing his clutch on her bony wrist. "The rage you feel derives from the Blood-Akkan. It yearns to override your pallid human impulses… You must learn to govern your newfound impetus, young one."

Calla's fearsome sneer softened, and she lowered her

armored fist, releasing her grip on Barry. The terror in his eyes sobered her, re-conjuring her genuine nature as if it were a long lost memory.

"What's happening to me, Acean?" she asked, afraid.

The cleric placed his palm atop her shoulder. "I wish I knew, young one. Your hybrid biology makes answering such a query most—challenging."

"What do you mean?"

"Mixing two violent genetic codes together can yield—unpredictable outcomes," Acean replied, helping Barry to his feet. "All I can offer in the way of wisdom is this: Do not let the Blood-Akkan augment your humanity, and vice versa... Fail at this task—and darkness shall reign."

A guttural thrum rattled the grating beneath Emthy's feet as she crossed the walkway. Her worrisome gait betraying her feigned surety upon coming to her father's broad back.

Vulgrell stood before the largest Hydro-Pod in the medical bay, leering at its contents. "I'm glad your mother was not alive to witness your failure, child... A royal—defeated by a minion of Kil'Dur!"

"She does not serve our world!" Emthy replied. The fire in her parent's eyes conjured a swath of lament on her stony mug. "Forgive me, my Khoth, I aspired to make you proud... To represent the Empire's strength... She was far tougher than I foresaw."

Vulgrell's hand grazed his daughter's scarred lip, slipping into a grip around her neck. "You failed, my Khath. I no longer believe I can depend on you to carry out the plainest of my demands." He heaved his child off the grated floor. "If I cannot trust you, my daughter, then I do not need you. Do I?"

"All I undertake is for you, father."

"So your failure was for me? I recall making no such demand! You were to bring the Leevahn!" Vulgrell bellowed, his grip growing tighter.

"She is not like the others. She's strong."

"Stronger than my child? Impossible!"

Emthy clutched Vulgrell's fist with pleading and frightened eyes. "If you believe I failed you on purpose, *kill me now*, but know I bled for my fallen mother as I shed blood for *you*, father."

The princess' words pierced the giant alien's hatred like a blade of reason.

He would have snapped his sole offspring's spine had they not.

The Khoth released his grip around the Khath's throat, falling to one knee as she hit the ground.

Emthy massaged her neck, "I shall not forget your benevolence, I swear it."

"Spare me your speeches," Vulgrell said, rising to his feet. "Your vertebra remain unbroken because you are all that survives of my beloved Unda." He reared his head toward the Hydro-Pod. "When is this one fit for combat? Perhaps it may prevail where my blood has proved so inefficient."

"Father, please…"

"*When* shall *it* be *ready*?" Vulgrell's manner was anything but amicable.

"The Thrakra-Krikari is an E-Class vessel, a luxury Xilan. Its power draw cannot sustain invasion-scale operations. It will take *years* to mature without the benefit of a War-Slyka's amenities."

The large alien belted out a derisive laugh, "Praise the Strodha for such—fortuitous news."

"She does not have control over the Akkan yet… I can crush her before it's too late. We must seize this world."

Vulgrell extended a palm to his child, hoisting her off the ground with a searing scowl upon his scaled face. "You had your chance, Khath. You did not defeat her… Be grateful your loss has not pressed my *usual* proclivities, young one."

Emthy's shivering gaze met her father's feet, "Would you have me search for her, my Khoth? In your eternal wisdom you realize she could be anywhere by now." She gagged on her remarks, "Not that I cannot locate her."

The lording alien trotted toward a war-portal in the chamber's center. "Spare your tongue, daughter. I know you cannot recover her—but *the Akkan*—will."

They were his eyes and ears

They were everywhere.

Chapter 26: Wrong Way

May 16th, 2047
5:35 AM

Wild ambled up the steps to the recreation deck, stopping to check the temperature in the jacuzzi as she yawned deeply. It was chilly outside, and the billowing steam looked inviting to her tired brain. She could feel her body heating just looking at it.

"I'd think twice before dipping my fingers in that water," Calla said, leaning over the guardrail, staring off into the sandy dunes flowing past the convoy.

"It's calling to me, honey."

"Yeah, well," Calla's head reared, "is the used condom floating in the filter-trap calling to you too?"

Vera's hand recoiled in disgust, "Whoa! I'm not that cold!"

"What are you doing up so early?"

Wild wiped her fingers dry on the billiard table beside Shepherd, "Had a chat with our oh-so-gracious host... He seemed a little shaken up."

Calla crossed her arms, "And? What of it?"

"I'd like to know what happened, for starters."

"I lost my temper."

Something at the hybrid's side caught the woman's eye.

"I can see that," Vera said, taking a few steps backward.

"Why are you stepping away? You think I'd hurt you?"

Wild glanced at Calla's forearm, "Not consciously."

Shepherd looked down, mortified to discover her arm had taken its alien form without realizing it. "Shit," she whispered, massaging her palms. "It's like it comes out when I'm thinking about it or something."

She shut her eyes, breathing deeply.

"What are you doing?" Vera asked, puzzled.

"Testing a theory," the hybrid said, feeling the dark ooze retreat into her pores. "There, it's going away."

"You can control it? Extraordinary."

"Barry would disagree."

Wild inched closer, a little wary, "Somehow, I get the sense he deserved it… He's a bit of a—cock."

Calla put some distance between herself and Vera, "What if you're wrong and I can't control it? What if it's not a conscious decision?"

"There you are. Been looking everywhere for you, Vere," Max interrupted, climbing the staircase with Vadim close behind.

"We're talking here, gentlemen."

Vadim perused the deck, spotting a mounted scope bolted to the guardrail. "I ain't seen one of these in years," he said, peering through the lense. "Yep, just like the old days at the beach. All sand and no nipples." He swiveled the telescope across the vista, pausing when he came across something that turned his lighthearted tone sour. "Wait a second, what the hell's this?"

"What is it?" Max asked.

Volkov leaned away from the telescope, "We got a building out here, boss." He looked skyward, shielding his eyes from the harsh rays. "It ain't Verenberg either… Sun's in the wrong spot. We're heading northwest, not west."

Amhearst rushed to the telescope.

The structure he saw through the desert haze was massive.

Almost biblical.

"Where the fuck are we?" he asked.

"Sonofabitch," the Mayor growled, frantic in his struggles to run the command-console. "Where the hell's the god damn override? Shit!"

Billy poked her head out of the grated hatch a few feet back, painted in soot.

"Fantastic," Barry groaned. He'd been wrestling with the controls for an hour. The last thing he wanted to do was deal with this little turd.

"How goes it, Mr. Conductor?" Kojimatsuo asked, pleasant enough.

"Beat it, brat! Go on!"

The girl's kind face turned bitter and fiery, "That's the last time I check on your miserable ass, ya old jerk! Thought you could use some cheering up after my girl made you look like a bitch, but forget it now."

"Now you're askin for it!" Strunk roared, swinging around to lash out at the girl, freezing in his tracks when he saw Acean standing behind her. He relaxed his balled fists. "Anybody on this fuckin train ever hear uh knocking?"

The alien's eyes were flinty and deploring, "It would behoove you to learn from your mistakes, would it not? Why show this adolescent female such unwarranted animosity?"

"Get off my back! Stress makes me pissed, I dunno! Just get the hell outta here and let me handle this!"

"Handle what, kraith?"

The Mayor trembled in a blubbering stupor, hobbling

toward the command-console in shame, "I screwed up bad, okay?"

Billy leered at Strunk, "How?"

Acean nudged Kojimatsuo aside, lording over the scared man like a hissing cobra. "Your inflections show remorse... Dishonor... What have you done?"

Barry erupted, "These people ripped me away from my Muriel! They didn't give a shit about me, just my goddamn train!" He grew more furious the harder he cried. "They used me, stretch! So I made a choice, and it was a mistake," he kicked the command-console as hard as he could," and now I can't get this fucking thing to change course!"

"Where have you elected to transport us, kraith?"

Strunk exhaled a guilty breath, "The promised land."

"What-the-hell? Were you even gonna say anything, you prick?" Billy exclaimed, kept at bay by Acean. "What'll happen when they find out who Calla is? We're dead!"

"I know that, ya little shit! That's why I'm trying to change course!"

The cleric stared daggers at this poor excuse for a man, confused by the complexity of human reasoning. "Why attempt to rectify your vacuous decision now?"

Barry slumped against the console, embarrassed and racked with guilt, "Of everyone on this fuckin train, you gotta be the one I owe my life to... Why'd ya have to save me from the girl? Why couldn't you just let her kill me?"

The alien looked down at the child in his care one moment, digging his slender forefinger into Strunk's chin-blubber the next. "You are not alone in regretting this, kraith."

"Out of my way, Ace!" *KAPOW!* Amhearst's knuckles crashed into Barry's face like the flat end of an anvil. "Where are you taking us, you fat sonofabitch!" He cocked his fist again, "Answer me!"

Vera grabbed Max's wrist, "He can't respond if he's

comatose."

"She has a point, boss," the Russian added, bringing up the rear.

A gob of bloody spit erupted from Strunk's swelling lips, dribbling down the side of his jaw. "Shoulda left me with my Muriel, pal. Everybody woulda got what they wanted." *WHACK!* He kneed Amhearst's balls, stealing the gun tucked at his waist. "Stay *the fuck* back! All of you!"

"We rescued you," Amhearst wheezed, cradling his manhood.

"You... You *what?*" Barry couldn't curb his wan smile, aiming the gun at Max's head, trembling with rage. "You think you're decent people? Dragging a husband away from his dead wife?"

"We were trying to help," Wild interjected.

"I may be a goddamn criminal, a prick even, but at least *I* wouldn't do what you cocksuckers did to me!"

"You're a monster, that's what you are," Max growled.

"I'm not the monster here, but I was wrong, I'll give ya that." Barry looked Acean in the eyes, "Don't know anybody who'd do what you did for a cutthroat bastard like me... I am sorry for whatever happens to you when we arrive, but it's outta my hands now."

"Where? When we reach where?" Max asked, still catching his breath.

"Jack Tanner's compound," Calla said, stepping through the hissing doorway. "I heard him talking about it with Muriel."

The Mayor pointed the gun at the hybrid, "Keep back, freak!"

Shepherd stepped closer, "You'd murder Lance Shepherd's daughter?"

"You gotta be shitting me," Strunk whispered, falling into

his chair, dumbstruck. "You're Lance-fucking-Shepherd's kid? Your dad made me who I am today."

Calla smirked, "He was also the one who ate your son."

"Jesus Christ, no!" Barry whimpered, cradling his sweaty head in his palms. "The thing that killed my Larry… That was him?"

Shepherd nodded.

The next few seconds became hours to Strunk, who tried to piece together the tragic irony of his existence as a room full of enemies watched on. Decades-worth of memories came and went like speeding cars on a bustling highway to nowhere, vanishing as fast as they manifested. Some, he was happy to forget, but there were a select few recollections he treasured, and they too faded the more he understood how meaningless his life was in that moment.

All his loved ones were dead, and he owed it all to Lance Shepherd.

Barry wanted to laugh about it, but he couldn't.

He put his gun in his mouth instead, pulling the trigger in a glorious eruption of brains and black-hearted blood.

Nobody seemed to care.

Chapter 27: The Last Stop

Cara Alovick lit her cigarette like someone about to shake hands with death, checking the monitors above her desk with vacancy behind her almond-shaped eyes.

She was a tall, attractive bad-ass, and the outpost's Chief of Security. A satin rose with many thorns; the type of woman who forced men to tremble in self-doubt despite looking like a tomboy most of the time. The Reverend appreciated her willingness to reject her innate sexuality in favor of the modesty he imposed on the rest of his flock. It made her more authoritative, which is exactly what Tanner wanted.

"Border-cam-numero tres," a voice cooed through the hand-radio at Alovick's midriff. "Handle it."

Cara checked camera-three, squinting to make out the train moving toward the compound.

"Don't sound like Jackie wants to roll out the ole welcome mat, do it?" asked a pleasant but withered tone behind the woman.

She extended a sympathetic grin to an elderly man in Cell-A-Thirteen. "It appears not," she replied, reaching for her hand radio, "I need two blues to main-gate. Safeties off."

"Hospitable."

"Only doing my job," she said, switching to another

frequency. "Headed to the entrance, Reverend. Awaiting further orders."

Tanner's mouth breathing bled through the radio speakers, "Good girl... The old man giving you any lip?"

Cara looked back at the elderly fellow in the cell, "No sir, the detainee hasn't spoken a word."

Jack chuckled, low and sinister, "How bout that? Satan's serpentine charms know no bounds, do they?"

Alovick pursed her lips around the cigarette wasting away in her hand, "Whatever you say, sir."

Tanner didn't like that response.

"Carry onward, my Christian soldier," he hissed.

If Tanner's flock found God through misery, these were the Godliest people alive. The promised land was an unfinished prison left to decay in the harsh Nevada sun. A casualty of budget cuts twenty years earlier, lacking all but the bare minimum to sustain human life, and even that was too charitable an appraisal.

This place was hell.

"Set up behind me," Cara ordered. "You see anything unusual, or worse, those things skulking around, you open fire."

Her underlings nodded with the surety of two virgins confronted by their first piece of ass.

It didn't inspire her trust.

"Is that fucking understood?" she barked.

"Yes, ma'am," the short one muttered, turning to his taller, skinnier partner with a timid nod. "You heard the boss. Weapons live."

The tall one scratched the side of his head, embarrassed. "How do you take the safety off, Percy?"

Cara reared her stony mug toward her underling with

crossed arms that made her biceps pop. "Are you kidding me, Numbnuts?"

The tall guard straightened his back, "Name's Hue, ma'am… And no, I'm not, ma'am."

"Jesus christ. Pussy and Numbnuts? This is what I'm working with?"

The short one raised his hand, "I'm Percy, ma'am."

Cara gave the little guy a tired once over. "Of all the professions you could've drawn outta the hat, you took the one you know dick about? Praise the fuckin Lord," she moaned.

The trio came upon the train. It stopped in the middle of the abandoned construction lot outside the compound walls. Its condition was a stark contrast to the corroded pipes and beams littering the site. It definitely wasn't from around these parts.

"Commercial?" Percy whispered.

"No," Alovick said, removing her shades and tucking them into her tac-vest. "Luxury transport. What it's doing here—that's the million dollar question… Take point, Hue."

"Ma'am?"

"Get in *front* of us—and move your ass toward the *train* with your *weapon* pointing *forward*… Can you do that?" Cara asked, nudging Percy's soft shoulder with the backside of her shotgun. "Form up behind him. He takes car-two, you handle three… I got the first one."

The Chief of security advanced. The hair on the back of her neck stood up, but her breathing was steady and measured. A byproduct of life in the Russian Army.

A shadow skittered past the portholes.

Alovick tucked her Benelli tight against her collarbone, "You're encroaching on private land. Come out—hands up—and we'll *consider* considering you friendly." She chambered a slug. *CHA-CHACK!* "Or you can choose not to, but I wouldn't do that."

"Easy! Don't open fire!" a voice hollered behind the shifting control-car door. A raised palm slipped out of the convoy, followed by Max's uneasy face. "This place is a sanctuary, right?"

Cara adjusted the butt of her shotgun, "Any weapons aboard?"

Wild and Volkov cleaned the blood off the console while Max stalled the guards, motioning for them to hurry with his hidden hand. "Wouldn't be alive if we didn't, ma'am," he replied, doing his best to occlude the doorway as Calla and Billy dragged Barry's corpse away behind him.

"*We*, huh?"

"Strength in numbers, ma'am."

"*Stop* calling me *ma'am*, wise guy. How old do I look to you?"

"Strength in numbers—*miss?*"

"Step aside," Alovick barked, snapping her fingers. "Watch my six, guys."

"What—what happens if they resist?" Hue sputtered.

Cara sighed, "Go stand behind Percy, Numbnuts."

"Right away, Chief."

"We're not looking to start trouble," Max said, glancing over his shoulder anxiously.

The woman set her dusty boot on the creaky steps to the control-car, "You seem—nervous."

Amhearst swallowed air down his dry throat as he guarded the doorway. "Wouldn't you be if three armed strangers walked up on you and your family?"

Cara's free hand crept to her hip as she rested the barrel of her Benelli against her clavicle. "There... Shouldered my weapon. Feel safer, manly man?"

"You're still kinda scary. It's the muscles, I think."

"Step aside. *Now*," Cara ordered.

"Gonna shoot me if I don't?"

Alovick pressed her shotgun against Max's sternum, "You make a better door than a window."

Billy and Acean hid in the vents underfoot beside Strunk's corpse as the Chief of Security and her goons boarded.

"He shat himself," the child whispered, crinkling her nose.

The alien raised a finger to his scaled lips, observing the armed kraitho above.

The one with the shotgun ran a hand across the console, "How many others are with you again?"

Max leaned against the wall, mulling over her question. "Well—there's me, my girlfriend, my best buddy, and uh—two girls. Er, one... One girl."

"You sure about that?"

"Been a long trip."

The woman stepped uncomfortably close to Amhearst, "The guy who runs this place isn't as easygoing as me... I suggest you make a wonderful impression by being *honest*."

Max nodded, "It's, um—two girls... One's eighteen, the other one is thirteen, I think."

Shit! Billy thought. *If I'm not with the others when this colossal bitch finds em, we're toast!* She looked at Acean, who was way ahead of her, pressing his body against the shaft so she could pass.

"We'll meet again," the alien hissed. "Go."

"Don't get captured," Kojimatsuo whispered back, pecking his amphibious cheek goodbye.

Acean touched the side of his face. But the fond sentiment was short lived.

The kraitho stormed through the hydraulic door above in a single-file line behind Max.

Hurry, child! he thought.

Cara trailed close behind Max, scanning the maintenance-hold ahead of her men.

Hue glimpsed something beneath the grating underfoot. "Anyone else see that?"

Fuck! Billy thought, shimmying through the vent. There was a secret compartment a few feet from a junction in the tunnel. She rolled inside, dodging three flashlight beams streaming through the grates.

The girl held her breath, looking to her right and seeing an aged brick of cocaine packed in cellophane by her head.

Thank God for dope traffickers, Billy thought.

Percy clicked off his light, satisfied. "Someone needs glasses."

"I'm telling ya, I saw something, people," Hue insisted. "It crawled straight down the car. It was a child."

Max let out a wary chuckle, "No kids in the vents, buddy."

Cara curved her fingers through the grated floor, "These are wobbly." She took a few steps forward and did it again, prying up a loose panel, thrusting her Benelli into the duct.

Hue hopped in place, "I told you!"

"Not so fast, stretch," she replied, reeling out of the tunnel with something in her fist. "No children," she murmured, tossing the dirty brick of cocaine at Hue, who stumbled to catch it. She dusted herself off, "Looks like we got us a drug smuggler, guys."

Billy poked her head around the t-junction ahead of the secret alcove. If she had stayed half a minute longer, the big lady would have spotted her for certain. "I'll level with you… The man who owned this rig was a criminal, but he's dead," she heard Max say.

"This keeps getting better," the woman retorted. "Where

are the others? Take me to them—now."

Billy needed to get topside. Fast.

Amhearst clenched his jaw, "Right this way—gentlemen."

Kojimatsuo was eating a fried drumstick when Cara and her lackeys entered the next-car. "Sup, Max?" she asked, wiping the crumbs from her red cheeks with her shirt sleeve. "Who're these assholes?"

Alovick smiled, "You got a lip on you."

"Um, chief?" Hue leaned in tight and whispered something in Cara's ear.

The woman's expression hardened. Her eyes glided along the grated path, stopping at a patch of steel facing the wrong direction. She glanced at the girl, "You winded?"

"Why?"

Cara tapped herself on the cheek, "Your face, hun. It's rose-red. Like you were—oh, I dunno—slithering through tunnels beneath our feet?" Alovick pointed the barrel of her Benelli at the out-of-place grate, "Were you rooting around under there, young lady?"

Kojimatsuo eyed Max, but it was obvious the guy had no answers, so she nodded in defeated affirmation, much to Hue's delight. "I told you guys!" he yapped.

The large woman lorded over Billy, intense and commanding. "Were you spying on us?"

"No ma'am," the youngster said.

"Well, if you weren't *snooping,* you were *hiding*... Why?"

Billy's shoulders slumped, "Have any family, lady?"

Alovick's throat tightened, "I had a little boy."

"Did the monsters get him?"

"No," Cara whispered. "Leukemia took him when he was seven."

Billy nodded, glancing up at the woman with sad but fierce eyes, "Well, a monster took mine... The man you work for murdered my family."

Alovick set the butt of her shotgun on the ground, "I'm —
sorry."

"You'd hide too if you were me."

"Knowing my employer," Cara said with a sigh, "yeah... I
would have." Her gaze grew cold and hopeless. "I hate him,
myself."

Hue turned to Percy, surprised. "Whoa. The chief's sane."

Alovick balked, "What the hell is that supposed to mean?"

Percy looked nervous, "We're atheists... Not exactly his
people."

"Secret's safe with us, chief," Hue added.

A boisterous voice with a regal drawl entered the car, "Why
are my two security saplings squabbling over their genitals in
front of a little girl?" Jack Tanner asked. He strutted into the car
with a smug swagger. It complimented his gaudy,
televangelist-looking, suit. "Do not have sexual relations with a
man as one does with a woman; that is *detestable*. They are to
be put to death; their blood is on their *own* heads. Leviticus,
twenty-thirty, ladies and gentlemen." He eyed his two male
guards up and down in an almost profane, hypocritical way.
"Am I to put you two to death, or is this some misunderstood
horseplay? I'm ever-so out of touch with as all the sinners," he
grinned.

"Chalk it up to two boys being foolish, Reverend. I have the
matter in hand, I assure you," Cara said, putting her arm
around Billy's shoulder. "I was just learning about what
happened to these poor people. Seems they were," she looked
down at Billy, "taken against their will by a drug dealer. In fact,
this was his train." She nodded to Max. "This man
overpowered their captor and took control of the train...
Right?"

Tanner walked up to Max and extended his jewel-encrusted
hand. "Who might this savior be?" he asked.

"My name's Max."

"Well ain't ya gonna shake my hand, Max? If anyone does not abide in me he is thrown away like a branch and withers; and the branches are gathered, thrown into the fire, and burned. John, Fifteen-Six."

Amhearst looked down at the Reverend's many rings, unimpressed. "I'm afraid I haven't washed my hands in a while. Last thing I'd wanna do is put dirt on yours."

Tanner cocked his head, amused, "A gracious gesture, young man. You and I are gonna be terrific friends."

"I'm sure."

The Reverend smirked. "Huh... I bet you are, Max. By God, I bet you are."

"This is my wife, Beverly, Billy's aunt," Max said. "Honey, this is Cara, Reverend Jack Tanner's Chief of Security."

"Yeah, auntie *Bev*," Billy added. "I was telling her how much I love spending time with you and stuff... Since you're my *aunt*."

Amhearst elbowed the girl's arm, nodding toward Vadim and Calla. "That's my best buddy, Ray, and our daughter—Emily."

Shepherd extended her hand to Cara, "I'm Beverly's little girl... Nice to meet you."

Alovick scanned her newfound acquaintances, glancing over her shoulder. "You guys wanna tone down the theatrics," she muttered under her breath.

"Well, get a load uh this hoyty-toyty palace right *here*," Tanner said, delighted by the Strunks gaudiness. "Was this drug dealer a fag? Cabin's so pink it looks like he painted the walls with Pepto Bismol!"

The Reverend strutted past Billy, who glanced at the

corkscrew on the bar across from the bed. She stepped toward it, but Cara grabbed her shoulder, shaking her head in stiff objection.

"Well, welcome to the promised land," Tanner said. "Ain't used to strangers fallin into our lap like this, but I understand y'all experienced quite the calamity. So what happened?" He trotted past Wild, brushing against her arm as he studied her features. "You look familiar."

"Not the most original come on I've ever heard," Vera responded, mustering as genuine a fake smile as she could.

"Oh, I'm not so odious as to charm a married woman right in front of her spouse, ma'am," the Reverend replied. He leaned close, "But when he *ain't* lookin—that's another matter altogether."

"How Abrahamic of you," Wild whispered.

Tanner snickered, inspecting her with hungry eyes. "I expect you'll find it nice here—Beverly." He moved on to Vadim, puffing out his chest with an impish grin. "What's your story, Roy? Get enough protein today, big guy?"

"Name's Ray, padre."

"Oh, I'm no priest—Ray," Jack replied, peering into the Russian's wintry orbs. "Strange... Your name don't fit your accent... At least not to me." He slapped Volkov's meaty tricep, "Then again, what do I know, huh?"

He set his sights on Shepherd next.

"You look *nothin* like momma, little lady," he declared, sneaking a peek at her barely legal curves. "I recognize y'all from somewhere though."

"Unlikely, Reverend," Calla replied.

Tanner grinned, waggling his finger at the girl, "It'll come to me, just you wait and see." He turned to Cara and his friendly demeanor hardened into stone. "Set them up in the big-house if you don't mind... I wanna show em something."

Chapter 28: No Heaven For Her

Tanner wasn't pretending when he called the indoor living area the big house. It was the defunct prison's A-Block. Minimum security, three levels, forty cells. Each unit crammed four individuals, and a dank, sour odor permeated through the air. It reeked of sweat, stale piss, and humidity-baked shit clogging the broken toilets.

They taped the toilet lids shut with duct tape to mask the stench, but it did little good. Some people even volunteered to return to life outside A-Block to escape the conditions.

Tanner considered their suffering beautiful.

KLANK! The door to Cell-Sixteen slid ajar and in walked Vadim carrying a pillow and bedding. "This mine? Oh, guys, ya shouldn't have."

Cara leaned against the cage, giving Vadim's ass a cursory glance. "Don't like your fresh digs—Ray?"

"My family was interned when I was a boy... Prison bars ain't my thing." He inhaled, reluctantly, "And I wouldn't call this joint fresh."

"Sounds like a sad story," Alovick said, scrutinizing the tall Russian. "Is it true?"

Vadim leered at the woman, having a seat on his creaky cot. "Don't expect I'll be doin any fuckin while I'm here, will I?"

"Not without W-D-Forty and a wedding license. The Reverend frowns on premarital—anything."

"Quite a fellow."

"You have no idea, Ray."

The Russian saw something in her face at that moment.

She was playing a part too, same as the rest of them.

"Name's Vadim… Vadim Volkov," he said.

Cara exited the cell, slid the bars shut. "Eyes. Ears. They're everywhere… Your name's Ray."

"I could've had that sonofabitch," Billy grunted.

Wild held her nose, securing a strip of tape peeling off the toilet lid. "I can't believe I'm suggesting this, but please—stop trying to kill the Reverend," she said, wiping her fingertips across her leg in disgust.

"The prick deserves to die."

Vera gave the child a tired hug, "Yes, he does, but we don't, do we?

"Catch you ladies at a bad time?" Cara asked, squinting through the cell-bars.

"We're fine," Wild snipped.

Alovick stepped into Cell-Eleven with a frosty stare locked on Vera, "Interrupting your girl talk?"

Kojimatsuo crossed her arms, "Care to chime in?"

"If only I could, kid," Cara replied, glancing over her shoulder.

"What's stopping you?"

Alovick looked askance at Billy, "Self preservation."

Wild leaned in close to the woman, "You've never once thought about it?"

Cara let out a melancholy chuckle, "Look around. You can't slay a Hydra, Beverly. Cut off one head, another one'll rise in its place.

"You can totally kill a Hydra," Kojimatsuo interjected, brushing past Vera. "Hercules did it with the help of his nephew... He lopped off it's head and the nephew, Iolaus, cauterized the wound before a fresh one could regrow." She shared an awkward stare with the two women looking down at her. "Teenagers still read, okay?"

"I'm not Hercules," Alovick said.

Billy backhanded Vera across her breasts, "Neither are we, but it ain't about being Hercules or Iolaus... It's about working as a team."

Cara grinned, "Reading pays off... Too bad this isn't a book."

Max followed Calla up to the third-floor, "What do you think this guy's planning?"

"That's anyone's guess," Shepherd replied, dispirited. "None of us need to be here long enough to see. Agreed?"

"If we get back to the train, I can plot a fresh course to Verenberg now that the nav-system's reset."

The duo reached the top of the steps to find Billy and Vera leaning against the guardrail, eyeing the open space below. Calla palmed the girl's shoulder. "Something's wrong," she whispered, turning to Wild and Max with an uneasy look on her face. "I can *sense* one of them... It's close."

"The things?" Kojimatsuo asked.

Shepherd nodded.

"Welcome!" Tanner's strident voice boomed as he pranced along the catwalk. Cara shadowed him like an assault-rifle-toting lapdog. "How y'all liking your new homes?" he inquired, clasping his palms together in gleeful anticipation of God knows what. "You'll get used to the odor, I promise. That's what they *tell* me at least," he grumbled with a hearty chuckle.

He halted mid-stride, eying Calla's exquisite features.

"You *positive* I don't know you from someplace?"

Shepherd's fingernails scraped across the railing, "I'd remember someone like you."

Tanner pretended to blush, "Such a darling."

"Didn't say that was a *good* thing."

"There's that teen spirit. You'll go far with that attitude." Jack cruised past the hybrid, giving Vera a cold wink. "Guess y'all wanna know what's goin on, right?" He leaned against the rail with a swagger, staring at Billy with unsettling tenderness in his glassy eyes. "What about you, kiddo? Wonderin why we're here?"

It took all the strength Vadim could muster not to shove Jack over the railing. "Will you spit it out already? None of us are mind-readers, padre."

Tanner waggled his finger at the Russian. "*You…* You're a party-pooper, I can tell." He swatted his Chief of Security's arm, "You two'll git along great."

"It's *Ray*."

The Reverend smirked, "It sure is, big fella." He nodded to Cara with a cocky grin. "Do the honors?"

Alovick's face turned a little ashen as she spoke into her hand-radio, "Let's go, gentlemen. Bring—bring in the girl."

"You feelin okay, honey-lamb? Looks like you saw the spirit of Judas himself," Tanner said. He yanked a handkerchief from his coat pocket and gave it to Cara.

"I'm fine, sir," Alovick muttered, patting down her forehead with the Reverend's cologne drenched rag. "Ladies and gentlemen, if you'll please make your way to the railing, the—show—will begin in a moment." Cara's tone was flat and unsteady.

The Reverend took notice.

SKREEE! Double-doors below shrieked open. Hue and Percy poured into the staging area, manhandling a steel-chain pulled taught by a hysterical young woman shrieking at the end.

"No!" the woman squealed, clawing at the chains as she dug her heels into the grimy concrete so hard they bled. "You don't have to do this! I'm a God-fearing girl, I swear!"

Her terrified stare tore away from her jailers, shooting skyward, toward the heavens, but all she saw was Tanner looking down on her with a motionless gaze that chilled her blood.

She stopped resisting.

There would be no reprieve.

No escape from her imminent death.

It was all in his eyes.

"I didn't do nothin," she whispered.

Hue pulled the girl to the center of the ground floor with a heavy heart behind his inhuman grimace. Percy's head was on a swivel, unlinking the steel chain fastened to her shackled wrists. She dropped to the concrete as the two guards removed her shackles and dashed out of sight.

"A sinner lays before you all," Tanner bellowed through the prison block. He raised his hands, his right arm descending with a heavy and ominous fingertip fixed on the young woman. "It is the wish of the Lord that this magnate of depravity sink into the flaming pits of hell for sins against our flock. Does anyone here doubt my conviction?"

"No Reverend!" the faithful cried as one.

"Is there any among you who prefer to see this girl spared despite her misdeeds?"

"No Reverend!"

"Then pray with me, brothers and sisters! That she may find harmony at His table! But if *not*... If I drive this harlot into the seventh circle of the devil's abode, so be it!"

"Amen, Reverend!"

"Amen!" Tanner shouted, digging into his jacket pocket, trotting out a remote control for all to behold. "Let judgment begin!" he yelled, pressing the large red button in his soiled fist. "May you find peace in death, sister! And may God absolve you!"

Cell-One opened with a heavy *CLANG.*

The flock watched from above like jackals thirsty for bloodshed.

The stillness was heavy and hateful, but the *CLACKING* of talons drawing out of the cage's abyss was much worse.

A foot jutted from the shadows, striking the concrete and rattling the girl's vertebra.

She didn't dare move, but her morbid curiosity led her stare toward the blackened cell.

The beast's claws raked underfoot, its shrouded body compressing into a lethal coil aimed at its prey.

The girl felt her own warm fluid trickling down her inner thigh. "Our father, who art—"

ROARRR! The Akkan-Rah was upon the woman in a famished rage, tearing through her breasts with its jagged teeth. It gnashed on her clavicle like an over-sized wishbone.

Crimson spewed from her mouth in thick spurts of senseless gore.

There was no heaven for her.

The monstrosity cleaved through her torso, spilling her gleaming entrails across the ground.

The girl's blood oozed from her once pristine skin, which was now a sickening grayish-blue hue.

Calla watched the woman thrash from side to side like a dying seal tenderized in the jaws of a great white shark. She stepped away from the stoop in self-disgust, much to Tanner's delight. The hybrid wanted to intercede, but when she glanced at Billy, she could feel the words the child couldn't say.

Don't do it. We're dead if you do it.

Calla's belly twisted when her ears picked up the woman's poignant death rattle below.

"Quite the sight, ain't it?" Tanner asked with a sadistic simper. "Gives the little ones nightmares, but the adults—they know the wrath of God with every swipe uh that abomination's talons... The children'll get there, with the correct guidance... Unless they wanna end up like the harlot down there."

Vera moved her cupped hand away from her mouth in nauseous awe. "How did you capture it?"

Tanner slid his fists into his pockets. "That's a marvelous question, Beverly. One I'll answer later." The Reverend stooped over the rail, reeling in amused disgust, "Holy shit in a shoppin cart! Ain't nuthin left is there? Whooo-eeeee!"

Amhearst white-knuckled the guardrail, fixated on Tanner's self-important mug. "That was someone's *daughter.*"

The Reverend's grin melted. He cocked his indignant head to the side. "I'm not *that* cruel," he replied, stepping close enough to smell Max's breath. "I made sure it ate her parents *first.*"

Max didn't flinch.

Jack gripped Cara's arm, "Get it back in the enclosure."

A piglet sounded off inside the beast's chamber, lowered through a hatch in the ceiling.

The monster's keen senses detected movement in its den, licking its chops as it drew closer.

Another snack.

The land-stalker hissed, leaping after the cowering baby pig. It dug into the helpless creature's supple flesh, latching on tight as it clamped down on the piglet's frail jugular.

Percy sprang into action, striking the cage door shut, springing backward onto his ass as the animal's gnarled claws erupted through the bars.

The beast's corneas shimmered in the dank blackness of its confines, locked on the delicious looking mammal just out of its reach, even as it swallowed the crushed piglet-brains gliding down its gullet.

Jack turned toward his visitors, and it was as if all the humanity drained from his face. "I can only imagine what you people must think of me... I guarantee you it's plenty worse than that if you cross me... Lie to me... I hope we understand one another."

"What did she do to deserve to die?" Billy asked, a little rattled.

The Reverend mulled for a moment, giving the child a wintry grin, "Nothing atall... Got my point across though, didn't it?"

Chapter 29: Kindred

"This is the only intact facility," Cara said, leading Vadim into the security station.

"Of course it is," the Russian sighed, spying an elderly man imprisoned at the end of the corridor. "What's his deal?"

Alovick tucked her palms into her pockets, "Why not ask him?"

"I won't bite, young fellow," the old timer said, perched at the edge of his dingy cot with his wrinkled hands dangling between his legs.

Volkov walked up to the cell, bending his fingers around the bars, curious. "Don't look like much of a lawbreaker, sir."

The aged man cracked a smile, "Whoever sheds the blood of man, by man must his spill, for God made man in his own image."

"You killed someone?"

"Yessir," the old timer answered, glimpsing at Cara with mournful eyes. "Had two children once. Daughter perished of natural causes," he hung his head, "the other one—he's dead because of me."

"Sorry for your loss," Vadim whispered, kneeling down to get an eye-level view of the elderly man. "I know what it's like, sir... I had a child of my own."

"That so?"

"Yessir."

"How old?"

"She—she was six."

"Pure age... I'm certain she's with the Lord now, son."

Volkov nodded with trembling lips. *Wish I was as sure after everything I've seen... Or* didn't *see,* he thought. "What happened to yours?" he asked aloud.

"My girl lost her battle with cancer a year ago... The boy died when he was in his twenties. Self-inflicted wounds, I'm afraid."

"Hold on a minute; you blame yourself for his death?" Volkov shook his head, "No, sir. We make our own choices."

The old man mustered a pained, cataract-laden glance at the large man beyond his cell. "I gave my boy the tools to destroy himself, friend. I assure you, it was my fault."

"And the Reverend found out and put you in here or what? That sonofabitch."

"For if you forgive others for their misdeeds, your divine Father will likewise absolve you... Jack's merely doing what someone *groomed* him to do, son. He can't help his convictions."

"Christ-like of you, but it won't change you not belonging in this fuckin cell, sir. I've seen what he does to prisoners around here."

The old man sighed, "Me too."

"Let him out," the Russian demanded. "I'm not watching another innocent person die."

Cara looked away in self-disgust, "Tanner has the keys, not me."

"You're the fucking security chief, aren't you?"

"This is his world! You think this man would be here if I could do anything about it? If you do, then fuck you! Not everyone is as righteous as you! And in case you haven't noticed, Ray, sanity's in short supply here, and those of us who have it do whatever we have to in order to fucking survive!"

Volkov's furious fists *CLANGED* against the old man's cell, "We gotta get him outta here, Cara!"

"And take him where?" Alovick barked back. "Where would he run? Not like there's a town outside these walls! He's in his eighties, he'd die out there in the desert!"

"Like *hell he will*," Vadim growled, looking for a way—any way he could—to set the old man free.

"You can't break him out… I tried," Cara whispered, defeated.

Volkov's grip on the steel loosened, and he turned to the woman, forcing himself to be calmer. "Look… No way me and my friends are sticking around after what we saw today. Get us to the train and we can fit this man, you, and anybody else who wants to escape this shit-pit aboard with the rest of us."

Alovick shook her head, frustrated by Vadim's ignorance. "Tanner doesn't open the main gates unless he has to, which is damn near never these days… If they're ajar and he finds out about it, he'll kill us all."

The Russian stared into the old fellow's tired eyes, "How can you accept this?"

The old man gripped his large fists, "Don't blame Alovick, son… You can't imagine how exhausting it is trying to keep these people safe when the one giving the orders asks you to do things that eat at your soul… Things you have to do to protect the many over the unlucky few… I don't envy her position at all."

"I don't envy yours, sir."

"Don't blame you," the old man said, grinning. His smile melted into somber reflection, "I belong in here, son. Too many suffer because of me… Too many."

Cara balked, "That isn't true, Homer. It's him. They suffer

because of Him... And If I could break you free, I would, I need you to know that."

"Yet, you can't... That's the Lord's will at work, my dear... And His will be done."

"Fuck the Lord's will!" Volkov turned to Cara, praying his next words would ignite whatever strength she had left. "You cried when you sent that girl to her death, I saw it... You gonna hide those same tears when it's time to murder this man too? Do the right thing... Open the gates and lets get him outta here —together."

Alovick said nothing, staring down at the cold concrete beneath her boots.

"Cara..." Vadim prodded.

"I'll —I'll see what I can do," Cara's voice hesitantly crackled through the intercom beside Tanner's leather armchair.

The Reverend grabbed the iron-poker leaning against his seat, stoking his fireplace with a gentle hand.

His vacant stare settled on the hellish blaze reflecting off his glass of Scotch as he lifted it to his lips, sipping.

It burned like a betrayal.

The chow hall was packed with eager mouths hovering over their trays in silent prayer as Tanner patrolled the aisles, bible in hand, while his flock gave thanks for their meager portions behind the outsiders and their lavish spread.

"This meat tastes like ass," Billy grumbled.

Calla nudged the girl's foot with the back of her heel, "Don't start."

"What? It's true."

Max leaned over the table, closer to Kojimatsuo, "Save the bitching for after we get outta here, kid."

Billy rolled her eyes, "Any of you see any livestock around here? I'm just sayin..."

"From the mouths of babes," the Reverend said with a snide chuckle, eavesdropping on the girl. "There are no cannibals here, young lady. We aren't savages. The promised land has enough frozen reserves to last us ten years."

"Yeah, well, I think some of it's expired."

"That's cute… Never stop being you."

"Why don't your people have as much food as we do on their plates?" Vera asked, glancing at the gloomy folks behind her. "Can we at least offer the children some of ours?"

"The God of grace, who called you to his eternal glory in Christ, after you have suffered, will restore you and make you steadfast. Peter, Five-Ten, my dear," Tanner replied, leafing through his Good Book as he plucked a grape from Wild's plate.

"These are developing minds. You're not making them strong by denying them nutrients. Where I come from, that's called abuse."

Annoyed, Jack clapped his tome shut, "We ain't where y'all are from though, are we—Beverly?"

"No, we aren't," Wild said, rising out of her seat, "because if we were, you'd get arrested for this."

Tanner's brows puckered in surprise, "Is that so?"

"Damn straight, padre," Vadim added, scarfing down a hunk of chicken with his mouth flapping open and shut. He let out a volcanic burp that made the children in the back giggle. "I gotta admit, you have me wondering if you ever read the bible, the way you carry on around here."

Tanner cocked his head, "And how's that, *Roy*?"

Volkov brandished an unanticipated grin, "I'm sure even Hitler fed the Jews a little more food than you give these folks for starters."

"Son, if my accommodations don't please y'all, you're more than welcome to leave."

That statement caught Vadim off guard, and he sat up

straight. "Wait… We are?"

Tanner palmed the wine-filled chalice resting beside Volkov's empty plate, raising it to his lips. "Absolutely," he said, wiping a smattering of purple fluid from his mouth with his hairy knuckles. "Course, there's a little something you and your friends gotta see before ya go though."

The old-timer was fast asleep when a metal stool CLANGED against the bars, startling him awake.

"You made new friends," Tanner said with sinister enthusiasm. "They seem like friendly folks, don't they?"

The elderly man sat up in his cot, unwilling to speak.

The Reverend's rings scraped along the steel bars, "Cat got yer tongue, ya ancient fart? C'mon… What do you think of em?"

"They're kind," the gray fellow, muttered. "That's more than I can say for others."

"Now, I *know* you don't mean *me*. I'm about to bestow the *ultimate* kindness upon your wrinkly ass—*despite* your betrayal."

The old man stood on his feet, "And that's my failure to bear, isn't it?"

"What does that even mean?"

"What's the saying? Do the crime, do the time? Yes, I believe that's how it goes."

Tanner grinned, "How you must hate me, old man."

"No," the elderly one whispered, sliding his frail, bony fingers over Tanner's knuckles wrapped around the bars. "I love *all* God's creatures…. And I forgive even you.

Jack recoiled from the cell in furious disgust, "Arrogant till the end!" A grisly smile slithered across his clenched teeth. "Let's just wait and see how forgiving *she* is, shall we?"

Chapter 30: Surrogate Gladiator

May 18th, 2047
6:59AM

The dawning sun scorched the bleachers lining the barbed prison yard by the time a crowd started forming. Tanner presided from the second floor of his security building, marveling over his makeshift fighting-pit like a Roman emperor hungry for a bloody spectacle.

The air was dry, and the winds were hot, but Calla's spine ran ice-cold, just as it always did when those things were around.

Maybe it was her unhoned senses, or extreme exhaustion, but whatever she detected, it seemed to meld together and then break apart, like two crossing wires melting into a single consciousness. Feral rage and hate drove one side, and the other was no less alien, and yet familiar.

Calla hoped it wasn't who she knew it was.

Vera swatted a cluster of flies away from her face, "This fucking heat is horrendous. At this rate, I'll be dead from dehydration before we even leave."

"Probably what that bastard wants," Billy grumbled. "Not like he's gonna keep his word, anyway. Watch."

A firm hand clutched the girl's arm. "Scootch over will ya?" Max asked, wedging Kojimatsuo between himself and Vera. "Got enough room?"

"Everything sucks out here. Who gives a shit?" the girl snipped. She looked over Amhearst's shoulder, "And here comes one more... Outstanding."

"I don't like this," Vadim said, plunking down beside Max, scanning the pit beyond the barbed fence. "Why do I have the feeling he's gonna try to get another point across?"

"That's not our problem, Vad," Amhearst replied, embarrassed by his own coldness. "These people *chose* him, they sought him out. Whatever happens happens because they let it."

"Not all of em," the Russian said under his breath.

"Looks like everyone's here! Welcome, brothers and sisters!" Tanner bellowed. "Is this not a glorious day?"

Uproarious cheering erupted from the bleachers.

"Who feels the Lord's spirit shining down on em this morning?"

"Praise Jesus for another day!" one devout child cried, prompting the entire flock to rise and applause.

Jack grinned, "That's the essence of Christ in that youngster, brothers and sisters! Praise God, that we may show such an innocent soul the way in this hour of Earthly peril! Today is a day of reckoning! Of justice!" He clapped his hands together twice, "Cara, get on out here, girl!"

Alovick stepped onto the balcony accompanied by the old man, shirtless and shackled. Her expressionless countenance belied her guilt as she searched for Volkov's face in the ranks below.

When their eyes met, Cara's lips quivered, and the Russian could have sworn he saw her mouth two words.

I'm sorry.

Tanner clutched the aged man's bony arm, shoving him to

the fore for all to see. "This vile degenerate stands before you so that none may endure his fate! A deceitful, selfish cretin with the hubris to challenge the laws of our Lord to satiate his own empty heart!" The Reverend lifted the prisoner's chin with a cupped palm, staring into his distressed, cloudy eyes. "This man dies today."

The throng burst into wild applause that made Cara's stomach turn with every gleeful cry.

In her silent anguish, she glanced down at her sidearm.

Use it...

Alovick's trembling hand crept toward her piece.

You can end this...

"Cara!" Jack barked.

"Yes, Reverend?" Alovick said, swiftly drawing away from her pistol.

"Have any siblings?"

"Half, yes."

"Where are they?"

"Gone, sir."

"Shame," Tanner replied, clutching his prisoner by the scruff of his neck, staring into the crowd. "When *I* was a child, I wanted a sibling of *my* very own. Tell you what, folks, I prayed harder than I ever did my entire life for the Lord to put another baby in my momma's womb. If you were an only kid, y'all know the struggle. The loneliness takes a toll on ya, specially when yer momma doesn't have time for ya because she's supposed to be in the kitchen."

The Reverend looked askance at his elderly captive, seething with a fiery heart so filled with rage it could have burned a hole in his chest.

"And *fathers*," he continued through grated teeth, "fathers are busy doing God's duty if they're worth their salt! So, where does that leave a youngin? Hangin on a prayer, that's where."

He released his grip on the old man, donning a warm smile, "Brothers and sisters, would you believe the Almighty answered my pleas? He sure did!"

"Amen!" the crowd jubilantly cried.

"Amen is right! One day I came home from school and there they were, my momma, my papa, and a shiny new baby!" Tanner paused, his eyes pooling as he composed himself. "I had my very own sister. Now—she was adopted, ya see—but she was still *my* lil sis... By God, we did *everything* together. My best friend in the world. There wasn't nothin I wouldn't have done for her... And y'all know what this animal did to her?"

WHACK! Jack slapped the old man as hard as he could, "He gave her straight to Satan, that's what he did!"

"Slay the heathen!" a nameless voice in the crowd wailed.

"Avenge her!"

"Yeah! Kill him!"

"Kill him! Kill him! Kill him! Kill him!" the crows cawed.

Tanner motioned for silence, "I ain't perfect. I've done things some wouldn't consider Christ-like, but I'd *never* do what he did!"

The throng stood on their feet in creepy solidarity, "Amen, Reverend!"

"I ain't even know she was sick, brother's and sisters!" Jack cried, pointing his spiteful finger at the man who helped give him life. "This degenerate watched my sister die of cancer and didn't even pick up the phone to call her only brother! I ask y'all, is that any way to treat a son?"

"My son died long ago, perverted by his own misinterpretations of everything I strived to teach him," the old man said, heartbroken. "I don't recognize who stands before me anymore than you'd recognize the good man you used to be."

Tanner's tone oozed with disgust, "See him before you, my

flock. The doting father… A man of God."

"If only you could say the same of yourself, Jackeriah Herman Tanner." The old man shook his head in pity, "I'll forever condemn myself for failing to protect you from yourself. And I pray my death brings you the peace that a life lustfully questing for power can *never* provide."

"I hate you!" Jack cried.

"I know, my child—and I love you as deeply as you adored Christine… Never forget that."

"Oh, there are so many things I'll never forget about you, daddy." Tanner pulled the old man close, planting a gentle kiss on his father's unkempt cheek, "Least of all your *weakness*."

The prisoner smiled, "Thank the Lord your sister was adopted then. Explains why she was always the stronger of the two of you."

The Reverend simpered, turning his back on his father, "Homer Alabaster Tanner, brothers and sisters! A fellow of conviction! One who brought a *clone* through these gates and said nothing! A man who made me embrace a ticking time-bomb-of-a-beast I thought was my beautiful sister! I opened my *home* to this abomination, and *this* is the repayment for my gracious mercy? I demand justice for this crime, my flock! The Lord *demands* blood!"

The crowd cheered in devout agreement.

Jack's scowl whipped toward Cara. "Open it," he hissed.

It paced through the dark with a ravenous craving.

The metal slats ascended, and the dawn's light stretched across its clawed feet.

It hunched like a threatened alley-cat, breathing heavy and hard.

The collective gasps of countless soft fleshed mammals triggered its lethal impetus.

It emerged from its holding pen with jaws agape and dripping with saliva.

"I ask you! How poetic is this man's justice? Slain by the abomination he, himself, brought into this world!" a softling shouted, high above the beast. *"A father executed by the offspring he should never have resurrected!"*

The prey beyond the barbed fence howled in unison, *"Kill him! Kill him! Kill him!"*

The Akkan-Rah's claws scraped across the concrete.

"Do any among you have anything to say before I cast this heathen into the pit?"

The creature's slathering-maw ascended toward the balcony above its scaled head. Its prey, so furless and frail, seemed familiar to the monster somehow.

They looked appetizing.

"Last chance, brothers and sisters! Speak now if you wish me to spare his life!"

"Take me *instead!"* a large mammal outside its confines roared.

The Akkan-Rah zeroed in on the only tall and muscular frame in the fray.

A hearty meal, indeed.

The softling on the catwalk chuckled in perverse malevolence, *"I was waiting for that—Roy."*

"Good luck," Percy said, handing Vadim a rusty machete and shield fashioned out of a mangled hubcap. Hue followed suit, giving the Russian a damaged riot-helmet, "Sorry about the blood in the cracks."

Volkov slid the headgear on, flipping up the cracked visor, "It's a little tight."

"Yeah," Hue shrugged, "Last head we pried out of it was on the smaller side, but it's all we have." He extended a hand to

Vadim, "Hope you fare better than that guy."

The Russian gave Hue's dainty mitt a firm shake, "Hell of a pep-talk."

"Let's hear it for today's martyr!" Tanner jeered with a taunting clap of his gaudy, ring-clad paws. "Homer thanks ya for yer sacrifice! Not that it'll make a lick uh difference after yer dead—*Mister Volkov.*"

Vadim's face paled, "What did you just say?"

The Reverend winked at Vadim, turning to Cara. "Ya shoulda shot me when ya had the chance, bitch," he said, shooting her in the gut with her own sidearm. Alovick dropped to her knees in shock, gasping and weakened as Jack clutched her by the throat, hoisting her off the balcony into the kill-zone below.

"Cara!" Volkov roared, dashing toward the pit.

Hue threw himself in front of the man, "We electrify the fence!"

"Fucking un-electrify the damn thing!"

"Help meeeaaackkk! Aghhhh!" Cara wailed as the beast bore into her, tearing her to shreds before the bloodthirsty crowd. Her nightmarish cries of pain would have been horrifying were they not overshadowed by the even more terrifying chanting.

"Sinner! Sinner! Sinner! Sinner!"

"Open the gate!" the Russian exclaimed. "Open it!"

"In due time, friend," Tanner cooed, fascinated by the carnage unfolding beneath his feet. He inhaled deeply, hoping to catch a whiff of Alovick's sweet smelling blood wafting through the humid air as the beast chewed on her face, digging at her entrails with its claws as it choked down her flesh.

"Christine, Cara. Cara, Christine," he fiendishly chuckled. "What am I sayin, y'all met plenty uh times before! Not as close up, mind ya." He eyed his father with a fiendish gleam in his blackened orbs, "It should be *you* next."

Homer shook his head in dismay, "I welcome death if it means freedom from the nightmare that is watching you become—this."

"You're not dying today, old man. Not if I got anything to say about it," the Russian growled.

"Y'all almost had me fooled, ya know that?" Tanner interjected, "Specially *you*, Beverly! I remember Dr. Vera Wild being much more homely! You clean up nice for an ugly woman, darlin!" He set his sights on Billy next. "Sorry bout the whole, makin ya an orphan thing. It was just business, kid. I didn't mean to kill yer chink-daddy and commy-mommy."

"I'll fucking kill you!" Kojimatsuo shrieked, leaping off the bleachers before being restrained by Max. "Let me go!"

"Yeah, Amhearst, let the kid go," Jack taunted. "She's had her stink-eye set on me since the moment we met, I wouldn't mind teaching her some manners."

"Neither would I, you sonofabitch," Shepherd growled, fighting to subdue the beast within as Tanner's surrounding sheep shied away in terror at the sound of her demonic voice.

The Akkan-Rah in the pit ceased its feeding, honing in on the Leevahn.

It watched her every move.

"Ah, the hellspawn uh the hour... Miss Shepherd. How you've grown, princess. In *all* the right places, I might add."

"Pig."

"Only to those who know me closest, sweetheart."

Calla turned to the scared crowd, "This is your leader speaking! This is who you go to for moral leadership! Wake up!"

"Enough! If you *fully* obey the Lord your God and carefully follow *all* his commands *I* give you today, the Lord your God will set you high above all nations on earth! Deuteronomy, twenty-eight one!" Tanner exploded.

"Amen, Reverend!" the flock cawed. "You are the way! Forever!"

"Hear that, freak?" Jack asked, outstretching his arms in terrible triumph. "*I* am the way. What are y'all? Just another gaggle uh sinners tryin to destroy everything we God-fearing folks have built! I had y'all figured out eventually... I see *everything*." He stared daggers at Vadim, "*Hear* everything." A cold smile overtook his hateful expression, "Cara's death is on your hands, Volkov. That's what happens when selfish pricks get in the way of the Lord's plan."

"What do you know about any of us?" Calla interjected.

"Not much, but maybe yer—*tall*—friend can fill in the gaps. Or did ya think y'all could hide him forever? Like I ain't gonna notice a seven-foot lizard skulkin around my compound."

Shepherd's eyes glowed a hellish red, stoking the fear of Satan in Tanner's minions as she spoke. "Where is he?" she roared, clenching her taloned fists.

Jack wrapped an arm over his father's weak shoulders, "Hey now... That ain't the right way to come at someone holdin all the cards, girly. You need information, and I demand a show... So, lets make a deal. Tell yer big Russian friend to take this old piece-uh-shits place in the pit *as planned*, and I'll tell ya what you wanna know when it's over, but not a moment before."

"Fine."

"*If* he survives."

Calla and Vadim exchanged a knowing glance, then she looked up at the despot on the balcony once more with a sly smirk. "Deal."

Alovick's body was so mutilated, it barely registered as human, but The Russian didn't have time to seethe over it now. Instead, he looked upon her carcass driven by pure hate for the

Akkan-Rah inching toward him like a starving lioness. Nothing else existed at that moment but he and his prey.

He clutched his machete tight, "Sure you wanna do this after the week I've had? Already killed a handful of your friends."

The creature let out a heavy and deep hiss, arching its back as it drew closer, stalking the softling's every move as it licked Cara's flesh from its cruel chops.

"Meh. What's one more?"

SHWACK! Vadim's weapon plunged into the Akkan-Rah's side with a twisting CRUNCH of its breaking ribs. The beast yowled in agony, its baleful eyes locked on the Russian's blade reeling from its torso. It lurched forward, clawing at the hubcap affixed to its prey's arm. Volkov wrestled the writhing creature off his bulging bicep, punching the monster in the face with his shield. WHACK! The Russian cleaved the dazed Akkan-Rah's shoulder with a ferocious slash of his rusty machete.

ROARRR! The beast's musings rattled the concrete beneath the softling's feet. Its taloned digits wrapped around Vadim's blade like a vice. It clawed the weapon out of the Russian's hand with a mighty swipe, biting into its prey, launching him across the pit. CRASH! Vadim nosedived into a bench to the south. He shook himself off, prying a two-inch nail out of his meaty thigh. "Sonofabitch!" he growled.

The smell of his blood sent the Akkan-Rah into a death-charge.

Volkov dashed for his shield.

SLASH! The monster sowed three deep gashes into the human's back, sending him rolling across the gravel in agony, coming to a stop on his side, battered and bruised.

"Yes!" Tanner cried from on high. "See what hubris looks like, brothers and sisters!"

His flock burst into cheers, but Volkov couldn't hear them.

All his attention rested with the mutilated woman mere feet from his bloody face. So little of her flesh remained, but the Russian could still make out the terrified expression on her skinless countenance.

From behind, the beast drew toward its prey, bearing down on Vadim's spine with a wet CRUNCH. Rivulets of blood pooled around the monster's talons as it lorded over the fallen champion, ready to strike a killing blow with its unhinging jaws stretched agape.

POW! A sea of teeth exploded from the Akkan-Rah's mouth as Volkov's vengeful fist crashed into the beast's face. It laid unconscious as its prey loomed over its hideous, limp form.

Conspicuously uninjured.

The crowd gasped in awe, watching the Russian's wounds heal before their fearful eyes.

"What in the name of God?" Tanner hissed.

Vadim removed his armor, tossing it at his feet as he cracked his neck in vexation. He tore his tattered shirt away from his hulking torso, looking up at the bewildered Reverend. "You owe me new clothes," he said, driving his heel into the beast's collar with a savage CRACK that vibrated up his leg in a satisfying wave.

"Yesss!" the outsiders cheered as one, unabashed by the faces zeroing in on them in contempt. "I knew you could do it!" Billy declared.

"Thanks kid," the Russian replied, staring down at the broken beast at his feet. He raised his shield skyward, ready to sever the beast's head, when the creature's claw drove deep into Volkov's torso, exposing the glistening entrails dangling from his gut.

"Vad!" Max cried, shielding Kojimatsuo from the gore. "Get off me!" she bawled, tearing away from both he and Wild. "Calla! Do something!" You gotta do something!"

Bloody spit oozed from Vadim's lips as he eyed the gaping hole in his abdomen, collapsing to his knees..

"Praise Jesus!" the Reverend shouted, waving his hands toward the heavens. "Ask and ye shall receive, brothers and sisters!"

"Go to hell!" Billy fired back. "You'll be praying for a closed casket by the time I'm done with you, you ignorant shithead!"

"This isn't helping matters!" Vera said, doing her damndest to restrain the girl.

"Nobody's trying to help shit, I wanna kill the guy!" Kojimatsuo exclaimed, ceasing her thrashing when she looked into the pit, wide eyed.

"No," she whispered.

The beast circled the prey beneath its flaring snout, reeling its scaly lips as Vadim cradled his exposed intestines. The stalker clamped onto the back of Volkov's neck like a feral dog, stripping flesh from bone as the Russian gurgled in protest. His vision blackened, but he could hear the beast's obscene, throaty gulps, unable to feel or sense what part of himself it was eating.

The man wanted to shriek, but he made no sound.

He couldn't even breathe.

For a moment, Vadim thought he had gone deaf, until his bloodshot eyes drifted past his chin and he realized his head was clinging to his neck by a single strand of glistening sinew. His sight blurred, but he still saw well enough to stare into the spasming throat-stump winking at him like half a pig's snout as the Akkan-Rah fed on his entrails in the background.

Fearing he was about to succumb to phantom nausea, Vadim shut his eyes.

"Get away from him!" an inhuman voice screamed in the darkness.

A slender figure vaulted over the electric fence, dive-bombing into the mutant. It gripped the beast by the scruff of its neck, hurling it off of Volkov. The creature slammed into the side of the balcony at Tanner's feet, rattling the security station as it crashed into the unforgiving concrete below.

It shook the detritus from its scaly hide, eyeing the slender, jet-black enemy before it. ROARR! It galloped after the hybrid, driving its fangs into the warrior's forearm. A crocodile's bite paled compared to an attack from an Akkan of any kind, yet the Leevahn didn't even flinch, locking eyes with the beast so desperately trying to break its bones. The creature's thrashing grew more lethargic with every passing second their stares met until its drooling jaws were motionless around the Leevahn's arm.

The hybrid withdrew its limb from the stalker's paralyzed mouth.

"What in the hell?" Tanner gasped.

The Leevahn's face, as seen by the catatonic beast in her clutches, enveloped the glowing war-portal in Vulgrell's chamber. He watched as the hybrid retracted its ebony claws, severing the Akkan-Rah's head from its body, thus ending the portal's connection.

If only the Leevahn had done so sooner.

The Khoth took a taloned finger to a button on his armrest, eager to claim what was always his.

For the Empire.

For his dear Unda.

"Ready my shuttlecraft," he hissed.

The creature known as Christine Tanner's head bounded over the balcony rail, *PLOPPING* beside Homer's bare foot in a pool of slime and gore, still twitching.

The Leevahn's alien features receded into Calla's flesh, "It's done! Now where's Acean?"

Tanner wrapped his arm around his father's shoulder, "What did I say earlier? Headless Horseman there's the one who had to come out on top if ya wanted answers. You broke the rules."

"No, she didn't," Volkov croaked, still splayed across the concrete, but with his hands compressing his head against his body. The crowd gasped as the Russian rose to his feet, releasing his hold on his regenerated neck and guts. "Wouldn't have some aspirin or Nexium on ya, would ya, padre?"

Jack's eyes widened in awe, "By faith in the name of Jesus, this man whom you see and know was made strong. It is Jesus' name and the faith that comes through him that has healed him, as you can all see. Acts, three-sixteen."

"Amen!" the flock echoed.

Tanner motioned for silence. "Even so, brothers and sisters," he said, eyeing the outsiders in the pit below him with a smug grimace. "If a man *vows* a *vow* to the *Lord*, or swears an oath to bind himself by a pledge, he shall *not* break his word. Numbers, thirty, two."

SHINK! The Reverend drove a dagger into the side of his father's neck, twisting it through the old man's esophagus. Homer's face paled in shock as he clutched the collar of his estranged son's shirt, smearing Tanner's chest in blood as he slid toward his eternal resting place at his child's hateful feet.

"You animal!" Shepherd cried.

"We had a deal, you bastard!" Vadim added.

Jack kicked his father's hand off his shined boot in disgust, "A life for a life; that was the arrangement! Got a problem with it, ya shoulda stopped fuckin breathin!"

"You're sick!" Calla exclaimed. "You never intended to keep your word at all!"

"I surely did! How *dare* you question *my* integrity! I never break a vow I make, you sinful little bitch!"

"How the hell were we gonna find out where Acean was

unless Vadim died, if him *dying* is what would save your father?"

The Reverend shrugged, frustrated by Shepherd's naivety. "It's called *hedging yer bets,* ya fucking idiot! I got what I wanted outta this, one way or the other!" He kicked his father's corpse, "I hated him more anyway."

"Come down here and I'll make you wish you had a father to cry to when I'm finished, you coward," Volkov growled.

Tanner leaned over the balcony, grinning, "Ya'll act like nun uh this was ordained from the beginning! This is the Lord's work, son! I'm just a vessel for his Divine justice, nothing more!"

"Homer didn't have to die," Calla asserted. "That was your doing! You took his life with your own hateful hands! He was your *father*! Your blood!"

Jack balked, "You're one to talk, freak. Killin yer own kind's *no* different. Why, you ripped that Hellspawn's head off without a second thought! That was yer *sister*! Yer *blood*!"

"The Akkan *aren't* my kind... They're weapons."

"Weapons? Weapons are tools," Tanner said, looking out into the crowd. "Dunno bout the rest uh y'all, but when I'm done with my tools, I put em away!" He gave Calla a cold leer, "Yet, these abominations are still wreaking havoc, ain't they?" He scanned the bleachers with a booming voice once more, "That must mean this beast before us has the power to stop these monsters, and *chooses* not to!"

"I stopped your sister, didn't I?"

The Reverend scratched his chin with the tip of the blade he used to kill his father. "That ya did, Calla. That ya did... Seems you weren't the only abomination with a grudge against my—baby-sister." He snapped his fingers, "Bring it out here."

The double doors behind Jack swung open, and out walked a toothless man wheeling Acean, blindfolded and chained to a yellow dolly, across the balcony.

"No!" Billy shrieked. "Lay one finger on him and I'll feed you your own balls, you crazy hick!"

Tanner brought a hand up to his ear, "What's his name? Acean?" He chuckled, "Looks more like Kermit the frog on steroids to me."

"Let him go," Calla demanded. "If you want this shit to end, he's the last person you should kill."

The Reverend removed Acean's blindfold, caressing the alien's gaunt cheek with the edge of his blade. "Callin it a person's a bit of a stretch... How bout levelin with me, Kermit... Y'all came here to assassinate me? That it?"

The cleric glanced down at the mammal, "If your death was my aim, there would be no opportunity for postulation."

"Us being here was an *accident*, Tanner," Shepherd added.

Jack shook his head, "Ain't no such thing as accidents! If you're here, it's God's holy judgment! What I wanna know is: why?"

Acean snarled, "Calla Shepherd's purpose far exceeds your feeble comprehension, kraith. She is an agent of balance your mind can never fathom. You speak of judgment? The Leevahn is the only judge your planet has now."

Something the alien said gave Jack divine pause. "What did you call her?"

Chapter 31: The Parable

8:10AM

"Move, will ya? Don't make this harder than its gotta be," Percy sighed. He dug his assault rifle into Max's back as he and Hue herded the group of outsiders into the commissary kitchen.

"They prepare food here?" Billy complained, tasting the rancid air wafting into her nostrils. It smelled of rotten meat and spoiled milk, and the tabletops buzzed with flies. "I'm gonna be sick."

Max snickered, staring back at Hue and Percy. "Yeah, these two make me wanna throw up too, kid."

Hue rolled his eyes, "We're not ending up like the Chief, buddy. It's nothing against you."

Volkov stopped in his tracks, "Cara had bigger balls than *both* of you."

A voice called out from the other side of the kitchen, "Play nice, Horseman." Tanner emerged from behind an industrial refrigerator door in a chef's smock and apron, pointing to his two guards. "Skedaddle before he beats ya to death," he said, cradling a handful of raw dough in his unwashed palms. "Pardon the stink... Joint didn't come with a crematorium

244

when I took over."

He glanced left, half-smiling as a duo of hickish minions hacked Cara Alovick's corpse to pieces on a butcher's block at the far end of the kitchen, tossing her limbs into an industrial oven. Homer's body laid atop the headless Akkan-Rah on the floor beside her.

Vera's mouth backed up with bile as she inhaled the pork-ish aroma of Cara's charred flesh. She darted for the closest sink, purging what little was in her gut as Max patted her on the back.

The Reverend smiled, "That reminds me—I gotta stick a note on that one," air quoting, "do not use for *food*."

Shepherd crossed her arms, "If you're trying to scare us, it's not working."

Tanner cocked his head, "I'm just enjoying a friendly chat with y'all, makin bread." He nodded to Billy, "Come closer, kiddo."

"She's fine where she is," Calla barked.

"I'm not scared of this blowhard," Kojimatsuo said, inching near the counter with an eye on the cleaver beside Tanner's rolling-pin. "What?"

Tanner stooped over the table, "Every little lady should know how to bake if they wanna please their husband… Can ya work an oven, Wilma?"

"The fuck do you think?"

Jack winked at the girl, "Suspected as much." He whirled around, grabbing an armful of ingredients out of the cupboard overhead. "Today, I'm gonna learn ya how to make the finest damn eats y'all ever ate!"

"What is this?" Calla growled. "Nobody gives a shit about your damn bread."

The Reverend sneered at the outsiders (especially Calla) exhaustedly. "I swear, y'all are the most impatient, miserable people I ever met. I've been nice as pie, ain't personally tried to kill any of ya, and all you do is bitch and bitch and bitch." He clapped his hands together, "Bring Kermit in here!"

The minions manning the oven behind him nodded, shuffling around the corner and returning with Acean, blindfolded and bound. They dragged him beside Tanner, who gripped the alien's shoulder as if he were an old friend. "Of all uh ya, this demon's the only one with fuckin manners. I haven't been the most hospitable to it, and do you think this lanky sumbitch's complained once?"

"You good, Ace?" Billy asked.

"Yes, young one," the alien replied.

"See? So polite!" Jack chuckled, discarding Acean's blindfold. "They *must* have finishing schools in hell or somethin."

"Are you finished?" Calla hissed.

"There's that impatience we talked about… Wilma, start takin notes." Tanner spun around and plucked a carton of eggs and a stick of butter out of the refrigerator, setting them on the counter. "Dunno if yer momma ever baked homemade bread, kiddo, but if so, I guarantee it was pure *shit* compared to my mammy's." He laid out the ingredients in a neat row, "Now then, we got water from the sink Dr. Wild puked in over there, we got our butter, eggs, flour, sugar, and salt." He raised his index finger like an engaging teacher, "Anybody know what we're missin?"

Nobody spoke a word.

"Calla, what's missin? Edify your rude little lesbian-ish friend here."

Shepherd stared daggers at the Reverend, tired of playing his little games. "Yeast."

"Louder, please."

"It's missing yeast!"

BAM! Tanner pounded the table, "Bingo! You can have the best herbs and spices and fats in the entire world, but if ya ain't got yeast, ya ain't got *bread*. It's about all the parts working together, but most important is the *yeast*." He leaned over the counter, scanning the outsiders with veiled contempt. "It's kinda like havin a buncha people tryin to work together with nobody to *lead* em… They fall apart… Or worse—die without that crucial component." Tanner kneaded his wad of dough, "So, why is yeast so damn important, Wilma?"

"I don't care," Billy grumbled.

The dough in the Reverend's palm smooshed through his clenched fingers. "Like a congregation without an overseer, without yeast, bread doesn't rise—doesn't ascend." He eyed Calla, "It doesn't *leaven*." His icy stare clicked into a warm, bipolar, grin. "Jesus knew this, once preaching of a woman who added but a *smidgen* of yeast to her meager dough, ending up with the most bountiful loaf uh bread y'all ever saw. A mountainous bounty, in fact!"

Kojimatsuo rolled her eyes, "Ooh… 'And the Colonel addedeth eleveneth herbs and spices to his chicken, and it was good, sayeth the Lord'… What in the hell is your point?"

"The point my Lord and Savior was trying to make, little Wilma, was even the biggest of things have microscopic origins. Like a humble congregation growing into an army of faithful Christian warriors." Tanner's pleasant grin faded into a stern grimace, "Or a single Podunk piece of half-alien trash growing into a threat to mankind."

"The Leevahn is not a threat, but a promise of ruination or salvation depending on the merits of your species," Acean said. "If you fear her, it is because you exemplify everything wrong with your species."

Tanner brandished a meat cleaver, "I don't remember asking for your input, Kermit."

"Touch him and I will kill you," Billy asserted.

"I second that," Volkov added.

"Me too," Shepherd said.

"You're in no position to threaten me!" the Reverend roared, swiping at Acean's neck, breaking just short of cutting the cleric's skin. "But you *will* serve me… Y'all being here's no accident. God don't have accidents! The Almighty *wants* you here, and I got this cleaver to his throat because that's what the Lord *wills*! I must rise to greater heights! Ascend! Leaven!" The Reverend's brow sank into a malevolent glare aimed at his young nemesis, "And you're gonna get me there, Shepherd."

"I can't stand to look at you, let alone help you," Calla retorted, defiant and self-restrained, well beyond human capacity.

"It's providence, freak! The signs abound if one's eyes are open! I've seen your gifts!" He turned to Volkov, wide eyed and hateful, "Witnessed the *miracles* you've bestowed upon the undeserving! The Lord obviously brought us together so you can strengthen me for the battles to come!"

Mechanical arms slithered along Vulgrell's frame, fastening his armor to his body. When the last piece clamped across his trunk, the machines receded into the roof of the battle-pod.

He exited the capsule, standing before a spire rising out of the floor. In the center sat his war-ravaged helmet. He held the headgear in his palms, thinking of how long it had been since he'd last donned it.

Emthy had not been born yet.

Unda had not even married him yet.

The memory of kissing his Qhan under the triple moons of Aurell'Kah, where they first met, brought a tear to his eye.

He tucked the helmet under his arm as his daughter idled in the hall.

"I can crush her," the Khath insisted, drawing toward her father, keen to atone for her failure. She bowed before Vulgrell in surrender. "Please, my Khoth, say I may pursue her—for mother."

"Rise," Vulgrell sighed, stepping past her on his trek to the armory at the other end of the corridor. "Nobody who bears my blood in their veins may beg, Khath. My answer is no."

"You'd refuse me the honor of avenging our Qhan, father?" Emthy asked, pursuing her armor-clad parent through the armory-bay's security checkpoint.

"Do not force me to remind you of my position again, lest I amend it—most unfavorably,*" Vulgrell growled, standing before the Scepter Of Elders floating in a secured levitation-cradle. He punched a code into a console beneath the cradle and attached a polarity-clamp to his wrist, drawing back his rippling arm.* CLANG! *The scepter sprang from the cradle and into his restless hand.*

Emthy eyed the scepter with a hidden longing, "I know what we discussed, father, but—"

"Then do not push me, offspring."

"At least let me join you! Together we can—"

"Silence!" Vulgrell roared, sweeping his child off her feet with the edge of his staff. He held the scepter's charged tip against Emthy's breast. "I lost one love, do not make me lose another, inexperienced, one! The Leevahn is mine!*"*

Acean *GASPED*, swallowing air in sudden distress, plagued by Vulgrell's telepathic rancor pulsing throughout his body like an injection of fire. "He knows you're here, Calla... He's coming."

"Who's coming?" Tanner inquired, still pressing his cleaver into Acean's gullet.

"How's that even possible?" Wild asked, misgivingly. "The only one who could have informed him was *you*."

"Inform who of what?" The Reverend prodded yet again.

"Incorrect, kraith," the cleric replied, nodding toward the dead beast at the other end of the kitchen. "He watched her through the eyes of the Akkan," he bowed his head in derision, "just as I feared would come to pass."

"Hold on a damn minute." Tanner's orbs bounced between Acean and the lifeless creature he once called his sister, "That's why you were skulkin around A-Block? You were tryin to keep your buddies from finding Shepherd by killin Christine?"

The alien gave the maladjusted man-of-God an ambiguous glance, "Correct, you miserable excuse for a vertebrate."

"Hey, no need fer name callin, Kermit."

"I disagree, kraith. By preventing the Akkan-Rah's death, you have wrought upon your people a consequence much worse than the hell you envision. The aforementioned title is befitting."

Tanner looked askance at Acean, "Ye of little faith."

"Faith will not prevent the havoc to befall this population, kra*ith*." The alien turned to Calla, "Only a seasoned Leevahn can stop the ensuing carnage if they so choose. Until then, the Akkan serve the Empire, spelling disaster for every human in this compound."

"How much time do we have?" Shepherd asked.

"Little," Acean deadpanned, looking down at the man holding the cleaver against his neck. "I am not the being to execute if you seek redress for that which has befallen your world."

Tanner's glazed-over orbs held steady, "It'd sure feel great to watch you bleed all the same, Kermit."

A hand touched the Reverend's shoulder, "Know what would make *me* feel good?" *TANG!* A cast-iron pan crashed into the back of Jack's skull. He crumpled to the ground, his cleaver sliding out of his palm and into Calla's hands.

Billy loomed above the dazed psychopath splayed across the filthy kitchen floor, twirling the skillet handle, "Golly, that felt good."

Calla cut Acean's binds, kneeling beside the Reverend with

the cleaver now pressed against his own throat. "Your people have enough firearms to defend themselves?"

"We're *Christians,* you dumb bitch. What do you think?" Tanner groaned.

"What do I think?"

KLANG! Shepherd drove the cleaver into the tile beside Jack's head, missing his ear by millimeters.

"I think it's time for *aggressive negotiations,*" she answered.

Chapter 32: The Storm

9:38AM

The faithful lined up outside the armory as Tanner jostled the first locker open. He pulled out a loaded M-Sixteen, passing two more to Max and Vadim.

"Know how to shoot?" he asked, squinting down the iron sight.

"We'll ignore that stupid-ass question," Volkov chuckled, pulling back the charging handle.

Jack studied the weapon in his hands, turning to the crowd outside the doorway. "Got a few scopes to pass out, but only to those who can snipe. Y'all take to the guard towers." He elbowed Max, "Let's get these guns passed out."

Amhearst took a friendly hand to Jack's shoulder, "Touch me again and I'll break your arm."

"I feel the love, brother," Tanner said, turning to his flock. "Man the parapets. No less than ten at a time. Hit the north block, then south, west, then east. Those left move to ground level and take a gun-port fer yerself. Those remaining hold the gate. We got riot-gear on the tables in front of ya. First come, first serve. If any women and children wanna fight, let em. Those who don't, I want holed up in the chow hall with chains

252

around the exits.

"Such a caring, protective guy," Volkov grumbled.

"I ain't protecting shit, big man," Tanner replied. "Gonna burn it down when this is over."

Max cornered the Reverend, "You plan on *incinerating* a building full of women and children?"

"You wanna pick up their slack, be my guest, but we're all the same in God's eyes. All subject to the same rules and judgment. No room for cowards here, son. If they refuse to take up arms against the wicked, they *are* the wicked."

"You're even crazier than I thought," Amhearst said, dumbstruck.

Tanner leaned closer, keeping his voice low, "Don't *press* me, boy. I can still have my men kill you and your big boyfriend if I felt like it... Keep pushing."

Vadim brushed Max aside, hoisting the Reverend off the ground by his shirt-collar. "Roy doesn't appreciate your *tone*, padre. Threaten my friend again and I'll shove that dusty M-Sixteen up your pious ass in front of your sheep... Got it, baaa-baa, bitch?"

Tanner's neck fat scrunched beneath his jaw as he fake-smiled, "I was only joshin, Volkov."

"Fuckin right, you were," Vadim growled.

Jack straightened his shirt out as best he could, still dangling against the wall, "Mind putting me down?"

"The women and children come with us," Amhearst interjected.

"That *wasn't* the deal." The Reverend's tone was uncompromising.

"I'm revising the terms on Calla's behalf. We help your people get through this, you return our train, we leave with them... Don't agree, and see how long you last."

Tanner's loathsome stare darted between Max and Vadim.

"Fine."

"Give your word," Volkov said.

"I will not violate my covenant or alter the word that went forth from my lips. Psalm, eighty-nine thirty-four."

"Shut up with the quotes! *Promise* us, Tanner!"

The Reverend gritted his teeth, "I promise."

Vera peered through the telescope bolted to the convoy's recreation deck railing, "Nothing on the horizon, honey."

"I feel them," Calla insisted, scouring the vista with her own extraordinary vision. "Keep scanning the dunes. They're out there, I'm sure of it."

Acean ascended the staircase, slithering beside the Leevahn, "What is the female doing?"

"Looking for the Akkan."

"Vera of earth, the first charge will not come from the sands, but the skies. Begin your search skyward," the cleric said, peering down at Calla. "The kraith does not appear scared, a byproduct of your leadership, young one."

Shepherd brandished a shaky grin, "I'm just a farm girl."

The alien placed his arm around her shoulder, "Large things have small beginnings, do they not?"

"Calling me fat?"

"I was echoing the only reasonable thing the Reverend has ever said. I would never pass judgment on a being for their molecular misgivings."

"It was a joke, Acean. A laugh."

The cleric cocked his head, "Ah. Humor… Yes."

Calla leaned over the railing, staring out into the infinite sky ahead. "Hope we spot them soon so we can get the drop on them."

"Get the drop?"

"Yeah. Surprise them. Ambush them… Have the upper

hand."

Acean's face writhed with unease. "You miscalculate the—*size*—of an impending onslaught, young one. This is not a battle the kraitho are likely to win. Vulgrell does not launch an offensive unless he is confident of triumph. To reach this end, he will employ the entirety of his arsenal.

"All the Akkan?"

Acean nodded with solemn gravitas. "You are the kraitho's sole hope for survival, child. Shed your nascent state and allow your pure nature to rise... It calls to you... Surrender to your better instincts and you *can* save these mammals.

"Nice speech, Ace," Billy interjected, scaling the steps clutching a Remington-Eight-Seventy. "Like my new toy? Vad gave it to me."

"Honey, that thing's bigger than you are," Calla balked, spotting a strap slung around the girl's chest. "Is that a bandoleer? Who are you? Rambo?" The hybrid rolled her disapproving eyes, "I got some words for Vadim."

The girl grinned mischievously, "Okay, maybe I *suggested* he let me have it."

"Suggested?"

"As in... He said something like hell-no at *first*—and then *later*—I sorta grabbed it anyhow?"

"Wilma Kojimatsuo."

"All those cultist pussies had were rock-salt shells! It's cool!"

"Not the point."

"Hey, unlike you two, I'm not a goddamn superhero. A shotgun levels the playing field."

Calla smirked, "Uncle Hare taught you how to handle yourself, right?"

Kojimatsuo racked the slide, "Nope."

Acean knelt before the girl. "The pervasive and vestigial figment of delusion your species adheres to broke the mold when producing you, Billy of Earth. You are an admirable soldier who will live on long after you are deceased, which may be rather soon."

The girl simpered, setting her weapon at her feet and draping her arms around Acean's neck in a dear embrace. "I see why you have no friends now, Ace," she said, pecking his cheek.

The alien's stoic mug trembled as he mustered his first human-like grin. "Why do you think I became a cleric?"

Billy's jaw dropped, "Was that a joke?"

"One wishes it were so, my friend."

"You got us—Kermit," Kojimatsuo replied, touching her forehead to his.

The alien leered at the kraith, "I will disregard that epithet."

"Totally calling you that from now on."

"Guys!" Wild exclaimed, peering through the telescope. "I see something! It's huge—and fast."

Acean set his sights skyward, "Vulgrell."

Kojimatsuo picked up her Remington Eight-Seventy, scanning the deck beneath her feet. "You guys feel that?"

Calla took a hand to the guardrail.

It trembled.

"Vera… Take Billy to the compound," she said.

"Hold on a sec, lemme see!" Kojimatsuo barked, looking through the telescope. After a moment, she backed away from the lens, pale faced. "I don't think we got enough ammo."

The shuttlecraft rattled in the Nevada wind, soaring toward triumph.

Vulgrell leaned back in his cockpit, bristling as the Akkan-Kah glided beside his ship.

He rode his vessel's accelerator with an unquenchable blood-thirst as his enemy's stronghold grew larger in his windshield.

Try as you may, kraitho.

Bring your surest wrath against my sickle-fanged monstrosities.
You will fail.

Nothing on this miserable planet is more ravenous than the Akkan.

We are coming for you.

Max hugged Vera tight, holding his lips against hers atop the northern parapet. She held her head against his chest, tuning in to his racing heart. "If you die, I'll kill you," she whispered.

Amhearst kissed her forehead, "Take Billy and wait for us in the chow hall with the others."

"No, I can treat the wounded. You need me."

"I remember when asking you for a *band-aid* was an imposition… You've come a long way, ma'am."

"Evolution is a beautiful thing."

"I'd like to think it was *love*."

Wild looked up at the man she adored, "I'm sure that had a little to do with it."

Everyone manning the parapets trembled as the shrill thrust of alien engines slowed on the horizon, ushering an alien craft that cruised to a stop upon the dunes below their feet.

Vera should have been terrified, but Max's beating heart sedated her. His devotion made her feel invincible, even if she was anything but. Like she was in a dream she knew was not real but refused to wake from.

If these were Wild's last moments, she was grateful to spend them in Amhearst's arms.

The hourglass was about to empty.

And she wasn't alone.

It was all up to Calla now.

Calla's forward stare was blank, but her mind was not as she stood beside Acean and his dual war-blades on the battlefield.

"Your unease is infectious. What troubles you?" the alien asked.

Shepherd looked askance at her friend, "You mean *aside* from the *thousands* of creatures stampeding after us?"

"A soldier without dread is no warrior at all. We may yet live to see another day, so long as you use your feelings to your advantage."

"How?"

"Do what humanity does best… Turn your fear into *anger*."

SCREEE! Vulgrell's engines howled as the shuttlecraft one-eightied its tail. A typhoon of sand rained to the earth, the hermetic rear-seal popping open as a ramp descended with a faint *HISS*.

Calla's carapace trickled from her pores as the Akkan-Rah stampeded past her and Acean as if they weren't there.

"What are they doing?" Shepherd asked.

Acean surveyed their formations, "It is a tactical calculation. By unleashing the entire Akkan divisions upon the kraitho, he means to distract you."

"I can't stand by and do *nothing*, I have to help them!" she cried, fixed to rush toward the compound.

"No!" The cleric barked, catching her by the end of her arm. "Leave the mammals to their own defense. Vulgrell *wants* you to go to them, child… To thwart him, we must act as *one*."

"Is that you, dear brother?" The Khoth asked. "Praise the Strodha I have found you!" he bellowed with a hearty grin. "I was so worried about you, vacating my Xilan so sudden as you had." The rippling alien eyed the hybrid, half grinning as his dark orbs drank her image. "At last we meet, my precious Calla… I must confess, I expected more. Such a paltry, feminine frame… To think—you—beat my Emthy?"

Shepherd gave Vulgrell a taloned middle finger, "And now I'm about to kick her daddy's ass too."

The Khoth sneered, clenching his fists with cracking knuckles. "You exalt yourself, girl. Such insolence will not go unpunished."

"Yeah?" Calla balked. "Eat me, you big sonofabitch."

Vulgrell waved his palm through the air, "I prefer *they* partake instead of I," he replied with a fiendish smile.

ROARR! Ten Akkan-Rah bounded past the Khoth, circling Shepherd and Acean.

"The teenage *mouth* is a dangerous component," the cleric grumbled.

DHAK! DHAK! DHAK! "Target their wings!" Max brayed, firing his M-Sixteen as death-gliders soared toward the sanctuary, some carrying sea-creeper payloads. "No! No!" he backtracked. "The legs! Aim for their legs!"

DHAK! DHAK! CLICK! CLICK! "Shit!" Vadim screamed, swapping out his magazine as an Akkan-Kah dove after him. He ducked as the creeper in its clutches decapitated the guy to his left as it dropped past their defenses.

"Booger on ground level!" he shouted, but the piling land-stalkers beyond the wall overwhelmed the forces below, who didn't see the Akkan-Yah slithering up behind them. Tendrils belched from its mass, strangling five men. Their agonizing shrieks went unheard as necrotizing fluids melted their throats.

The remaining fighters dispersed, abandoning their posts below the north parapet.

"They're coming in too fast! We need ground support, or they'll break through!" Max hollered.

"I'll do it! I'll go!" a man in a red plaid shirt said. *CHOMP!* A land-stalker scaling the wall lurched over the barrier, driving its jaws into his neck. The man's aorta spurted in all directions as the beast thrashed from side to side. It swallowed his head like a crocodile gulping down a raw chicken, descending its throat with a nasty crunch.

Vadim set the barrel of his rifle flush against the creature's skull. *DHAK! DHAK! DHAK!* The Akkan-Rah's brains burst from the other side of its cranium as it plummeted to the earth in a plume of crimson grit.

"Any of you fuckers goin down there *now*, or ya wanna end up like the headless guy?" the Russian asked.

WHOOSH! A death-glider barreled down upon Volkov, hoisting him skyward, beyond the compound walls.

"Vadim!" Max exclaimed, firing at the winged hell-beast clutching his oldest friend.

"Downstairs is good. I—I'll go down there," someone muttered.

Elsewhere in the sanctuary, Vera tended to the wounded as the carnage unfolded all around her. "You! Tear off your shirt sleeve!" she barked, creating a tourniquet out of a woman's tattered garments, tying off an older man's gushing thigh. "Keep pressure on it!"

"I told you to wait in the chow hall!" Max shouted from the parapet.

"I can't leave these people this way!" she countered, nudging to the woman beside her. "Help me with his arms!" She looked up at Amhearst, "I'm sorry, but they need me!"

"So do I!"

SQUAAAAAAK! A death-glider's claws sank into a plump, bald fighter to Max's right, hoisting him off by his clavicles with a thrash of its huge wings. "Dear Lord, Jesus Christ, save me!" the man cawed, flapping his flabby legs in a panic.

Max bear-hugged the man's gut, tugging him downward, but the Akkan-Yah's grip was too strong for one person to handle. "*Fucking* help me!" he shouted to a young guy on his left who was spraying his AK-Forty-Seven across the sky in a panicked flurry. *"Dammit*, kid!" Amhearst groaned, deadening his weight as much as he could, feeling his feet lose contact with the ground.

"No!" Wild screamed below.

Max swiftly glanced down, horrified by the prospect of losing Vera. He watched on as the sea-creeper mutilated the man she struggled to save, whipping its tentacles across his flesh like a rope coated with razor blades. She tried to drag him to safety, but the creeper's tendrils slithered through his corpse like burrowing snakes.

And they were making their way toward Wild.

"Run!" Max yelled, letting go of the fat man, about to fall off the parapet. He clung to the inner ledge, climbing atop the ridge as the sea-creeper thrashed after Vera.

She sprinted toward the prison-chapel on the east side of the compound with the slimy beast slithering at top speed after her.

"I'm coming, baby," Amhearst huffed, ambling down the stairwell, tripping down the last five steps and landing on his back.

CHA-CHAK! BOOM! CHA-CHAK! BOOM! Billy unloaded her Remington through the gun-port to the left of Max.

"Come here," he said.

Kojimatsuo rushed to his side, helping him sit upright, "What the hell happened to you?"

"Gimme your shotgun."

"No way! You got a fuckin M-Sixteen, man!"

Max shoved his rifle into Billy's hands, "Not anymore."

Billy inspected the rifle with wild-eyed glee.

"Fuck—yes," she hissed.

The door to the chaplain's quarters opened a sliver. Tanner's shiftless eyes scanned for danger, but he only found scared souls trembling in the pews.

WHACK! Vera dashed through the exit-way in a spate of sunshine and deafening chaos. She locked the doors as something heavy crashed into them from outside, scraping the wood in search of a fissure to invade. The oak bowed under the beast's heft as muddy blobs of slime seeped underfoot.

Wild backed herself against the exit, facing the pews.

Nobody moved a muscle.

"What the hell are you people doing? *Hide*," she hissed.

An older mother with maroon hair shook her head, "The Almighty will shield us, tramp. Mind *yourself*. Perhaps your science will save you."

"Excuse me? Tramp?"

"That's right."

"Does everyone else feel the same?"

Nobody spoke a word, but their scowling faces suggested they did.

Wild scoffed, "Are there children in here?"

"No," the woman declared with a curt snicker.

"Alright then... Fuck you all, I guess," Vera retorted, dashing toward a row of confession booths along the south corridor.

CRASH! The Akkan-Yah splintered the doors with a lash of its fattest tentacle. It sloughed into the chapel, rolling its fleshy body over the pews after the scattering sheep. Most of the people escaped through the busted door, but not the maroon-haired spinster. The monster seized the woman by the midsection, braiding its whip around her waist. Her gut-churning gurgles rang through the church.

"Dear lord, Jesus! Help me, please!" she wailed, watching her fingers melt off as she wrestled with the acidic whips boring into her body. Her deafening cries stopped when the tentacle severed her in half. The corpse's torso slid one way, the lower end, another, tethered by a film of melting flesh bubbling on the tile.

The creature lapped its proboscis across the crimson slop pooling between her entrails.

Its limbs sensed a vibrating cadence thrumming around the corner.

A pulse.

A heartbeat.

Vera hugged her legs, stooping against the back of the confession booth as the beast stalked her.

The source of the vibration was close.

GRRRRR. The Akkan-Yah's beak belched a throaty rumble as it slid up and down the tile.

Then there was nothing.

Not a sound.

Acean's war-blades dispatched their fifth stalker. The remaining beasts circled the cleric and his half-human partner with caution.

"Have you the energy to finish the rest? If all else fails, you can try stabbing them in the back as you did your empire," Vulgrell said.

"Such bravado coming from a conspirator to the Kil'Durian throne," Acean countered.

The Khoth stepped toward the Leevahn and her accomplice, as jaunty as his arrogance allowed him to be. "Listen… Do you hear it? The *pleas* of your putrid humans beyond that barricade?" the alien gave the hybrid an evil smirk, "You have failed, little one, and in *brilliant* fashion."

Calla's superhuman hearing honed in on the havoc within the compound walls. She heard Billy's war-cries, but it was a shrill shriek and the slimy sound of a creeper's limbs that wrenched at her soul.

Vera was in danger.

"No!" Calla screamed.

You are the kraitho's sole hope for survival, child. Shed your nascent state and allow your pure nature to rise... It calls to you... Surrender to your better instincts and you can save these mammals.

Acean's words awoke something furious deep in her consciousness, ignited like a hidden fire stoked into a raging inferno with every terrified scream she heard. Her heart raced with adrenaline, breaking in two as she pondered the genuine possibility that those she cared for were dying at that exact second. As she idled there, so far from them, yet so close, Calla made her choice.

It was so clear.

Her people needed her, but she needed them more.

Even if they were but a handful of loving souls in a sea of hateful enemies.

Big things came from small beginnings.

"Stop!" the hybrid roared, waving her palm through the air in a blast of telekinetic rage. *ARRRRRRGG!* The circling Akkan whimpered and howled as their skulls expanded and contracted. *POP!* A brutal gush of brains and bone erupted from their necks as their headless bodies collapsed in the sand.

Vulgrell's countenance was awash in astonishment. "Remarkable, hybrid, but your feeble abilities won't sustain you now."

Calla's eyes burned bright red, and her tone dropped further than the devil's. "I'd get back on that ship if I were you."

The Khoth sneered, "Who are you to threaten me? A puny pest! An instrument of *my* making, *nothing* more!"

"You *wish*, asshole."

"Spare me your juvenile attitude, girl. You do not

understand what you are."

"Yes, I do." The girl's bones cracked and shifted as her frame transformed. "I'm Calla Shepherd, daughter of Lance and Elle Shepherd… And I'm the mother-fucking Leevahn."

RAHHHHHH! Glowing crimson-ooze snaked across the hybrid's feminine silhouette. The sentient lava burned her clothes off, enveloping her body in molten bio-armor. It cooled into a reddish-black hue as a crown of horns radiated out of the top of her head, gleaming in the sunlight.

Calla's evolution into maturity was complete.

She was ready for war.

"Holy shit," Acean muttered.

Wild cupped her lips, peering through the confession booth's wicker vents. There was a streak of slime leading from the pews to the row of confessionals, but no monster. If she hadn't fixated on the ooze, Vera may have seen the enormous limbs descending above her door.

THWACK! The beast's pincers punched through, clamping after its prey. Wild sank as low as she could, howling in dread as the Akkan-Yah's lobster claws strained to reach her. She shuddered in terror, motionless and breathless, hoping the animal would lose track of her if she didn't stir.

The creeper continued its search for a moment, but then it withdrew its pincers from the booth and out of sight. Vera made no sound as a thin tentacle crept along the roof of the confessional like a gossamer worm, coiling around something unseen below.

The doorknob jiggled.

Then it twisted.

"Shit!" Wild bawled, clinging to the knob with all her might. *CRASH!* The monster's claws broke through the sides of the booth, gnashing in a blind frenzy. They missed Vera by mere inches as she clung to the handle, crouching as low as possible.

Even with all the adrenaline coursing through her veins, Wild's grip failed.

Time was running out.

CHA-CHAK!

"Get away from her, you, you lumpsucker!" Amhearst shouted.

BOOM!

The beast retracted its claws, shielding its body from Max's Remington as its skin bubbled and boiled in viscous pockets of gory goo above Wild's head.

"Like the taste of rock salt, bitch?"

CHA-CHAK! BOOM!

"Ever see what happens to a snail when you dab a dash of Morton's Salt on it?"

CHA-CHAK! BOOM!

CHA-CHAK! BOOM!

The Akkan-Yah fell off the booth, thrashing across the tile as Amhearst pushed his barrel into the spasming creeper's center mass.

CHA-CHAK! BOOM!

Max rested the Remington against his shoulder as he nudged the monster with the tip of his boot. "It's dead."

Vera burst out of the confessional, leaping into her man's arms with tears cascading along her cheeks. "I love you so fucking much!"

Her lover smiled, "Next time I tell *you* to stay inside, you gonna?"

"One question…"

"Yeah?"

"What the hell is a lumpsucker?"

Max kissed Wild, "An ugly fish." *WHIKASH!* The sea-creeper's whip wrapped around Amhearst's ankle. "Get it off me!" he wailed, clutching his leg as he collapsed to the floor. "Shoot it!"

Vera pawed the Remington. *CHA-CHAK! BOOM! CHA-CHAK! BOOM! CHA-CHAK! CLICK. CLICK.* She kicked the dead beast's tendril away from her man's leg.

Max's head fell back against the tile, exhausted by the pain. "Yeah… I really, *really* love you so fucking much too."

CLANG! Acean's blades struck Vulgrell's forearm in a spark of Kil'Durian alloys. The Khoth deflected every savage swipe the cleric threw at him. *POW!* He parried a lunging attack, side-kicking Acean to the sand as he ducked a punch from Calla, uppercutting the Leevahn off her feet.

"Not even when fulfilling your life's purpose can you overwhelm me in battle!" Vulgrell roared. "Submit and I may let your mammals live one more day!"

RAHHH! The hybrid coiled, dashing after her enemy, arresting his hooked fist as she jabbed the enormous alien in the gut, head-butting him with her spiny forehead. He stumbled, smashing against the shuttlecraft and dropping to a knee.

Nobody had ever forced Khoth Vulgrell of Kil'Dur to kneel.

The warmonger felt a pulsing pain radiate from his mouth, passing a taloned thumb along his scaly lips.

It was the first time he'd tasted his own blood.

Vulgrell spat across the sand, "I will enjoy seeing your world *burn*." He activated the polarity clamp on his wrist, sweeping his arm toward his ship. *WHOOSH!* The Scepter of Elders rocketed into his waiting clutches with a thunderous *CLANG.*

"Calla, get back!" the cleric shouted.

"No!" she exclaimed. "He's not taking me with him! This ends now!"

Acean stepped in front of the hybrid, shielding her from Vulgrell's staff. "The Scepter of Elders is the only weapon you can not recover from… If he wields it, he means to *slay* you."

The Khoth cackled, cracking his broad neck from side to side. "With you lifeless, my sweet Calla, I will command the Akkan for all time! They'll be mine—and *mine* only!"

The Leevahn brushed Acean aside, her spiny alien face contorted by vengeance. "You've taken enough away from me! You want my life, you better be ready to bleed for it!"

Vulgrell smiled, "With pleasure."

"They're gonna get through! Pick up those barrels!" Percy wailed, scuttling an oil-drum toward the fortress doors on a rusty hand truck. He slipped the container off the dolly and punched his knife into the top, booting it over. Gallons of crude gushed over the sand, pooling at the monumental entrance.

Hue pushed his second canister over, rolling it across the ground to start an ignition trail.

WHAM!

The gates buckled as hundreds of stalkers crashed into them. Some scaled the walls, but the snipers in the guard towers shot them down before they could get over.

WHAM!

It wouldn't be long before they breached.

"Billy!" Vera cried out, helping Amhearst hobble toward the chow hall. "Where are you?"

"Here!" Kojimatsuo replied, sprinting after them carrying her M-Sixteen like a seasoned soldier.

"We need the keys," Wild said, nodding to the chained entrance. "Max can't stay out here."

WHAM!

"The doors won't take much more!" Percy shouted.

Billy watched Percy's men stack boxes of dynamite in the pooling oil. "Are they nuts?" she balked.

"Honey!" Vera interrupted. "The chains! Please!"

"Hold yer horses! Look what they're doing over there! They're gonna blow us to kingdom come!"

"Would you rather be indoors when it blows or standing out here?" Max asked, wincing in pain.

Kojimatsuo mulled, "Point taken." She yanked an overstuffed keyring out of her pocket. "This'll be a minute."

WHAM!

CRACK!

Hue looked up at the gate, "This piece uh shit's gonna crumble any second."

CRUNCH!

Percy pursed his lips, offering his friend his lighter. "Do the honors?"

"Nope," Hue replied.

"Don't wanna go out in a blaze of glory?"

"I mean we *could* light the dynamite and run away like *sane* men."

Percy shook his head, "After everything we've done for the Reverend... We don't deserve to run away."

Hue sighed, "Suppose not."

Percy ignited his lighter, "Here's to no more running."

"No more running."

KA-BOOM!

CLANG! TANG! CLING! Acean's blades crashed against the Scepter of Elders, but Vulgrell was too skilled. The Khoth swept the cleric off his feet, pressing the tip of his weapon against his brother-in-law's abdomen. "Your life for his!"

The Leevahn's fiery eyes darted between Vulgrell and the war-blade beside her clawed foot.

Acean gave Shepherd an almost indecipherable nod.

"You know what the problem is with guys as *big* as you?" the hybrid asked.

"Stalling will achieve nothing, but I shall indulge you, given your inevitable demise... Regal me," the Khoth replied.

"You're too slow." *KA-TANG!* Calla punted the war-blade into Acean's waiting clutches. *SLASH!* The cleric sheared Vulgrell's staff-clad hand off at the wrist, tossing the scepter to his ally.

PITCHOO! She blasted Vulgrell in the rib cage, knocking him to the earth in a shower of sparks and plasma.

The Leevahn helped Acean to his feet as their enemy panted in the sand.

"You're on the wrong side!" the Khoth moaned, choking on his own blood. His lingering hand was tight against his damaged chest armor. "They are a plague among the stars, Calla. *Murderers.* Primitive *animals* that must fade from the cosmos... Your Khoth demands it! For my dear, Unda!"

Acean balked, "You think your wife wanted this? She did not!"

Vulgrell sneered, his breathing becoming flat., "Irrelevant! Her kindness was her downfall! Love, her weakness, and it cost my Qhan her life! I would have murdered everyone for her! Every old woman! Newborn baby! I would have spared none, because that is what this species deserves! We are superior to them!"

"I have heard such rhetoric before," Acean said, pointing toward the towering sanctuary behind him. "From the insidious kraith beyond these walls... You believe you are superior, yet echo his cruelty so soundly... If my time on this planet has taught me anything, it is that evil is not a species, but a state of mind... That you both had a hand in Unda's death is no coincidence."

"Silence, filth!" Vulgrell bellowed with the last of his

energy. "I am nothing like these *mongrels*," he panted.

The cleric sighed, "Expect lies from everybody, including those you care for. Do this, and you will never falter in battle."

"Wise words, to be sure," the seething alien hissed.

"Very *human* words, brother."

The Leevahn rested her foot atop Vulgrell's belly like a hunter posing with a trophy, "And I choose them."

The Khoth shut his eyes, "They do not deserve your mercy."

Shepherd twirled the Scepter of Elders, "That's what makes you no different from the Reverend." *CRUNCH!* The hybrid drove the tip of the staff straight through Vulgrell's beating heart.

Acean bowed his head, "At last, his reign is over."

Calla shook hers, "No…"

PITCHOO! She fired a burst of plasma through his corpse, vaporizing his body across the sands in a torrent of flesh and bones.

She smiled, "Now it's over."

Oh, dear Lord, they're coming through the gates!

What are we gonna do?

We can't take them all! There's too many!

The Leevahn looked over her shoulder and saw the Akkan-Rah swarming over the fiery debris.

They're breaking down the door!

Jesus!

God, please save us!

"You know what to do, child," Acean declared. "You are ready."

The Leevahn shut her eyes in concentration, linking with the Akkan, hearing and feeling them all at once, but this time was different. It was as though she not only saw through them.

She was them.

And every single beast on the planet was the Leevahn.

One entity with millions of moving parts all working in harmony.

Calla shuddered as she found her infinite conciousness devouring and slaying innocents across the globe, stopping their carnage with a mere thought, leaving them still and docile where they were once a plague.

Where there was boundless chaos, there was calm.

And silence.

Peaceful, obedient silence.

It was over.

Chapter 33: Another Way

The Akkan-Rah idled in the wrecked doorway, pliant and aloof, lumbering away from the building to everyone's disbelief.

"What the hell happened?" Billy asked.

"She did it," Vera whispered.

Kojimatsuo slung her M-Sixteen over her shoulder, tiptoeing outside. The dead surrounded her, ravaged and unrecognizable, but the land-stalkers showed no interest in the bodies.

Calla emerged through the flaming rubble, her nude body shrouded under Acean's hooded cloak as survivors climbed out of the woodwork, afraid to get too close to the Akkan. *SQUAAAA!* The flock cowered below a throng of death-gliders perched along the parapets. The wraiths flapped their wings, letting loose mighty *CAWS* that rattled the earth, every bit as docile as the stalkers.

What of the sea-creepers?

The heat killed a great number of them well before Calla put an end to the Akkan's ire. Those remaining broke into Tanner's grotto, basking in his Olympic-sized swimming pool.

And what of Tanner?

The crowd, so elated to have won the battle, didn't notice

the good Reverend wading through their ranks as they cheered to victory.

Neither did Max and Vera.

WHAM! Jack rammed Amhearst off Vera's shoulder, knocking the wounded man to the dirt. Tanner pressed his sidearm against Wild's temple, dragging her backward. "Back off or she's dead!"

"It's over, Reverend," Calla said. "Evil lost."

Tanner's shrewd eyes flitted toward the land-stalkers at his side, then at the Akkan-Yah above his head. "A fucking *farm girl* shouldn't have this much power! These beasts belong to the righteous!"

"Someone like *you*?" a forgotten voice asked, pushing through the crowd. A flood of relief overcame Max when he saw his bloodied best friend shuffling toward him. "Vad! You bastard!"

"Didn't expect a mutant bird to take me out, did ya? That woulda been just sad."

BLAM! Vadim crumpled to the ground with a hole in his forehead.

Tanner retrained his smoldering gun on Wild's skull, "I *loathe* that guy."

"You know he's not gonna stay down," Max said.

"Yes, but will she?" the Reverend gnashed, clutching Vera fast against his chest. "Maybe we need to find out!"

"Stop this, Jack!" Calla exclaimed. "I beat the Kil'Durians! Isn't that what you wanted, or have you been fighting so fucking long you've forgotten what peace is?"

"Far from it, darlin! I've been so wrong, thinking these creatures were demons straight from hell, but now I get it! They're a gift from God! As the Almighty's chosen prophet, I *demand* you hand them over!"

Shepherd shook her head, "Never. They'll never be yours."

KLAK. Tanner chambered his pistol, "Wild's life is in yer hands, bitch. She may be a good geneticist, but I doubt she can grow her *own* skull back… Give the monsters over to me."

Calla's eyes darted between Tanner's gun and Vera, who's knowing glance gave her pause. "You heard the man," Wild said. "Let him have it."

"Yeah?" Shepherd asked, reading between the lines.

The woman nodded, "Give him what he deserves."

Jack's devilish grin shined with anticipation, "Yes… Do as mommy says, girl."

A curled talon sprang from Calla's index finger, "You'll need my blood."

Tanner outstretched his palm, bearing the pain as her alien fingernail slashed across his hand. She then sliced deep into her wrist, dripping her precious life-source into the Reverend's wound.

One drop.

Two drops.

Three drops.

Done.

Jack felt an overwhelming rush as the Leevahn's blood coursed through his veins. The raw power was intoxicating, sending the man into a rapturous orgasm of the senses. He could feel himself becoming more, something greater than he had ever been before. This was his destiny. His Heavenly right.

And it felt so amazing it hurt.

Really fucking badly.

"What in God's name?" The Reverend's fiendish grin soured, realizing something was terribly wrong inside him. He wasn't growing stronger atall.

He was burning.

Deteriorating.

"What have you done to me?" he groaned, powerless to

draw air into his lungs as hellfire invaded every cell in his system.

Calla brandished a frosty smile, "I wished you death, Reverend. The same way I wished Vadim life."

Jack fell to his knees, choking on his own melting throat. "This isn't what the Lord wanted, you succubus! This wasn't God's plan!" A wet streak dribbled down his lips. He rubbed it away, thinking it was blood, when it was his nose itself, oozing off his stubbled face. He drew back his hand, mortified by his bursting veins spewing maroon muck across the sand in thick globs.

In his final seconds, Jack Tanner witnessed the genuine relief in his weary flock's eyes as they watched him shed his mortal coil.

They looked so happy.

It made him want to kill someone.

So he did.

BLAM! The Reverend's last shot filled the air as his body cascaded to the sand like melted ice-cream and raw hamburger. A viscous mass of pious evil nobody would commemorate.

Vera felt nothing, but the dolor on everyone's faces said she should have, Max's most of all. He couldn't talk, let alone move.

That's when the pain set in.

Wild's eyes sank as she slid a finger into the void in her bosom. Her finger tapped against her heart as its pulse cycled down to extinction.

Vera collapsed into Calla's arms, wide-eyed and breathless.

"Vera!" Calla sobbed, slashing open her wrist once more. "I can save her... I can save her!"

Vadim took a solid grip to the hybrid's arm before she could spill her blood into the gaping wound in her mother's chest. "Calla..."

"I can save her, Vadim! Let me go!" the Leevahn bawled, doubled over in heart-wrenching misery. "Let—me—go," she gnashed.

"Is this what you think she needs? Honey, I'll never forget what you did for me, but I'll never escape my nightmares because of it. I'm never gonna escape my little girl's corpse haunting me when I close my eyes when all I want to do is die and be free." The Russian lifted Calla's chin and dried the tears from her cheeks. "Honey, sometimes we gotta let people go—for *them*—not ourselves."

"He's right," Max whispered, powerless to turn away from his soul-mate's body. "She wouldn't choose this." He pressed a smile across his lips. "A woman as sharp as her would off herself if she lived forever."

Calla nodded, passing her fingers over Vera's eyes, shutting them forever. "I love you, mom… So much."

The Leevahn's head leaned upon Vera's cooling breast.

Acean knelt beside Calla, studying Vera's serene countenance. "Your friends possess a wisdom beyond their evolution. As a being who can live for a millennium, I can attest that said life can grow tedious at moments. One considers the finite nature of human experience an exquisite gift, young one."

"Tell that to Vera."

"I cannot. She is *dead*."

"She doesn't have to be, dammit!"

Acean could see the pain in Calla's heart would never abate knowing she had the power to do something and did not. A being who had sacrificed so much for these mammals did not deserve to live with such a dishonor in the cleric's mind. He searched his conscience for a solution.

"There is—another way," he said.

Chapter 34: Nothing More

June 16th, 2047

That's it, wake up. Open your eyes nice and easy, it's bright in here.

A hazy silhouette caressed Vera's cheek.

"How do you feel?" Calla asked, passing a moist cloth over Vera's forehead.

"My chest aches," Wild answered.

"What's the last thing you remember?"

"Well, you don't forget something like being *shot*, honey." Vera scanned the room. "Are we in the compound? This equipment looks too advanced for Tanner."

"No."

Wild rested her head against her thin pillow, "Where are we then?"

The Leevahn said nothing.

"Calla?"

"Last time you were here, you woke up my dad."

Vera looked down to find her arms dressed in sensor-pads and wires. "Why am *I* in a cloning bed, honey?"

Calla rested her hand atop her surrogate mother's, "Because —you're a clone."

Wild gasped, flooded by utter befuddlement. "How could you do this to me *knowing* what's inside me now?"

"The Akkan are dormant... They're gonna *stay* that way."

"How can you be sure, Calla?"

"Because *I am* the Akkan," the hybrid said, handing Vera some folded clothes.

Vadim slid out from under the generator in car-two, Billy manning the toolbox at his side. "You're a respectable helper, kiddo," he said, wiping the sweat from his brow with an oily rag.

"Used to help my dad in the garage," Kojimatsuo replied, nabbing the filthy towel out of Volkov's hands, handing him a clean one. "That's how you get eye infections, numb-nuts."

Volkov rolled under the generator, "Wanted to show my little girl how to fix shit... Thanks for sorta keeping the thought alive."

"That's what family's for, Tittyshits."

"Been a while since I had one uh those."

"What do you mean? *We're* a family, everyone on this train is your family."

The Russian nodded, "I meant *family* family."

"Right... Gotcha... Miss mine, too."

"I miss my Afanasia."

Billy glanced at the oily rag in her hands, "So, listen... You lost a daughter. I lost my parents and brother... Maybe we can —work somethin out?"

Volkov slid out from under the generator, "Like what? Adoption?"

"I mean, I've dealt with worse."

The Russian grinned, "Dadbro has a cool ring to it, I guess."

Kojimatsuo extended a palm to Vadim, "Way better than Tittyshits."

Vadim shook her hand firmly, "Family it is then, kid."

Billy hugged Vadim's thick neck, "Just so you know though… Lecture me on dating, and I'll cut you."

"We'll see, Daughtersis."

"No."

"No?"

"*Daughtersis* is fucking creepy. Listen to it… Daughtersis… *Daughter-sis*… That's some backwoods kinda shit. Dadbro sounds rad, but that?"

"You may have a point."

"Of course I do."

When Wild stepped into the master suite, it transported her to a world of lilac-scented candles, champagne on ice, and a bed covered in flower petals.

Max slipped out from behind the door bearing a single rose, "Like it?"

"Lilac is my favorite."

Max inhaled the rose's fragrance, "I remembered."

Vera plucked the flower from her lover's hand, uncertain what to say. Her belly fluttered, but she was not anxious.

She was in love.

"Do you remember our first date?" Amhearst asked.

Vera nodded.

"From the moment I spoke to you, I knew you were for me." He kissed his love's hand, getting on one knee. "I'm nothing without you in my life… Waiting for you to wake up proved it… I'm not about to throw away a *second* chance to love you with all my heart."

"Max…"

"Will you marry me?"

Wild cupped her mouth. She'd been through this eighteen years before, and it was no less scary now, but as her heart beat for the man before her, she knew the decision she had to make.

The right one.

The convoy chugged along the tracks as the setting sun caught Acean's eye. He gazed in awe as he pondered a future on his new home-world. Life among the kraitho taught him much, but the one thing he respected them for above all else was their resolve. Soon, the mammals would regroup and reconstruct more than they lost.

"The auburn glow is pretty, isn't it? The way it fades into all those beautiful blues," Calla said, standing beside her friend. "I used to park on my porch and stare into the sky with my mom and dad on evenings like this. We'd—*dream*."

Acean wrapped an arm over the hybrid's shoulder, "The capacity to wonder is a precious element."

Shepherd sighed, "Sure is." She glanced up at the cleric. "We've contacted Verenberg. There's a medical facility on base. Vera thinks she can use their equipment to further her research. Maybe even reverse a clone's mutation."

"A lofty ambition, young one."

"My dad taught me that if you *can* fix something, you *should*… It's worth a shot."

"That it is, Calla, that it is," Acean said in deep reflection. "Leave it to you to, yet again, justify yourself to be far more than this globe's salvation, but its moral beacon."

"I'm no savior. Just giving these people a fighting chance to save themselves, that's all."

The hybrid's words moved the alien. Curiosity etched into the cleric's reptilian countenance as his eyes met Calla's. "Your compassion for the mammals speaks volumes, child. I am a rational being, and I cannot look past all which I have experienced. Not without slight skepticism… But you—you have endured the dregs of their species for so long and still believe in them."

The Leevahn pondered Acean's words. "It's got nothing to do with *believing*, Acean." She reached into the cleric's robe pocket, holding the Strodha against his heart. "It's about faith."

Acean smiled, proud of his friendship with such a noble creature like Shepherd.

Neither of them spoke as they watched the setting sun usher in a pristine blanket of infinite stars overhead. They were simply two beings from two worlds, joined by a belief in vast possibility.

All her life, Calla yearned to know who she was, and as she gazed into the starry night sky, she finally knew her purpose.

It was to shine.

To cast hope where there was fear.

It was to love.

To leaven.

There is nothing in this world more human than that.

Epilogue

The transmission hurled through space, immortal and unrelenting.

A baritone specter of old, desperate for an audience.

You should have made sure I was dead, Vulgrell. I'm coming to reclaim what is mine.

The message swept across countless galaxies over thousands of years. At long last, an acknowledgment of the bloody and tearful sacrifices that preceded it was at hand.

It was only a matter of time before the broadcast reached the Thrakra-Krikari.

So would the voice who spoke it.